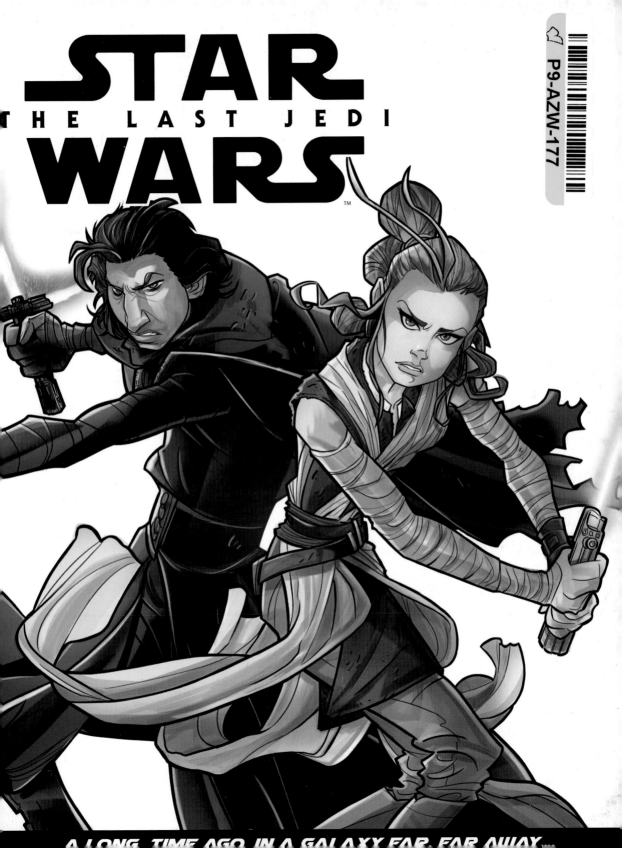

STAR WARS
THE LAST JEDI

A LONG, TIME AGO, IN A GALAXY FAR, FAR AWAY...

Meet the CHARACTERS

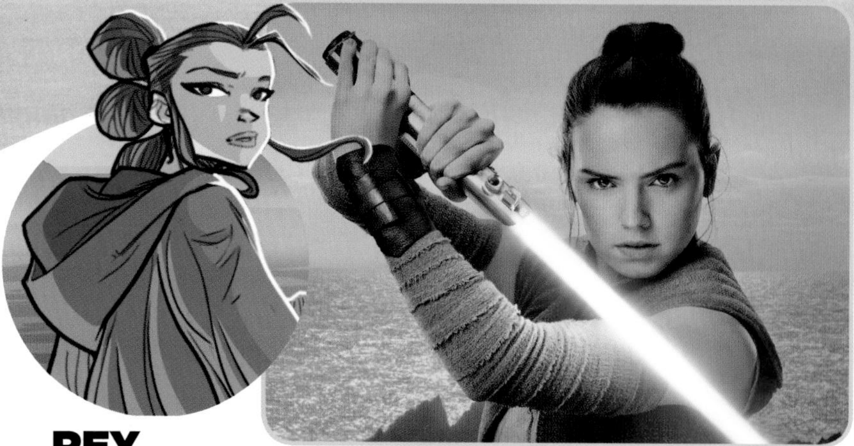

REY

Rey was **able to defeat Kylo Ren** on Starkiller Base and now shares **a Force connection with him**. She doesn't know if this bond will lead her to the dark side or **what her place is in the war** between the First Order and the Resistance. She just knows that the only person who can guide her along the right path is Luke Skywalker.

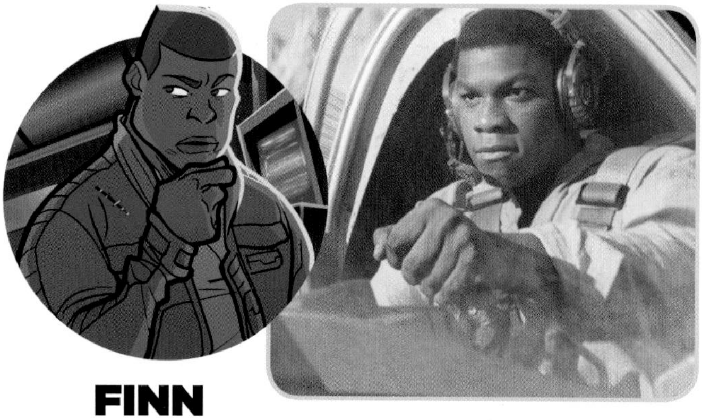

FINN

Every member of the Resistance knows the story of the hero called Finn, how he **left the First Order** and **helped destroy Starkiller Base**, how he was struck by a lightsaber blow in a **duel with Kylo Ren** and therefore fell unconscious. What they don't know is that Finn doesn't feel like a hero, he just wants to keep Rey safe.

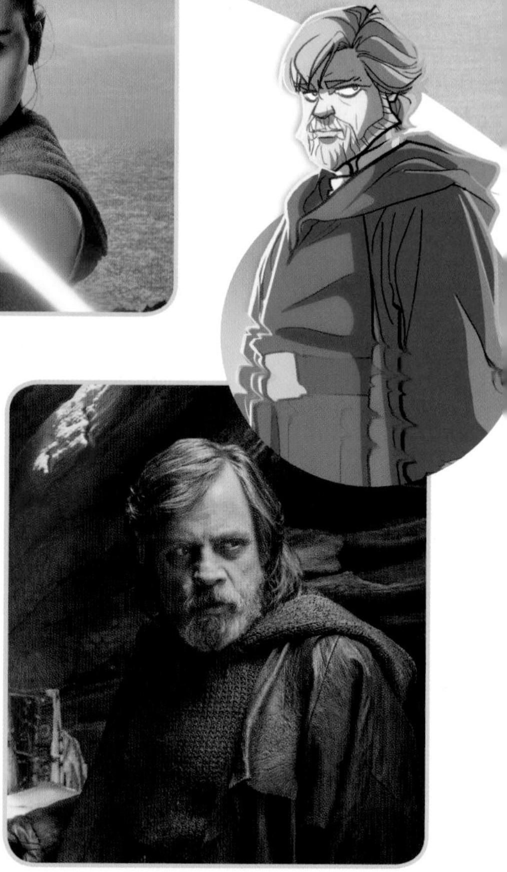

LUKE SKYWALKER

When Ben Solo, the son of Leia Organa and Han Solo, becomes Kylo Ren, Luke Skywalker, the **legendary Jedi Knight** who defeated Darth Vader and the Emperor, **exiles himself** on an uncharted planet. He wants to **end the Jedi once and for all**. But the past comes calling on him when a stranger hands him his old lightsaber.

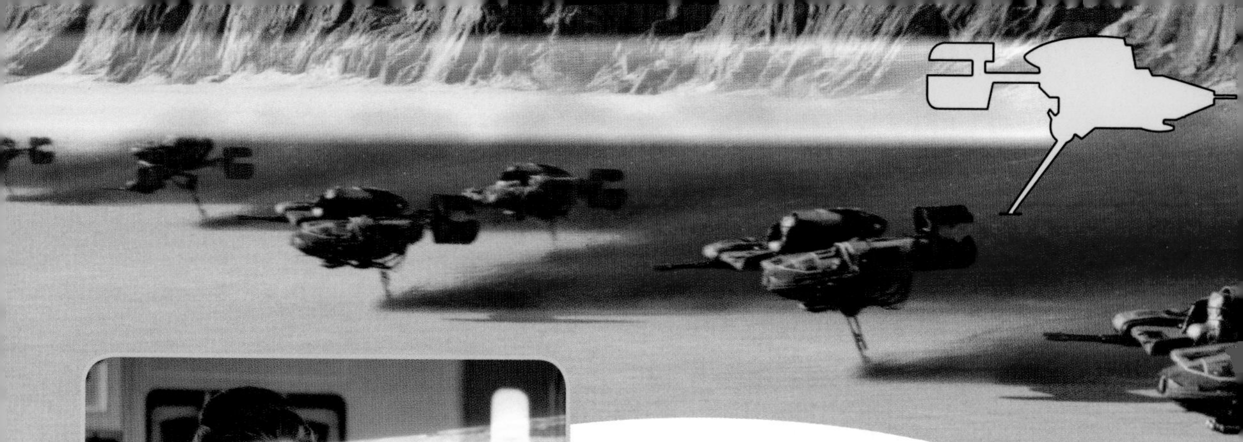

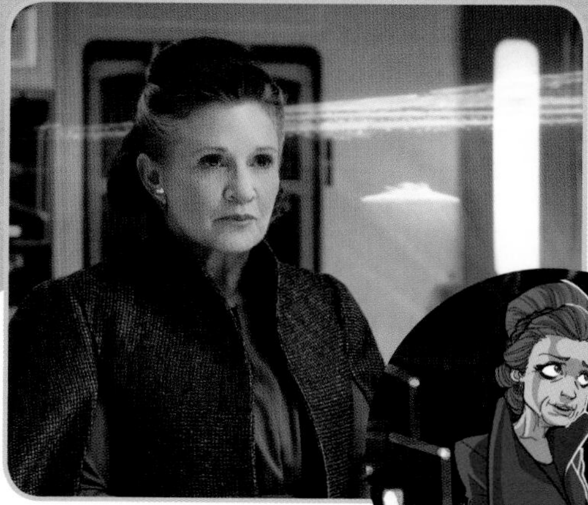

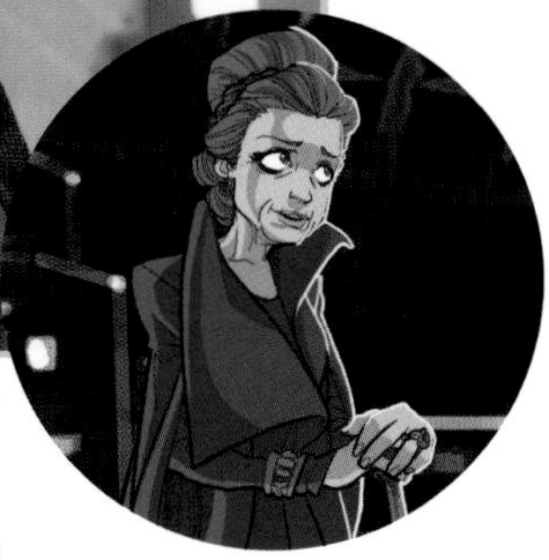

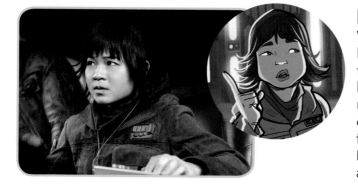

GENERAL LEIA ORGANA

Leia Organa **never loses hope**. She didn't when the Empire destroyed her home planet, not when Snoke turned her son to the dark side, not even when Ben killed his father and Leia's husband Han Solo. She has no choice: The Resistance needs **her tenacity and determination to survive**.

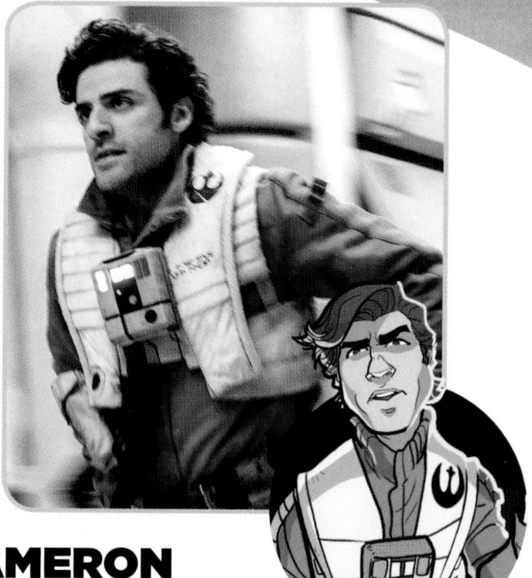

POE DAMERON

Aboard his black T-70 X-wing, Commander Dameron has been able to destroy the First Order's supreme weapon built on Starkiller Base. He's the **best pilot in the Resistance**, but he is also **too reckless**. A fault that might cost many lives.

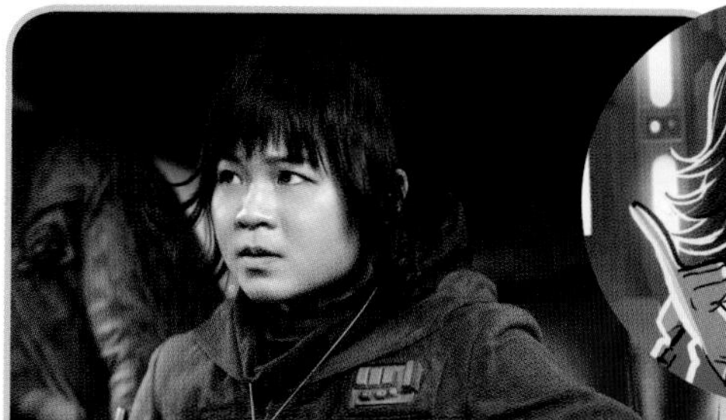

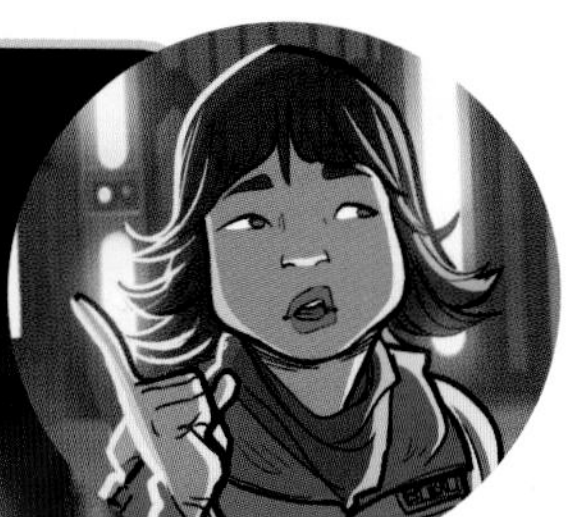

ROSE TICO

When the First Order razed her home planet, Rose joined the Resistance together with **her sister Paige**. A **talented mechanic**, Rose is now a member of the **support crew**, while Paige flies aboard one of the MG-100 Resistance's bombers, serving as a ventral gunner.

Meet the CHARACTERS

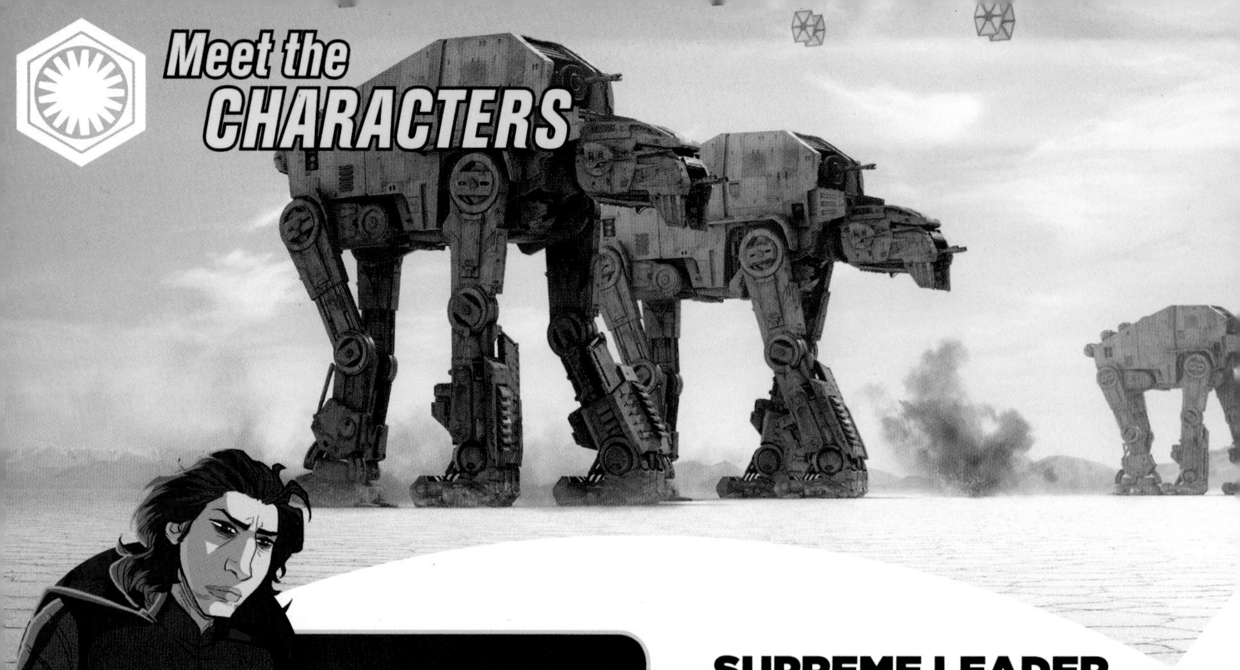

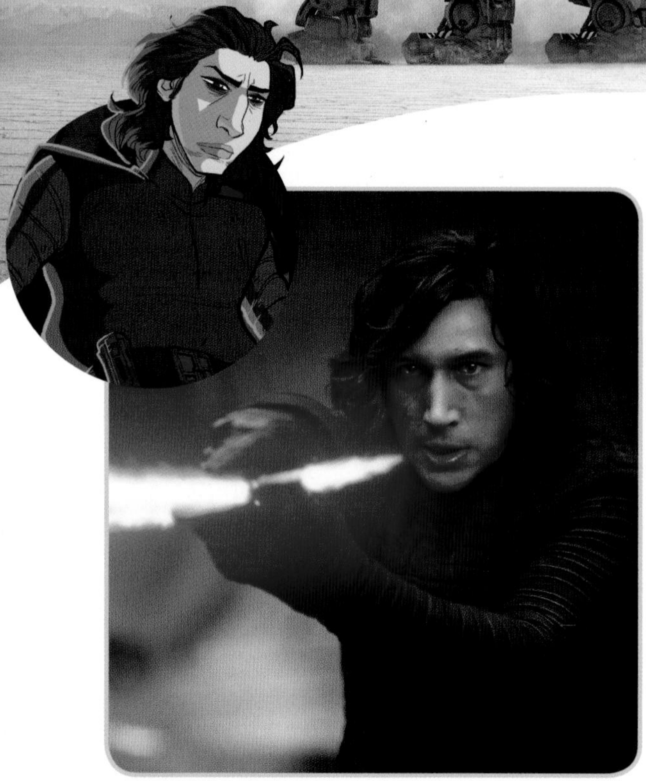

SUPREME LEADER SNOKE

The Supreme Leader commands the First Order from **his secret chambers**, protected by elite warriors—the eight members of the **Praetorian Guard**. But even though his body is frail, Snoke's authority and Force abilities have never been so powerful. He can **manipulate his apprentice's visions** and punish any of his generals even over stellar distances.

KYLO REN

Killing his father on Starkiller Base should have been the last step in becoming a dark lord, but then Kylo Ren let a young scavenger, a nobody, defeat and wound him in single combat. A disappointment his master Snoke cannot forgive, the source of **Ren's frustration and rage**, and, maybe, the proof that there's still good in him.

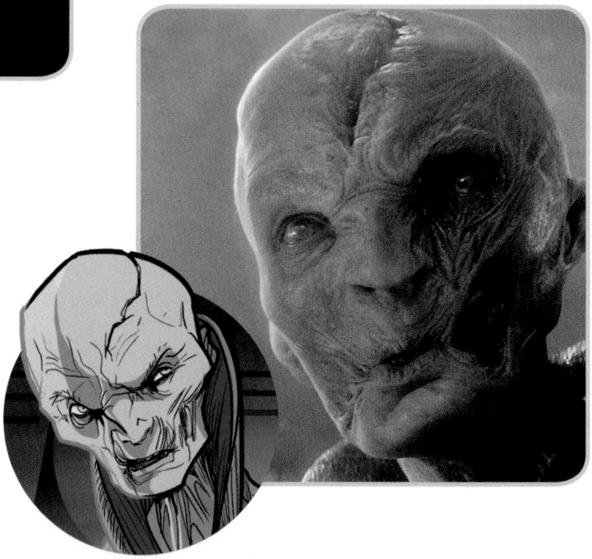

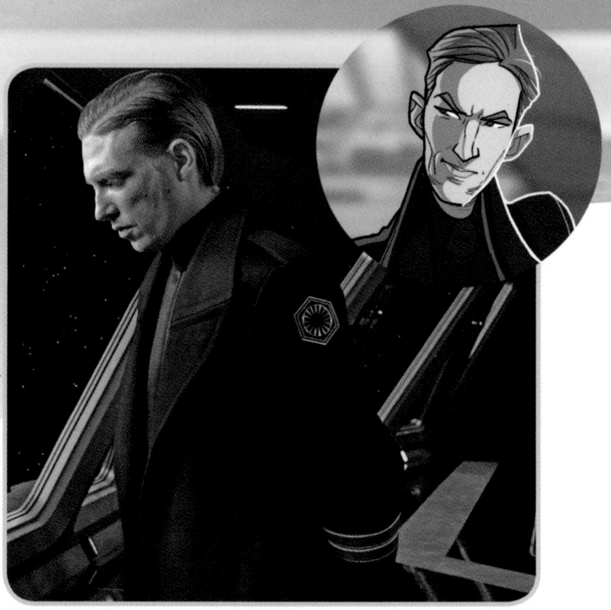

CAPTAIN PHASMA

Threatened by Finn (once the stormtrooper FN-2187 at her command), Phasma was **forced to take down the Starkiller Base shields**—unwittingly helping the Resistance destroy the base. To clear all the tracks of her treason, she killed the Lieutenant who could report her. Now she waits for an opportunity to meet FN-2187 again and **get her revenge**.

GENERAL HUX

The destruction of Starkiller Base didn't bother Armitage Hux. Now that the Republic fleet is no more, **the might of the First Order** cannot be matched by the Resistance—or any other rebel movement. It's only a matter of time before the Supreme Leader rules the entire galaxy, and Hux, the **key man in Snoke's military strategy,** knows that he earned a place of honor.

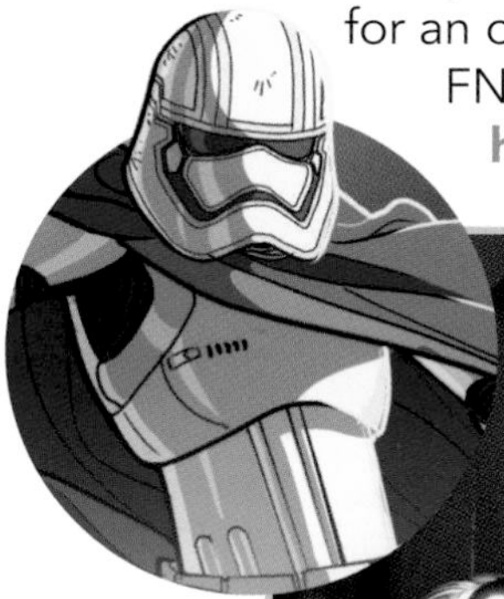
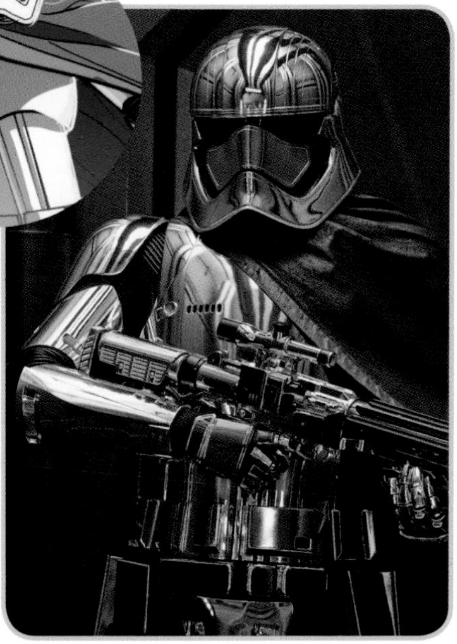
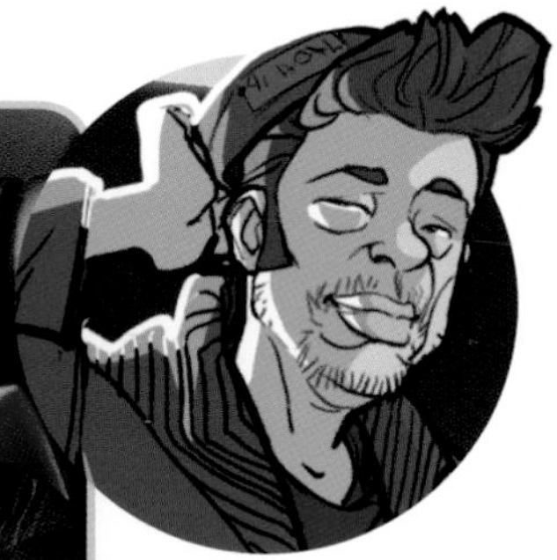
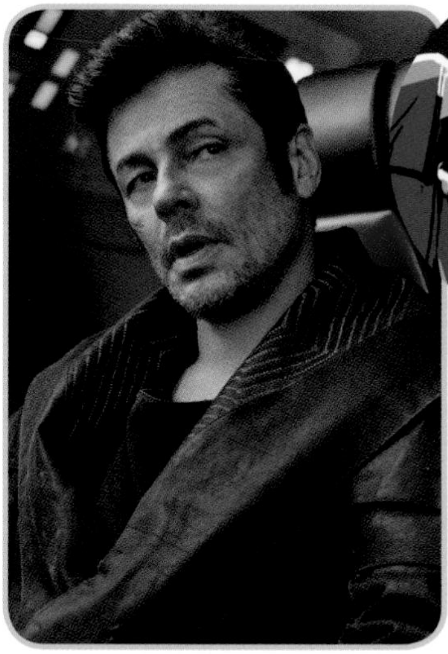

DJ

DJ is **one of the best codebreakers** on the market—he can open the door of any cell or easily steal any spacecraft. **Only caring about money and himself**, he would equally work for both the Resistance and the First Order. His nickname stands for "Don't Join," his motto and also his attitude towards any cause.

"LET THE PAST DIE. KILL IT IF YOU HAVE TO. THAT'S THE ONLY WAY TO BECOME WHAT YOU WERE MEANT TO BE."

KYLO REN

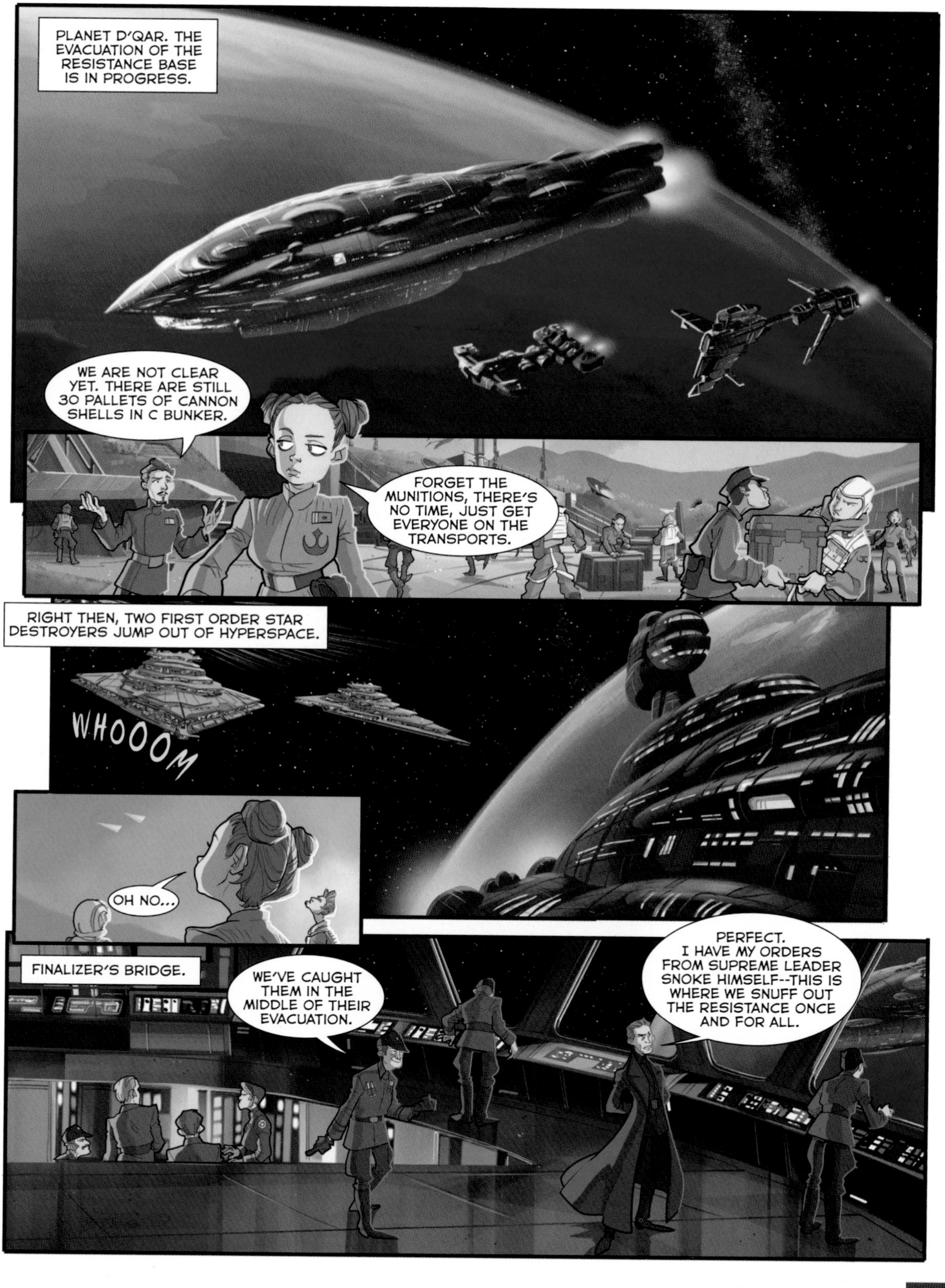
PLANET D'QAR. THE EVACUATION OF THE RESISTANCE BASE IS IN PROGRESS.
WE ARE NOT CLEAR YET. THERE ARE STILL 30 PALLETS OF CANNON SHELLS IN C BUNKER.
FORGET THE MUNITIONS, THERE'S NO TIME, JUST GET EVERYONE ON THE TRANSPORTS.
RIGHT THEN, TWO FIRST ORDER STAR DESTROYERS JUMP OUT OF HYPERSPACE.
WHOOOM
OH NO...
FINALIZER'S BRIDGE.
WE'VE CAUGHT THEM IN THE MIDDLE OF THEIR EVACUATION.
PERFECT. I HAVE MY ORDERS FROM SUPREME LEADER SNOKE HIMSELF--THIS IS WHERE WE SNUFF OUT THE RESISTANCE ONCE AND FOR ALL.

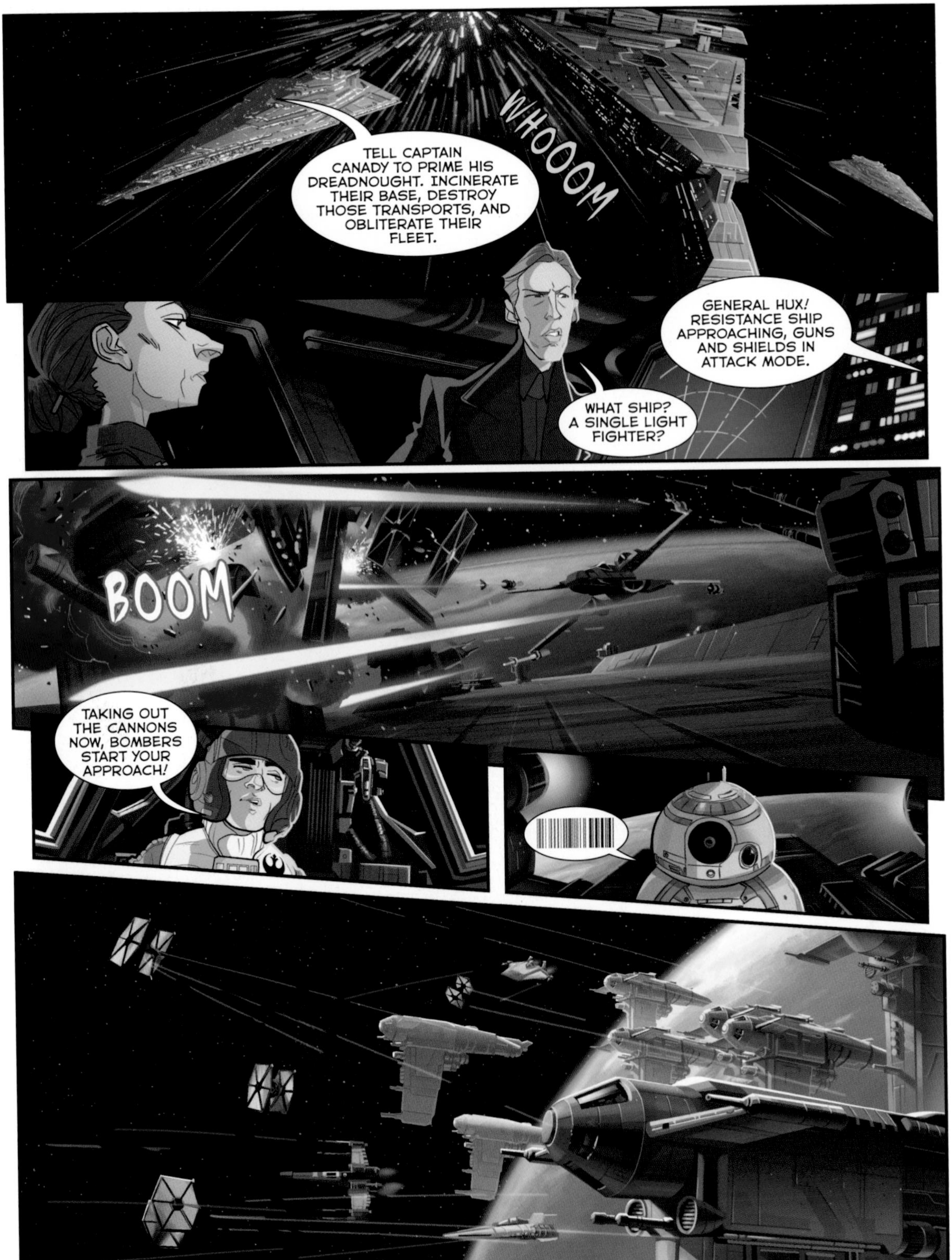
TELL CAPTAIN CANADY TO PRIME HIS DREADNOUGHT. INCINERATE THEIR BASE, DESTROY THOSE TRANSPORTS, AND OBLITERATE THEIR FLEET.
WHOOOM
GENERAL HUX! RESISTANCE SHIP APPROACHING, GUNS AND SHIELDS IN ATTACK MODE.
WHAT SHIP? A SINGLE LIGHT FIGHTER?
BOOM
TAKING OUT THE CANNONS NOW, BOMBERS START YOUR APPROACH!

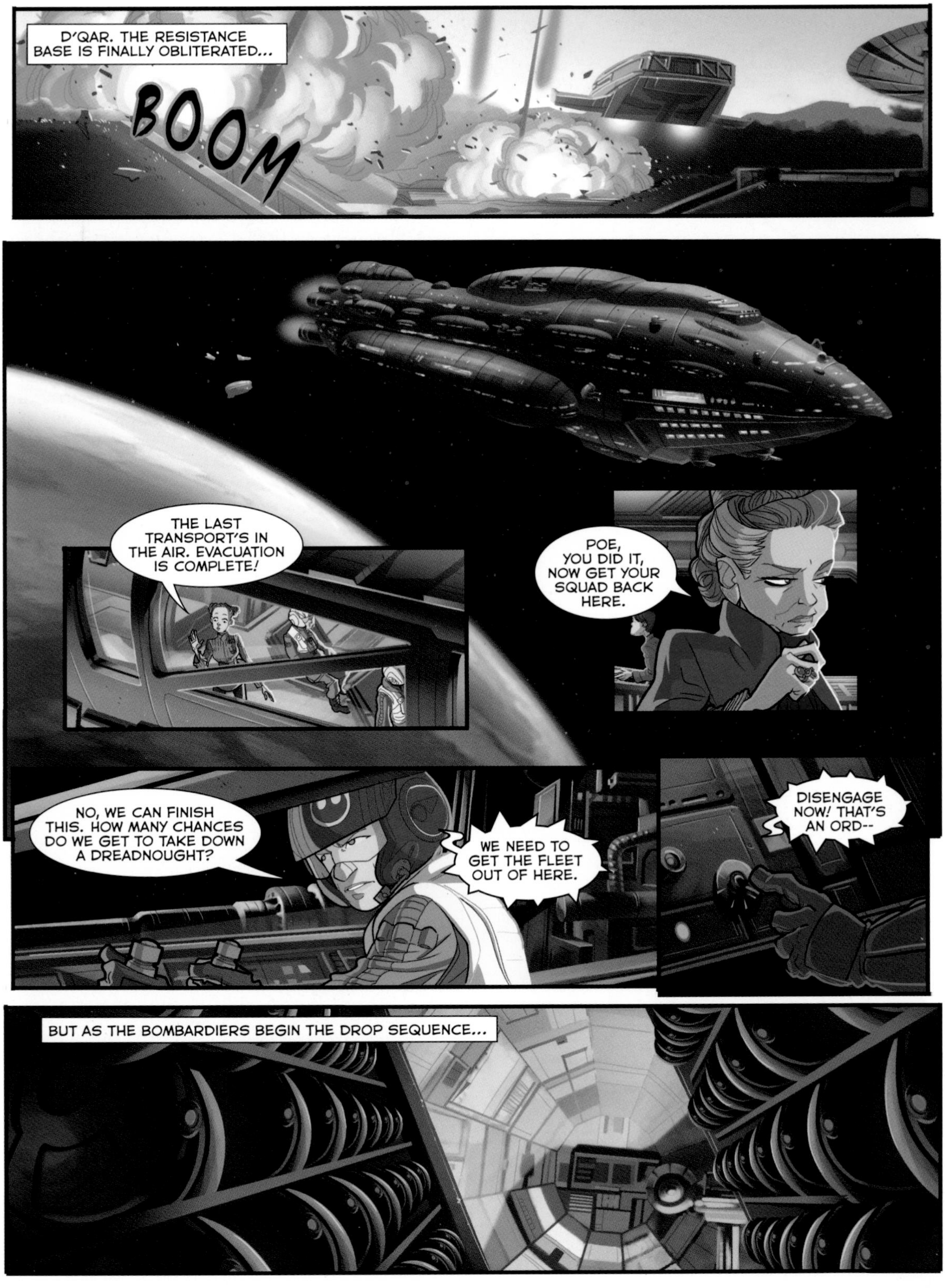

D'QAR. THE RESISTANCE BASE IS FINALLY OBLITERATED...
BOOM
THE LAST TRANSPORT'S IN THE AIR. EVACUATION IS COMPLETE!
POE, YOU DID IT, NOW GET YOUR SQUAD BACK HERE.
NO, WE CAN FINISH THIS. HOW MANY CHANCES DO WE GET TO TAKE DOWN A DREADNOUGHT?
WE NEED TO GET THE FLEET OUT OF HERE.
DISENGAGE NOW! THAT'S AN ORD--
BUT AS THE BOMBARDIERS BEGIN THE DROP SEQUENCE...

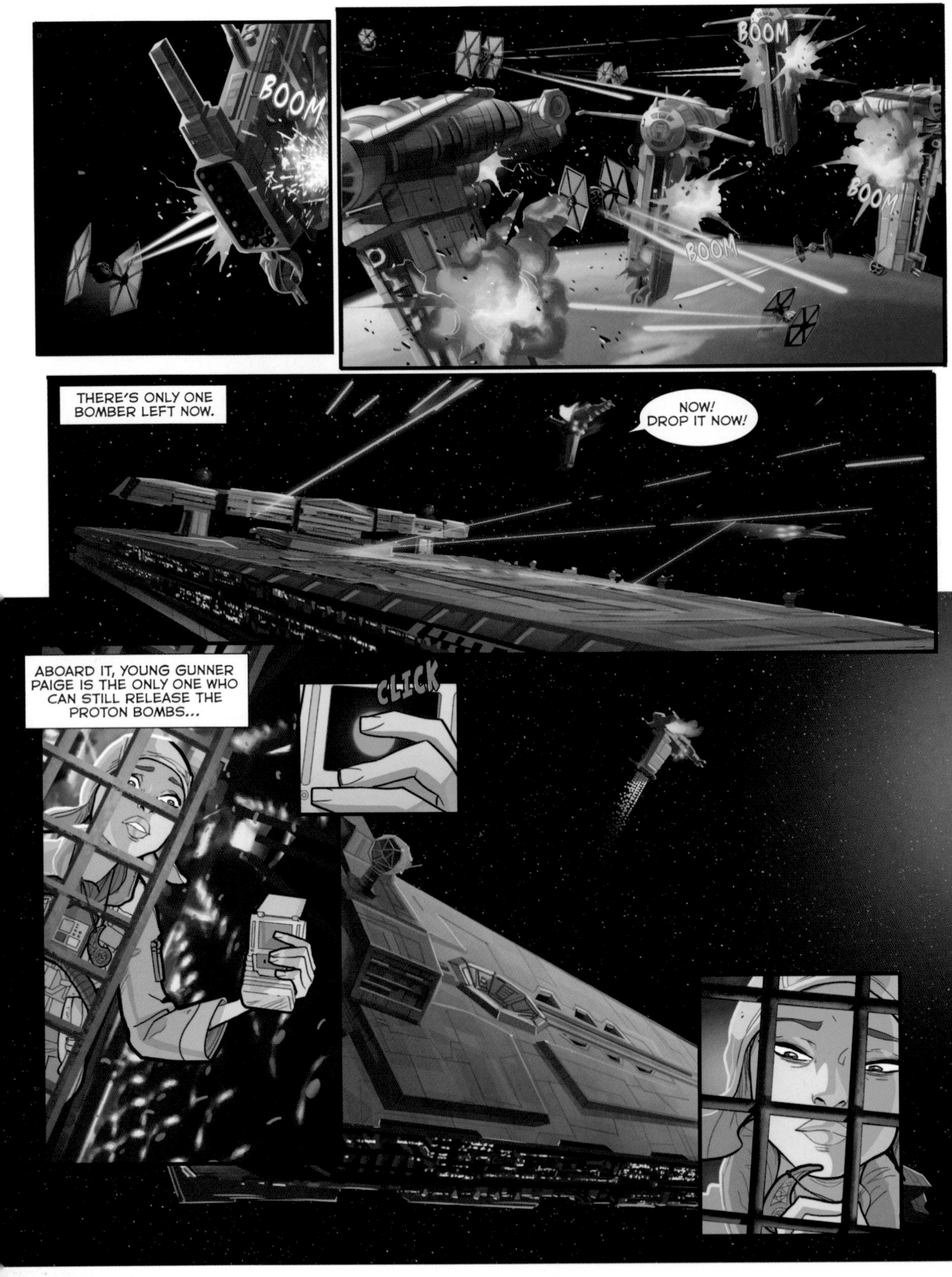

BOOM
BOOM
BOOM
BOOM
BOOM
THERE'S ONLY ONE BOMBER LEFT NOW.
NOW! DROP IT NOW!
ABOARD IT, YOUNG GUNNER PAIGE IS THE ONLY ONE WHO CAN STILL RELEASE THE PROTON BOMBS...
CLICK

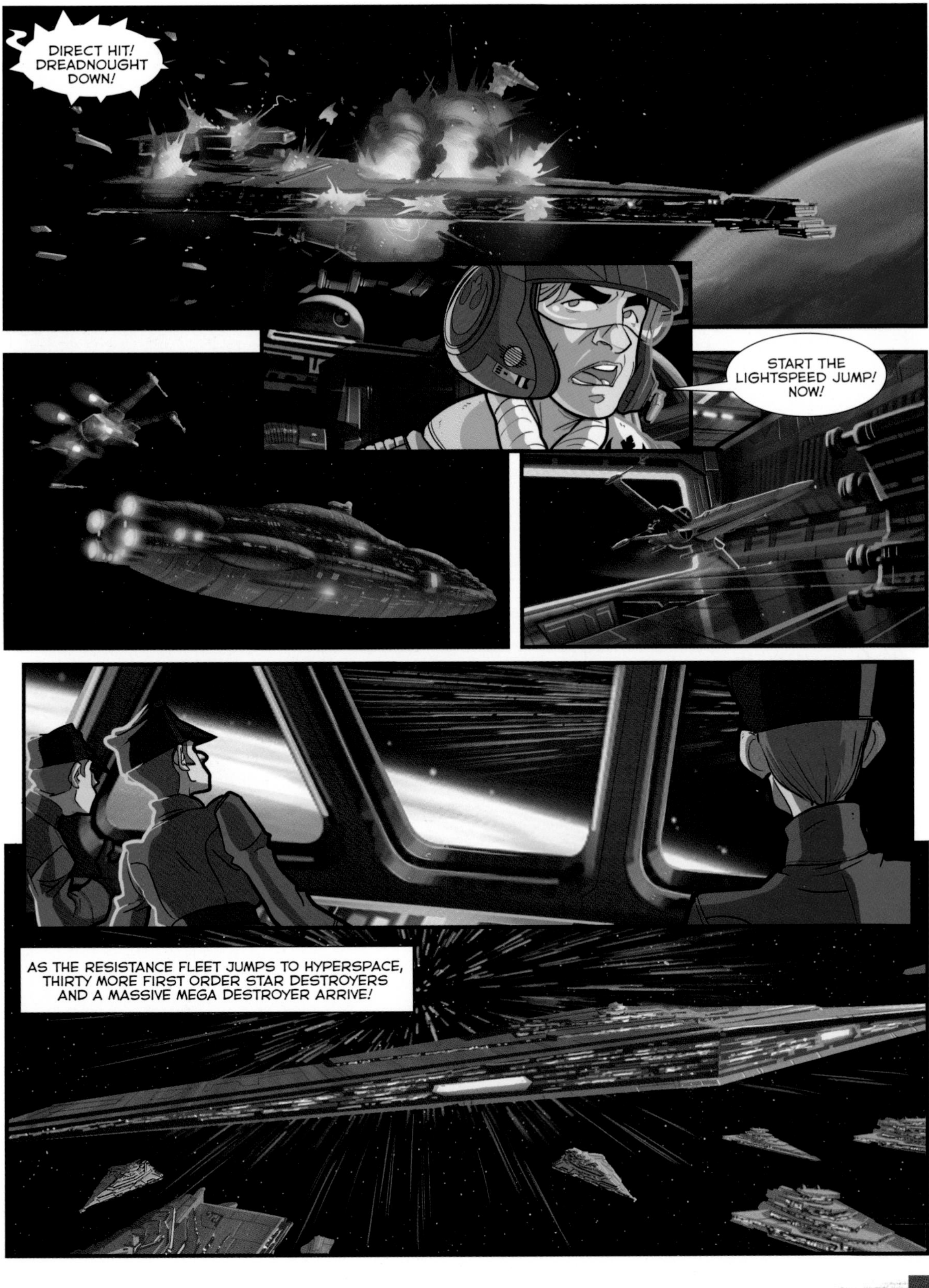
DIRECT HIT! DREADNOUGHT DOWN!
START THE LIGHTSPEED JUMP! NOW!
AS THE RESISTANCE FLEET JUMPS TO HYPERSPACE, THIRTY MORE FIRST ORDER STAR DESTROYERS AND A MASSIVE MEGA DESTROYER ARRIVE!

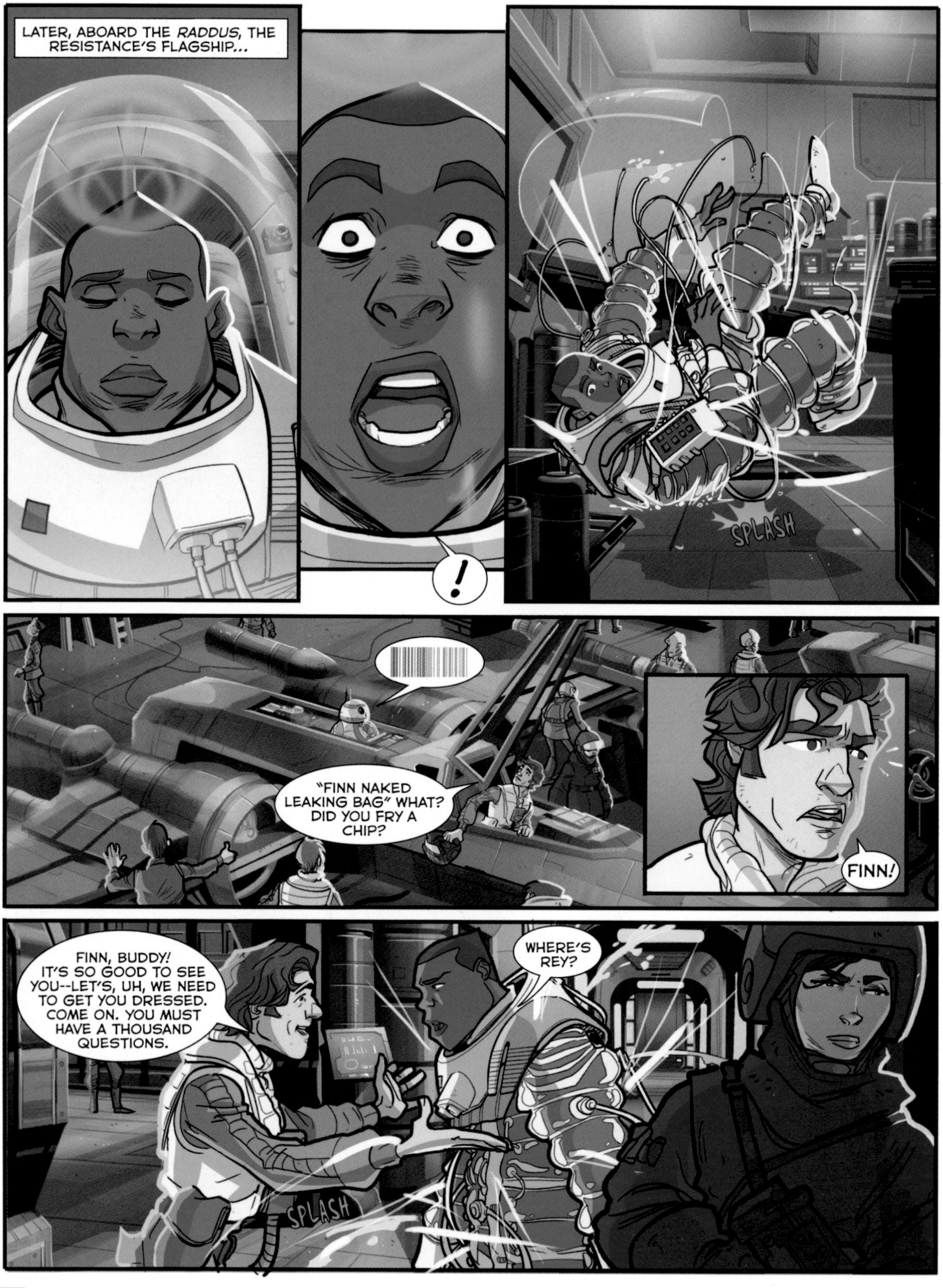
LATER, ABOARD THE *RADDUS*, THE RESISTANCE'S FLAGSHIP...
!
SPLASH
"FINN NAKED LEAKING BAG" WHAT? DID YOU FRY A CHIP?
FINN!
FINN, BUDDY! IT'S SO GOOD TO SEE YOU--LET'S, UH, WE NEED TO GET YOU DRESSED. COME ON. YOU MUST HAVE A THOUSAND QUESTIONS.
WHERE'S REY?
SPLASH

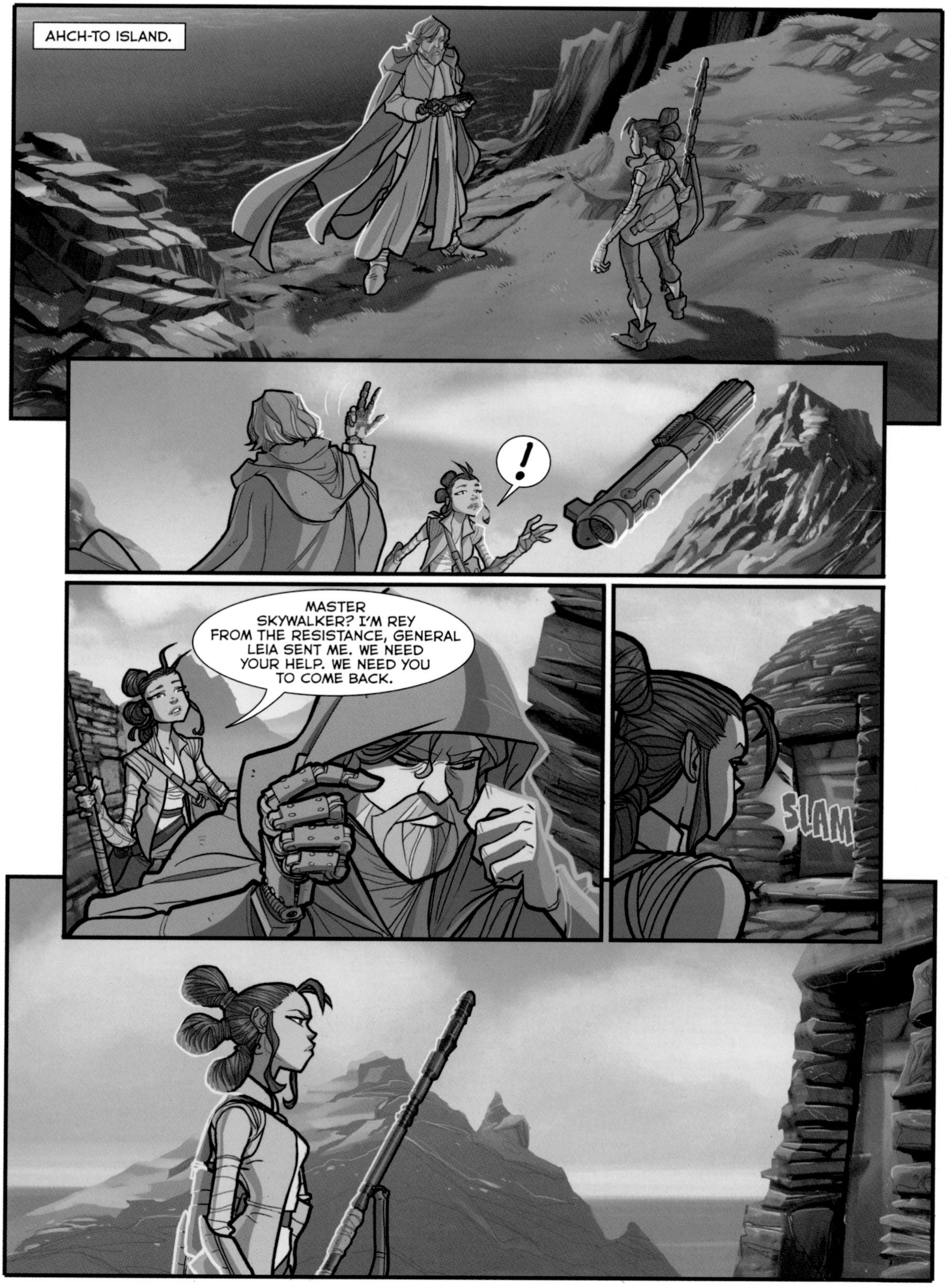
AHCH-TO ISLAND.
!
MASTER SKYWALKER? I'M REY FROM THE RESISTANCE, GENERAL LEIA SENT ME. WE NEED YOUR HELP. WE NEED YOU TO COME BACK.
SLAM

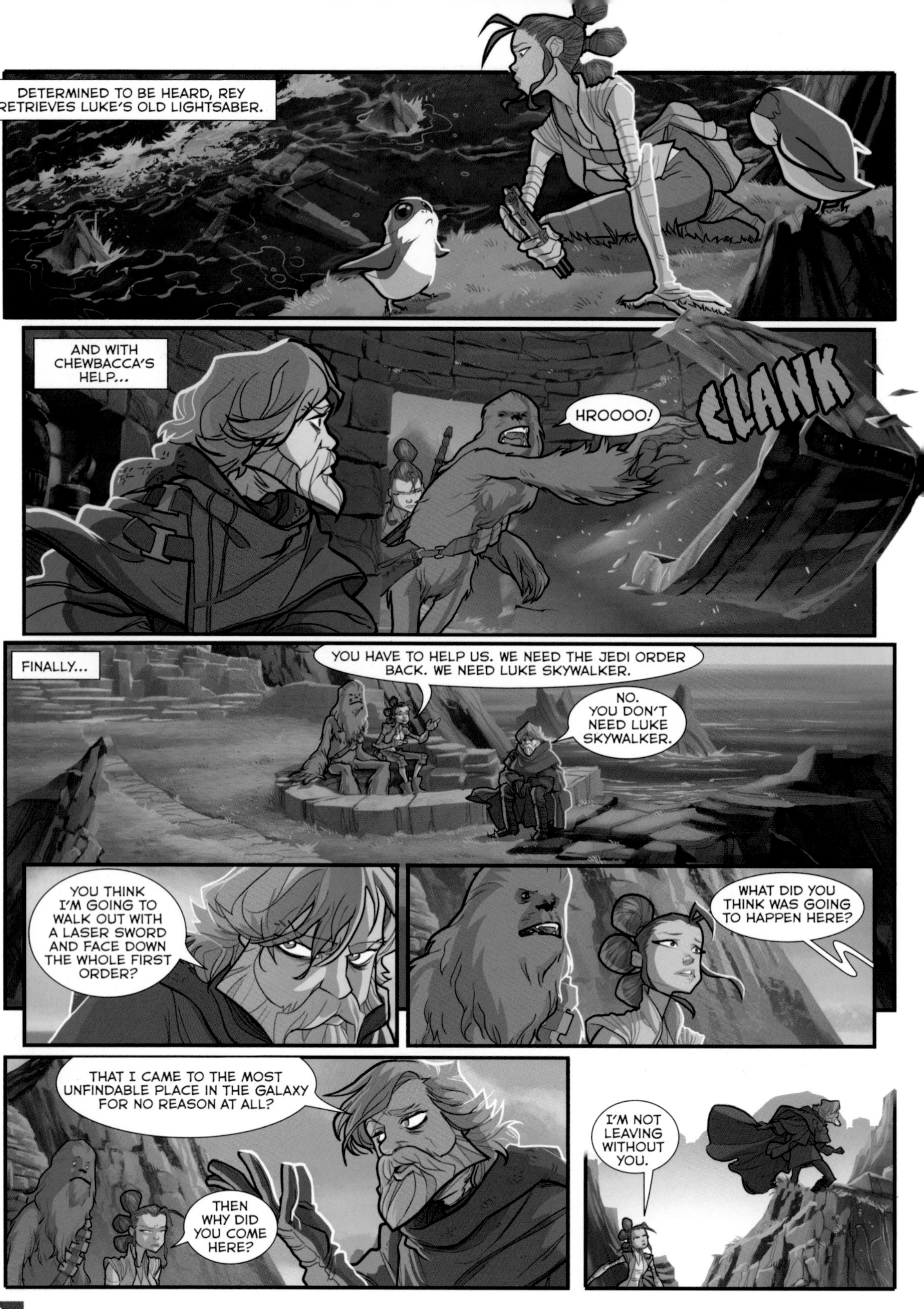

DETERMINED TO BE HEARD, REY RETRIEVES LUKE'S OLD LIGHTSABER.
AND WITH CHEWBACCA'S HELP...
HROOOO!
CLANK
FINALLY...
YOU HAVE TO HELP US. WE NEED THE JEDI ORDER BACK. WE NEED LUKE SKYWALKER.
NO. YOU DON'T NEED LUKE SKYWALKER.
YOU THINK I'M GOING TO WALK OUT WITH A LASER SWORD AND FACE DOWN THE WHOLE FIRST ORDER?
WHAT DID YOU THINK WAS GOING TO HAPPEN HERE?
THAT I CAME TO THE MOST UNFINDABLE PLACE IN THE GALAXY FOR NO REASON AT ALL?
THEN WHY DID YOU COME HERE?
I'M NOT LEAVING WITHOUT YOU.

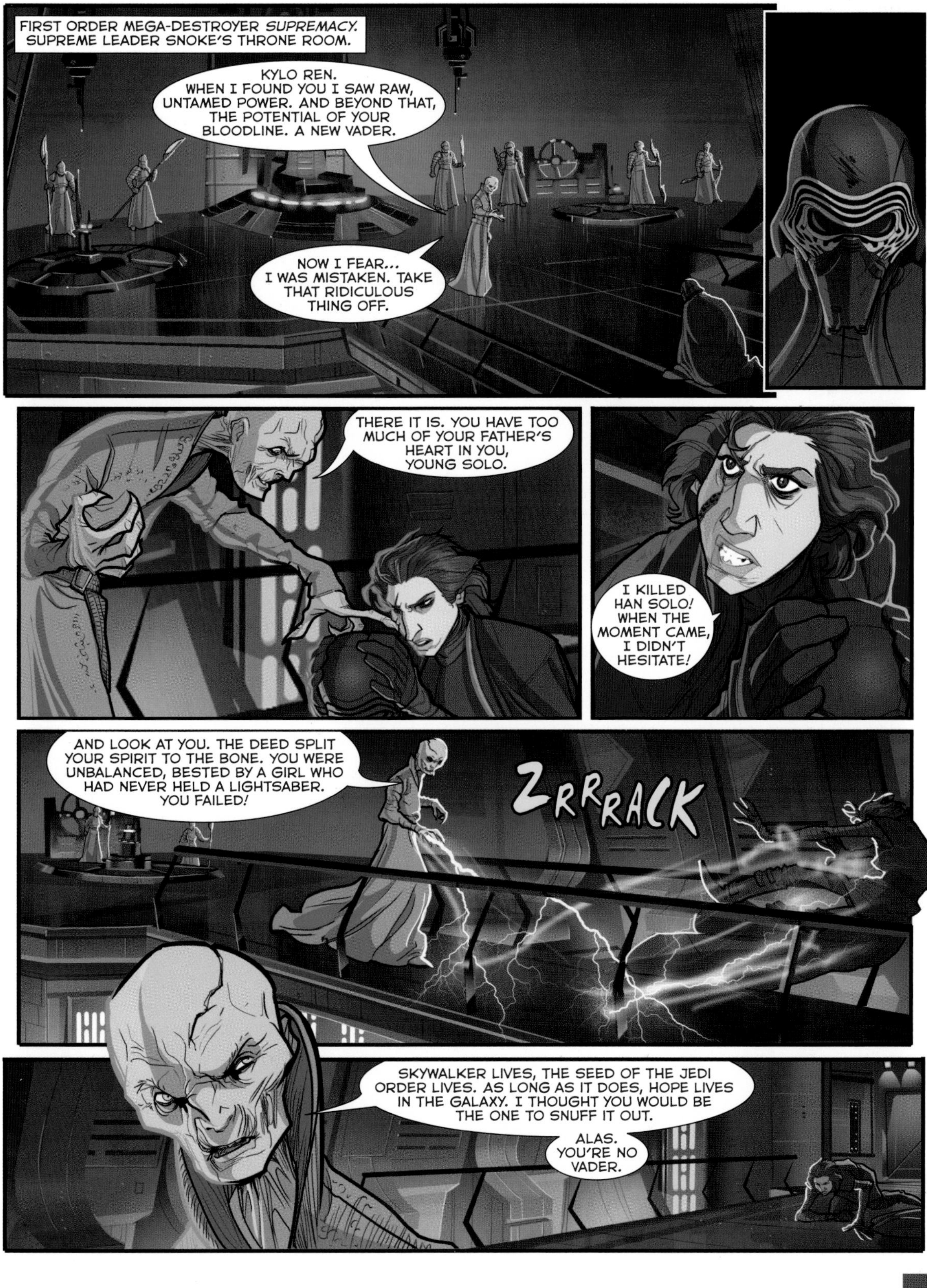
FIRST ORDER MEGA-DESTROYER *SUPREMACY.* SUPREME LEADER SNOKE'S THRONE ROOM.
KYLO REN. WHEN I FOUND YOU I SAW RAW, UNTAMED POWER. AND BEYOND THAT, THE POTENTIAL OF YOUR BLOODLINE. A NEW VADER.
NOW I FEAR... I WAS MISTAKEN. TAKE THAT RIDICULOUS THING OFF.
THERE IT IS. YOU HAVE TOO MUCH OF YOUR FATHER'S HEART IN YOU, YOUNG SOLO.
I KILLED HAN SOLO! WHEN THE MOMENT CAME, I DIDN'T HESITATE!
AND LOOK AT YOU. THE DEED SPLIT YOUR SPIRIT TO THE BONE. YOU WERE UNBALANCED, BESTED BY A GIRL WHO HAD NEVER HELD A LIGHTSABER. YOU FAILED!
ZRRRACK
SKYWALKER LIVES, THE SEED OF THE JEDI ORDER LIVES. AS LONG AS IT DOES, HOPE LIVES IN THE GALAXY. I THOUGHT YOU WOULD BE THE ONE TO SNUFF IT OUT.
ALAS. YOU'RE NO VADER.

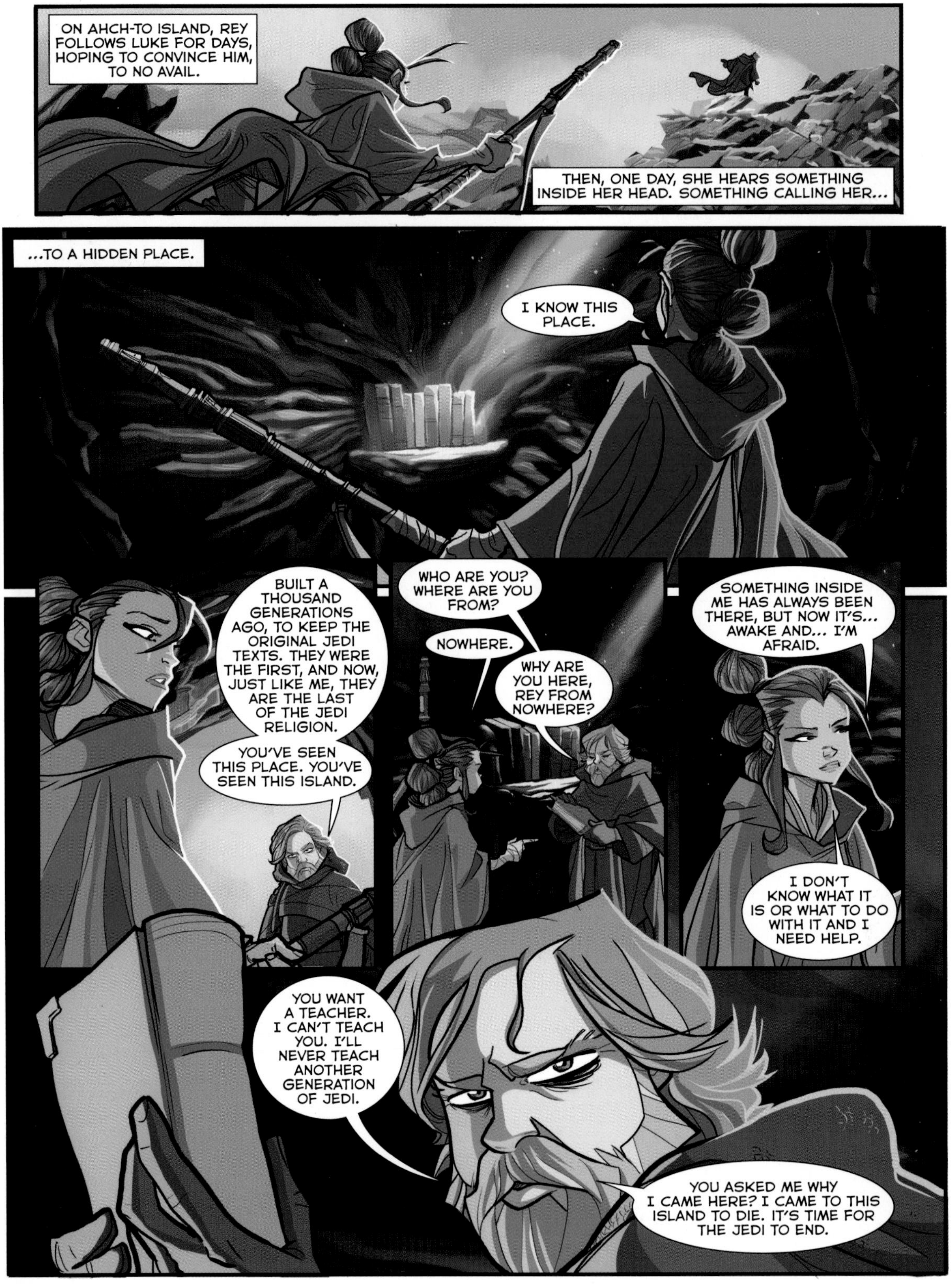

ON AHCH-TO ISLAND, REY FOLLOWS LUKE FOR DAYS, HOPING TO CONVINCE HIM, TO NO AVAIL.
THEN, ONE DAY, SHE HEARS SOMETHING INSIDE HER HEAD. SOMETHING CALLING HER...
...TO A HIDDEN PLACE.
I KNOW THIS PLACE.
BUILT A THOUSAND GENERATIONS AGO, TO KEEP THE ORIGINAL JEDI TEXTS. THEY WERE THE FIRST, AND NOW, JUST LIKE ME, THEY ARE THE LAST OF THE JEDI RELIGION.
YOU'VE SEEN THIS PLACE. YOU'VE SEEN THIS ISLAND.
WHO ARE YOU? WHERE ARE YOU FROM?
NOWHERE.
WHY ARE YOU HERE, REY FROM NOWHERE?
SOMETHING INSIDE ME HAS ALWAYS BEEN THERE, BUT NOW IT'S... AWAKE AND... I'M AFRAID.
I DON'T KNOW WHAT IT IS OR WHAT TO DO WITH IT AND I NEED HELP.
YOU WANT A TEACHER. I CAN'T TEACH YOU. I'LL NEVER TEACH ANOTHER GENERATION OF JEDI.
YOU ASKED ME WHY I CAME HERE? I CAME TO THIS ISLAND TO DIE. IT'S TIME FOR THE JEDI TO END.

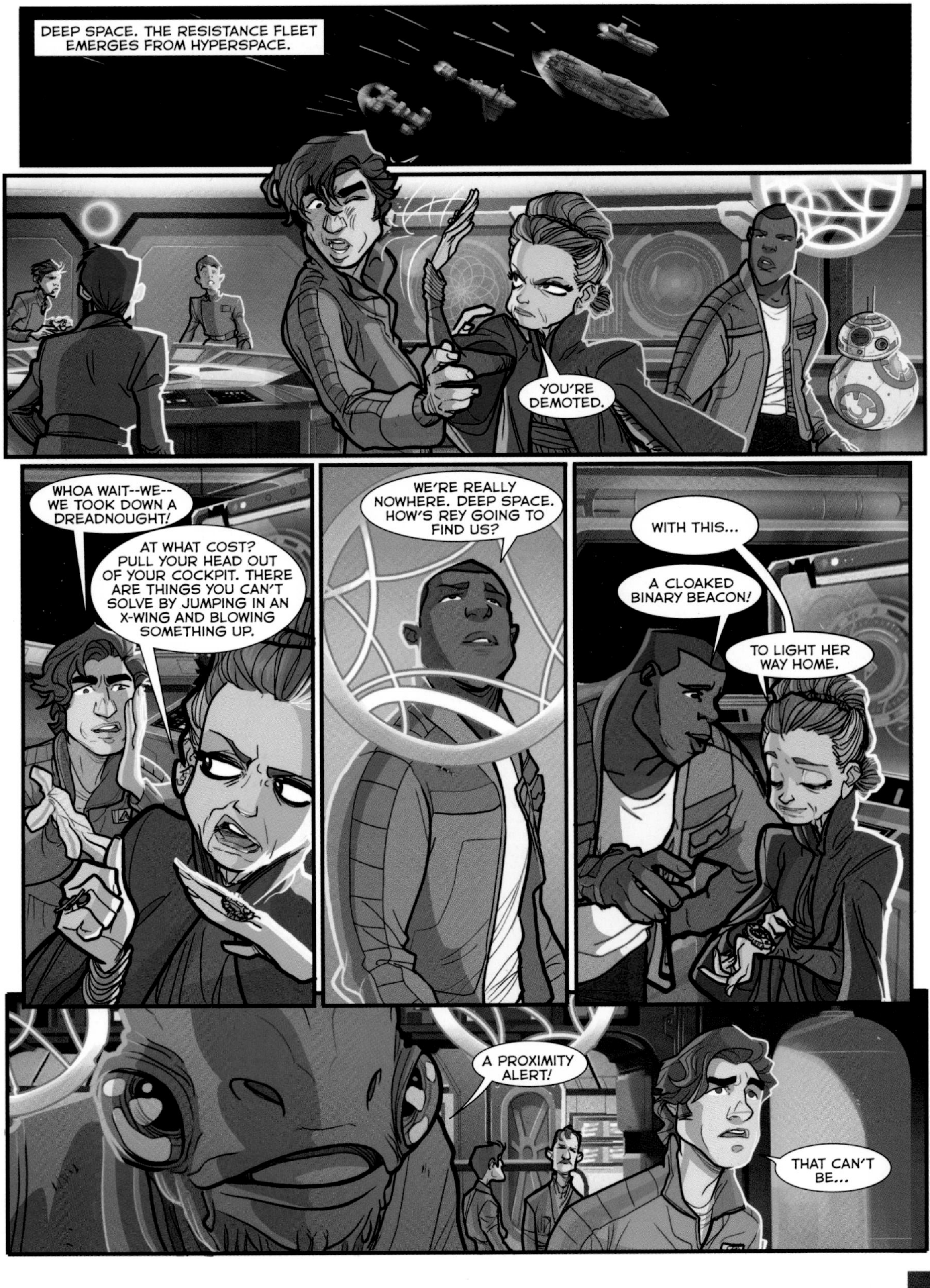

DEEP SPACE. THE RESISTANCE FLEET EMERGES FROM HYPERSPACE.
YOU'RE DEMOTED.
WHOA WAIT--WE-- WE TOOK DOWN A DREADNOUGHT!
AT WHAT COST? PULL YOUR HEAD OUT OF YOUR COCKPIT. THERE ARE THINGS YOU CAN'T SOLVE BY JUMPING IN AN X-WING AND BLOWING SOMETHING UP.
WE'RE REALLY NOWHERE. DEEP SPACE. HOW'S REY GOING TO FIND US?
WITH THIS...
A CLOAKED BINARY BEACON!
TO LIGHT HER WAY HOME.
A PROXIMITY ALERT!
THAT CAN'T BE...

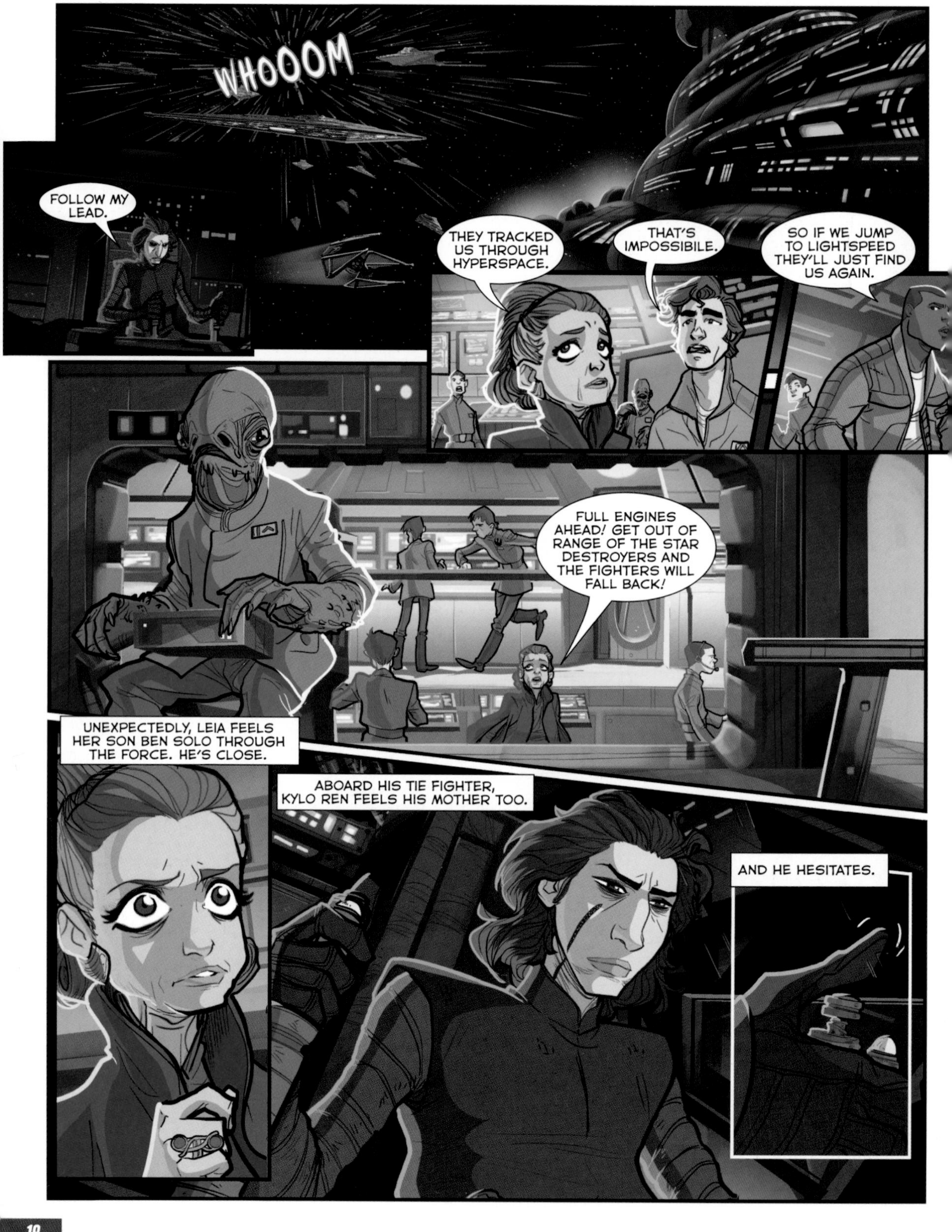
WHOOOM
FOLLOW MY LEAD.
THEY TRACKED US THROUGH HYPERSPACE.
THAT'S IMPOSSIBILE.
SO IF WE JUMP TO LIGHTSPEED THEY'LL JUST FIND US AGAIN.
FULL ENGINES AHEAD! GET OUT OF RANGE OF THE STAR DESTROYERS AND THE FIGHTERS WILL FALL BACK!
UNEXPECTEDLY, LEIA FEELS HER SON BEN SOLO THROUGH THE FORCE. HE'S CLOSE.
ABOARD HIS TIE FIGHTER, KYLO REN FEELS HIS MOTHER TOO.
AND HE HESITATES.

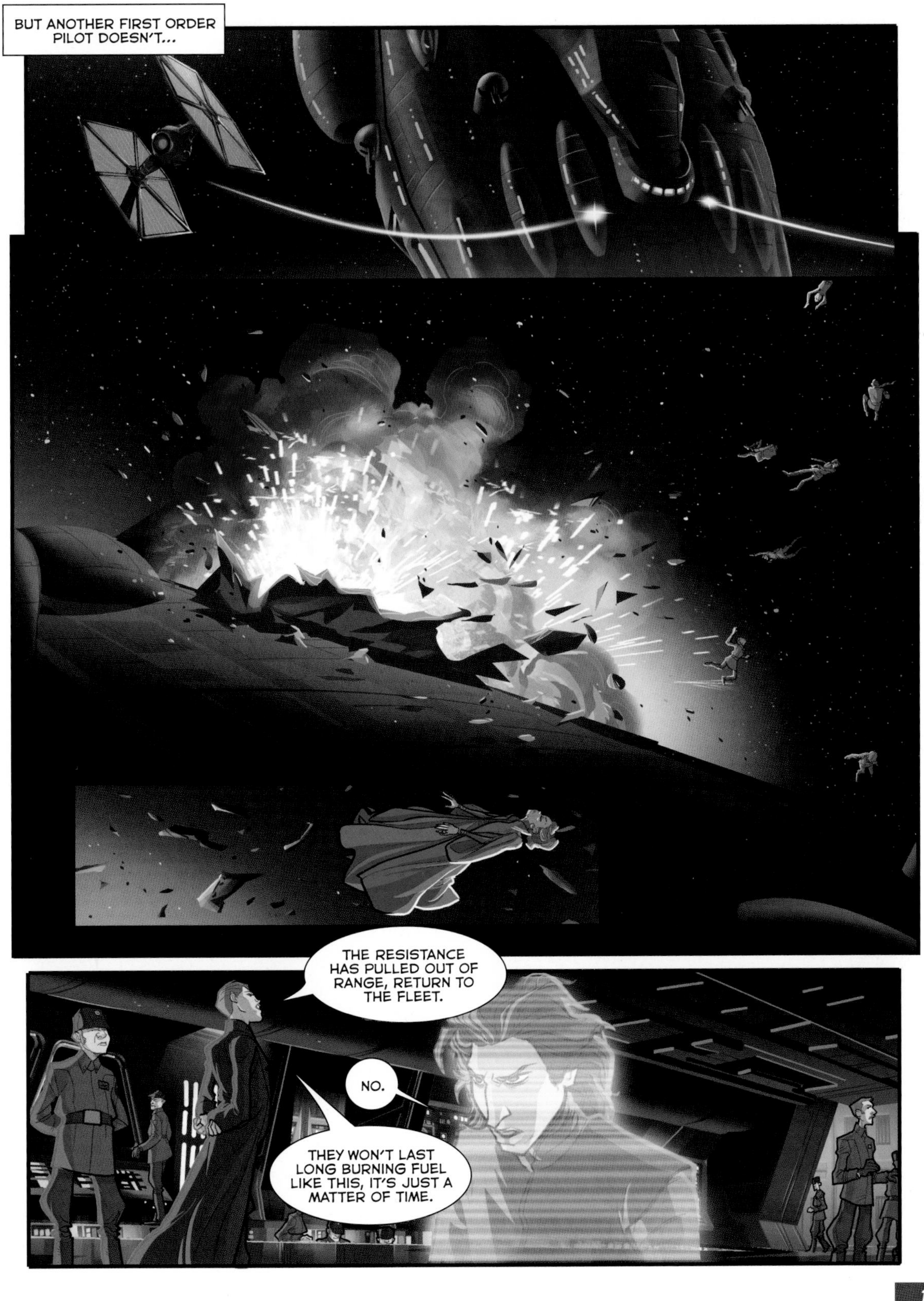
BUT ANOTHER FIRST ORDER PILOT DOESN'T...
THE RESISTANCE HAS PULLED OUT OF RANGE, RETURN TO THE FLEET.
NO.
THEY WON'T LAST LONG BURNING FUEL LIKE THIS, IT'S JUST A MATTER OF TIME.

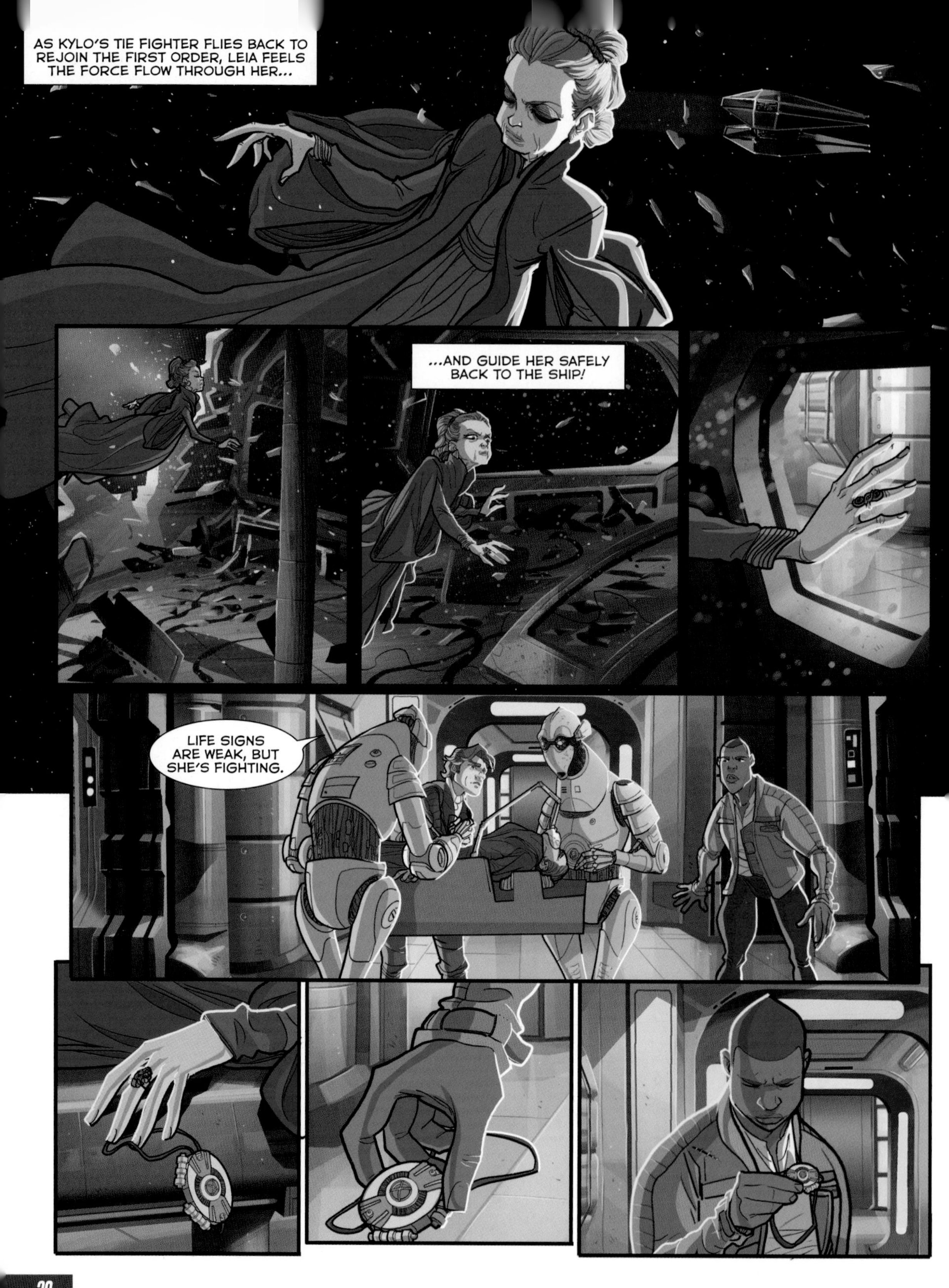
AS KYLO'S TIE FIGHTER FLIES BACK TO REJOIN THE FIRST ORDER, LEIA FEELS THE FORCE FLOW THROUGH HER...
...AND GUIDE HER SAFELY BACK TO THE SHIP!
LIFE SIGNS ARE WEAK, BUT SHE'S FIGHTING.

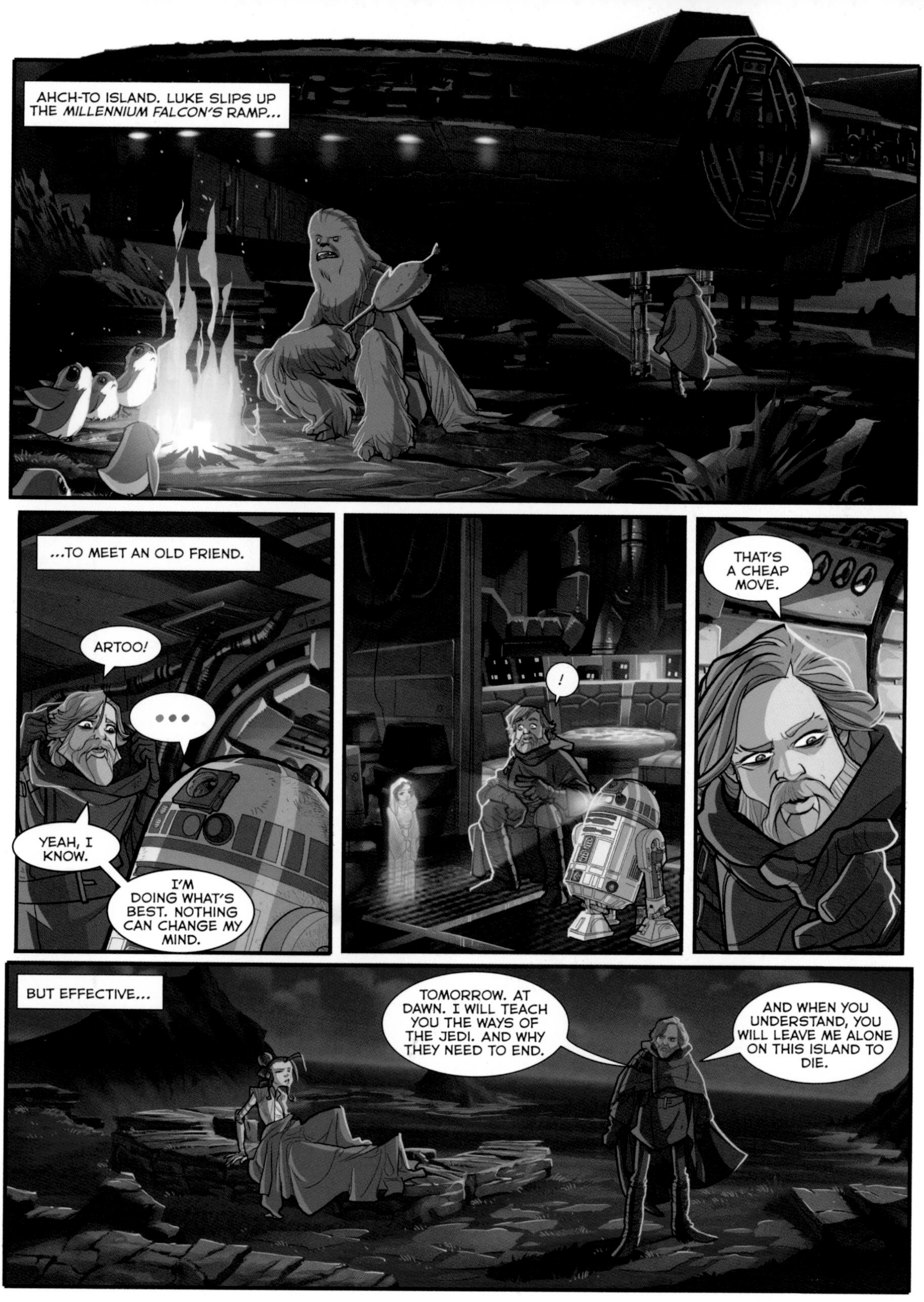
AHCH-TO ISLAND. LUKE SLIPS UP THE *MILLENNIUM FALCON'S* RAMP...
...TO MEET AN OLD FRIEND.
ARTOO!
•••
YEAH, I KNOW.
I'M DOING WHAT'S BEST. NOTHING CAN CHANGE MY MIND.
!
THAT'S A CHEAP MOVE.
BUT EFFECTIVE...
TOMORROW. AT DAWN. I WILL TEACH YOU THE WAYS OF THE JEDI. AND WHY THEY NEED TO END.
AND WHEN YOU UNDERSTAND, YOU WILL LEAVE ME ALONE ON THIS ISLAND TO DIE.

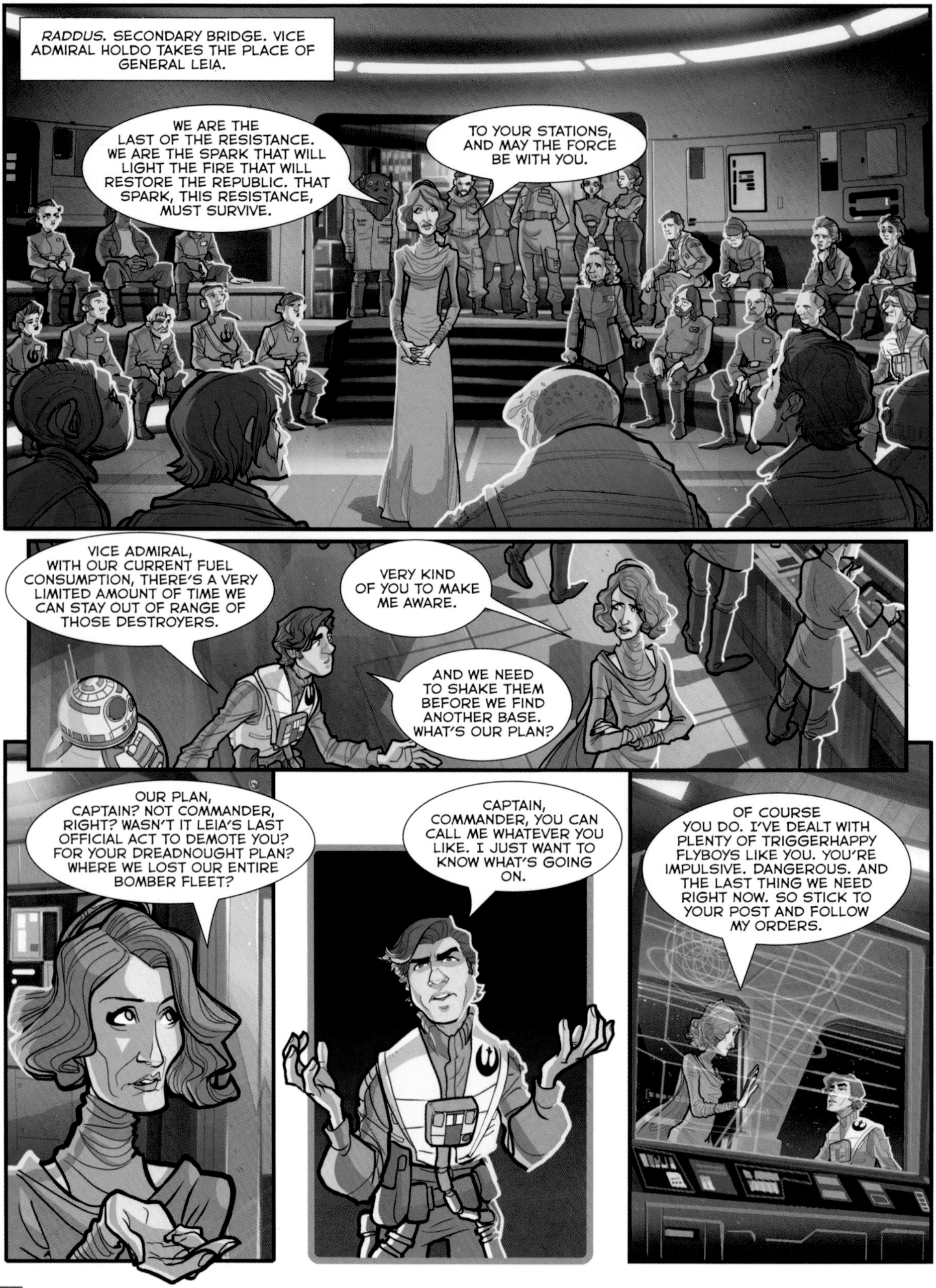
RADDUS. SECONDARY BRIDGE. VICE ADMIRAL HOLDO TAKES THE PLACE OF GENERAL LEIA.
WE ARE THE LAST OF THE RESISTANCE. WE ARE THE SPARK THAT WILL LIGHT THE FIRE THAT WILL RESTORE THE REPUBLIC. THAT SPARK, THIS RESISTANCE, MUST SURVIVE.
TO YOUR STATIONS, AND MAY THE FORCE BE WITH YOU.
VICE ADMIRAL, WITH OUR CURRENT FUEL CONSUMPTION, THERE'S A VERY LIMITED AMOUNT OF TIME WE CAN STAY OUT OF RANGE OF THOSE DESTROYERS.
VERY KIND OF YOU TO MAKE ME AWARE.
AND WE NEED TO SHAKE THEM BEFORE WE FIND ANOTHER BASE. WHAT'S OUR PLAN?
OUR PLAN, CAPTAIN? NOT COMMANDER, RIGHT? WASN'T IT LEIA'S LAST OFFICIAL ACT TO DEMOTE YOU? FOR YOUR DREADNOUGHT PLAN? WHERE WE LOST OUR ENTIRE BOMBER FLEET?
CAPTAIN, COMMANDER, YOU CAN CALL ME WHATEVER YOU LIKE. I JUST WANT TO KNOW WHAT'S GOING ON.
OF COURSE YOU DO. I'VE DEALT WITH PLENTY OF TRIGGERHAPPY FLYBOYS LIKE YOU. YOU'RE IMPULSIVE. DANGEROUS. AND THE LAST THING WE NEED RIGHT NOW. SO STICK TO YOUR POST AND FOLLOW MY ORDERS.

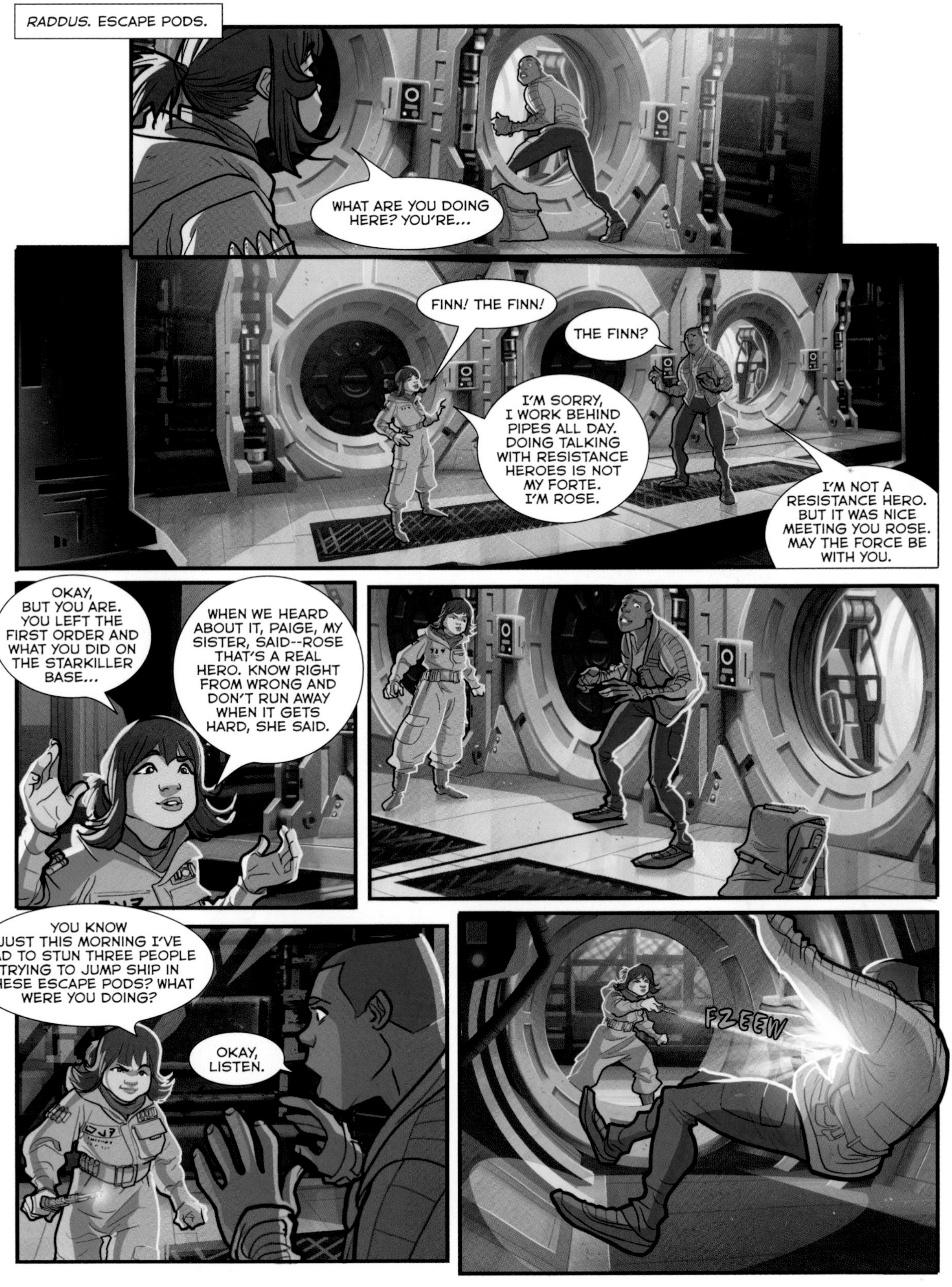
RADDUS. ESCAPE PODS.
WHAT ARE YOU DOING HERE? YOU'RE...
FINN! THE FINN!
THE FINN?
I'M SORRY, I WORK BEHIND PIPES ALL DAY. DOING TALKING WITH RESISTANCE HEROES IS NOT MY FORTE. I'M ROSE.
I'M NOT A RESISTANCE HERO. BUT IT WAS NICE MEETING YOU ROSE. MAY THE FORCE BE WITH YOU.
OKAY, BUT YOU ARE. YOU LEFT THE FIRST ORDER AND WHAT YOU DID ON THE STARKILLER BASE...
WHEN WE HEARD ABOUT IT, PAIGE, MY SISTER, SAID--ROSE THAT'S A REAL HERO. KNOW RIGHT FROM WRONG AND DON'T RUN AWAY WHEN IT GETS HARD, SHE SAID.
YOU KNOW JUST THIS MORNING I'VE HAD TO STUN THREE PEOPLE TRYING TO JUMP SHIP IN THESE ESCAPE PODS? WHAT WERE YOU DOING?
OKAY, LISTEN.
FZEEW

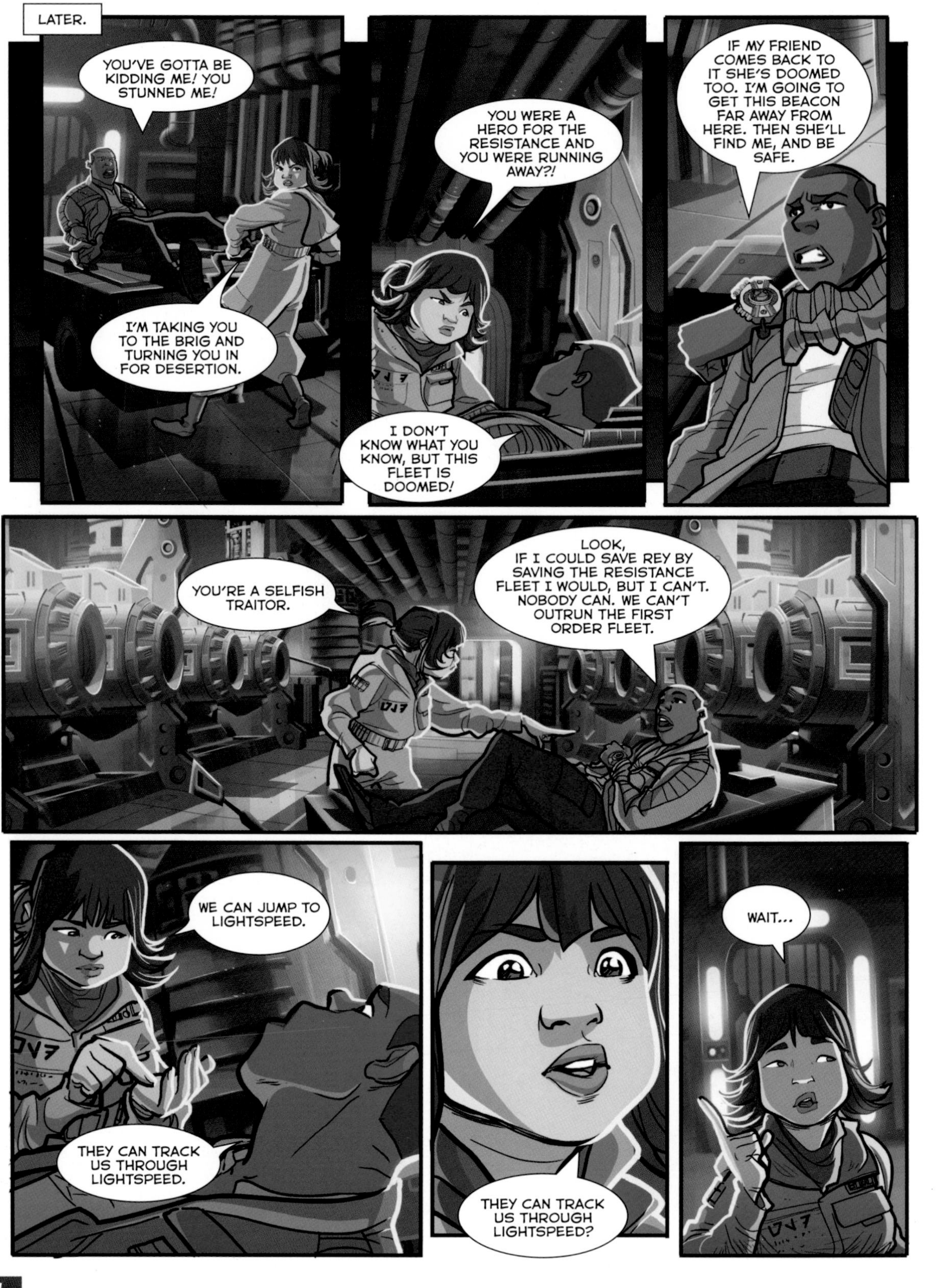
LATER.
YOU'VE GOTTA BE KIDDING ME! YOU STUNNED ME!
I'M TAKING YOU TO THE BRIG AND TURNING YOU IN FOR DESERTION.
YOU WERE A HERO FOR THE RESISTANCE AND YOU WERE RUNNING AWAY?!
I DON'T KNOW WHAT YOU KNOW, BUT THIS FLEET IS DOOMED!
IF MY FRIEND COMES BACK TO IT SHE'S DOOMED TOO. I'M GOING TO GET THIS BEACON FAR AWAY FROM HERE. THEN SHE'LL FIND ME, AND BE SAFE.
YOU'RE A SELFISH TRAITOR.
LOOK, IF I COULD SAVE REY BY SAVING THE RESISTANCE FLEET I WOULD, BUT I CAN'T. NOBODY CAN. WE CAN'T OUTRUN THE FIRST ORDER FLEET.
WE CAN JUMP TO LIGHTSPEED.
THEY CAN TRACK US THROUGH LIGHTSPEED.
THEY CAN TRACK US THROUGH LIGHTSPEED?
WAIT...

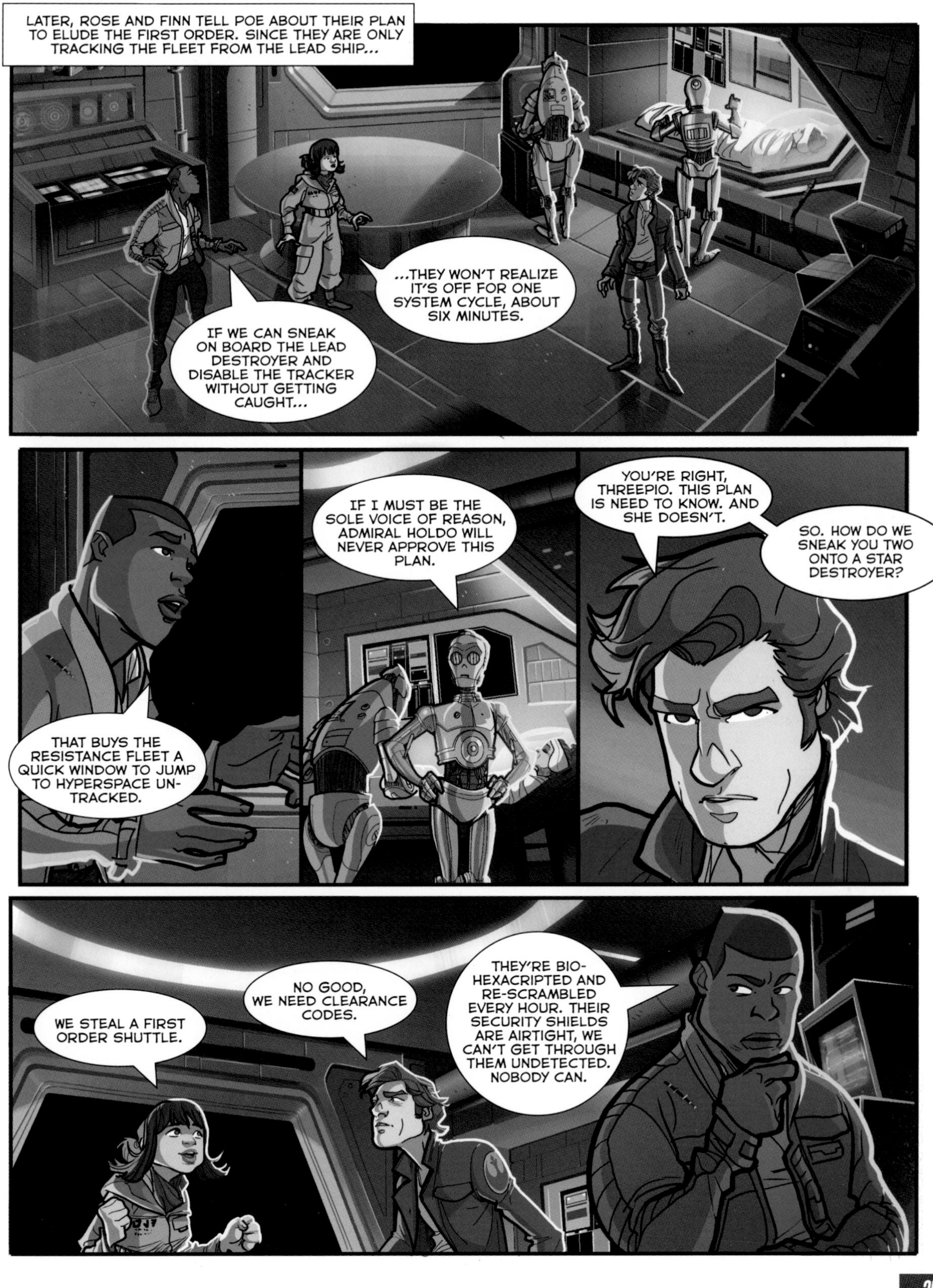
LATER, ROSE AND FINN TELL POE ABOUT THEIR PLAN TO ELUDE THE FIRST ORDER. SINCE THEY ARE ONLY TRACKING THE FLEET FROM THE LEAD SHIP...
IF WE CAN SNEAK ON BOARD THE LEAD DESTROYER AND DISABLE THE TRACKER WITHOUT GETTING CAUGHT...
...THEY WON'T REALIZE IT'S OFF FOR ONE SYSTEM CYCLE, ABOUT SIX MINUTES.
THAT BUYS THE RESISTANCE FLEET A QUICK WINDOW TO JUMP TO HYPERSPACE UN-TRACKED.
IF I MUST BE THE SOLE VOICE OF REASON, ADMIRAL HOLDO WILL NEVER APPROVE THIS PLAN.
YOU'RE RIGHT, THREEPIO. THIS PLAN IS NEED TO KNOW. AND SHE DOESN'T.
SO. HOW DO WE SNEAK YOU TWO ONTO A STAR DESTROYER?
WE STEAL A FIRST ORDER SHUTTLE.
NO GOOD, WE NEED CLEARANCE CODES.
THEY'RE BIO-HEXACRIPTED AND RE-SCRAMBLED EVERY HOUR. THEIR SECURITY SHIELDS ARE AIRTIGHT, WE CAN'T GET THROUGH THEM UNDETECTED. NOBODY CAN.

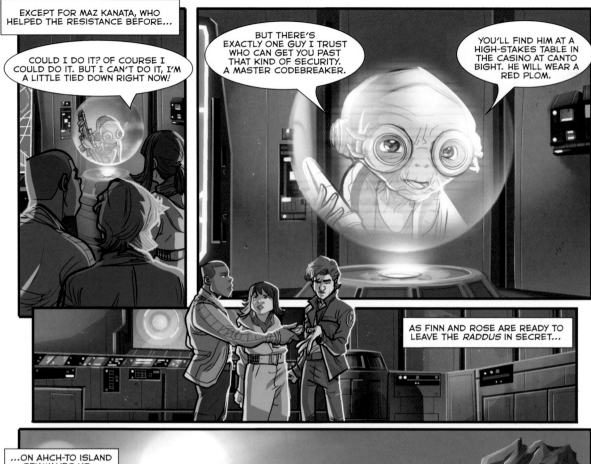

EXCEPT FOR MAZ KANATA, WHO HELPED THE RESISTANCE BEFORE...

COULD I DO IT? OF COURSE I COULD DO IT. BUT I CAN'T DO IT, I'M A LITTLE TIED DOWN RIGHT NOW!

BUT THERE'S EXACTLY ONE GUY I TRUST WHO CAN GET YOU PAST THAT KIND OF SECURITY. A MASTER CODEBREAKER.

YOU'LL FIND HIM AT A HIGH-STAKES TABLE IN THE CASINO AT CANTO BIGHT. HE WILL WEAR A RED PLOM.

AS FINN AND ROSE ARE READY TO LEAVE THE *RADDUS* IN SECRET...

...ON AHCH-TO ISLAND REY WAKES UP...

...AND SENSES SOMETHING...

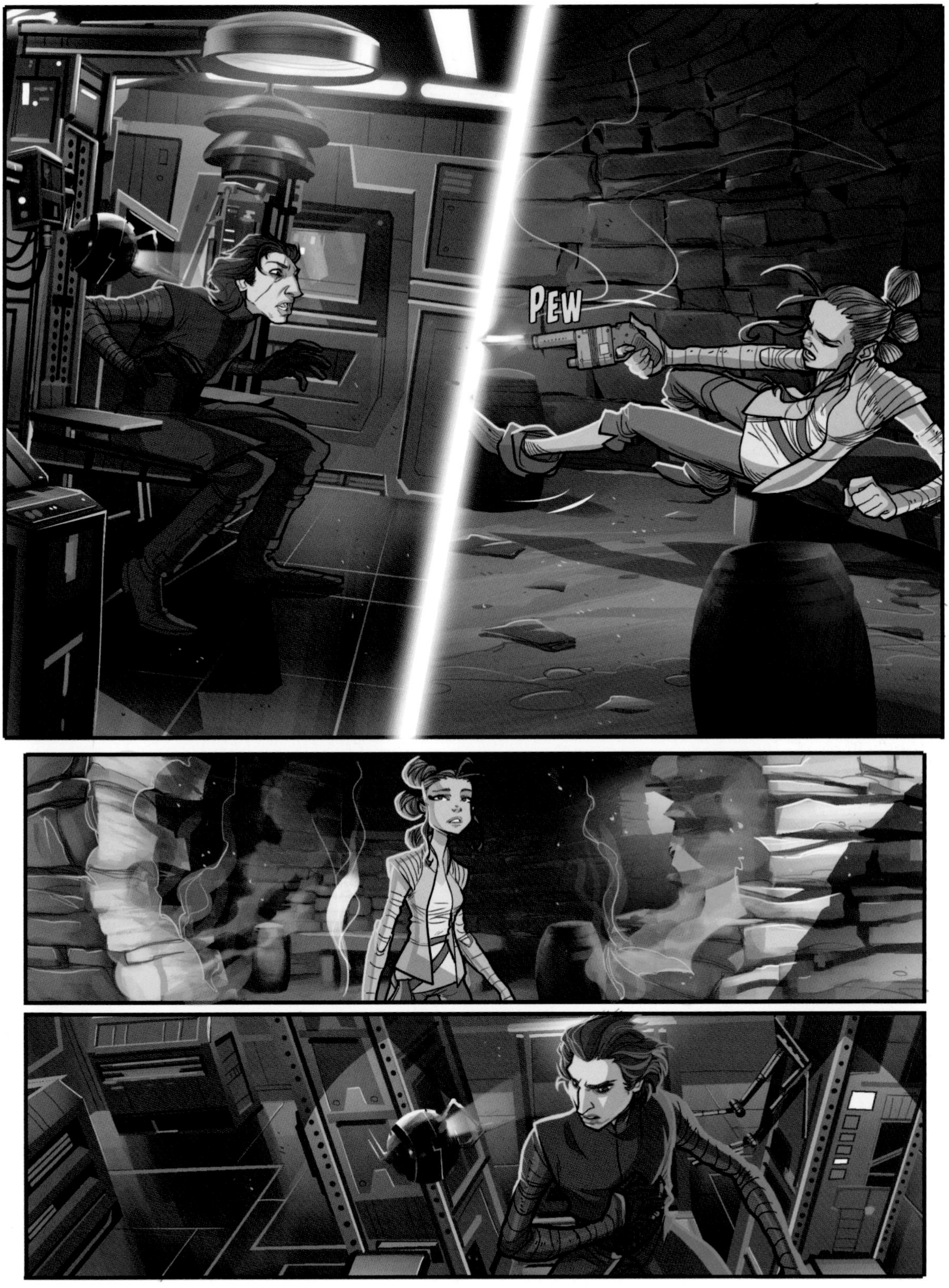
PEW

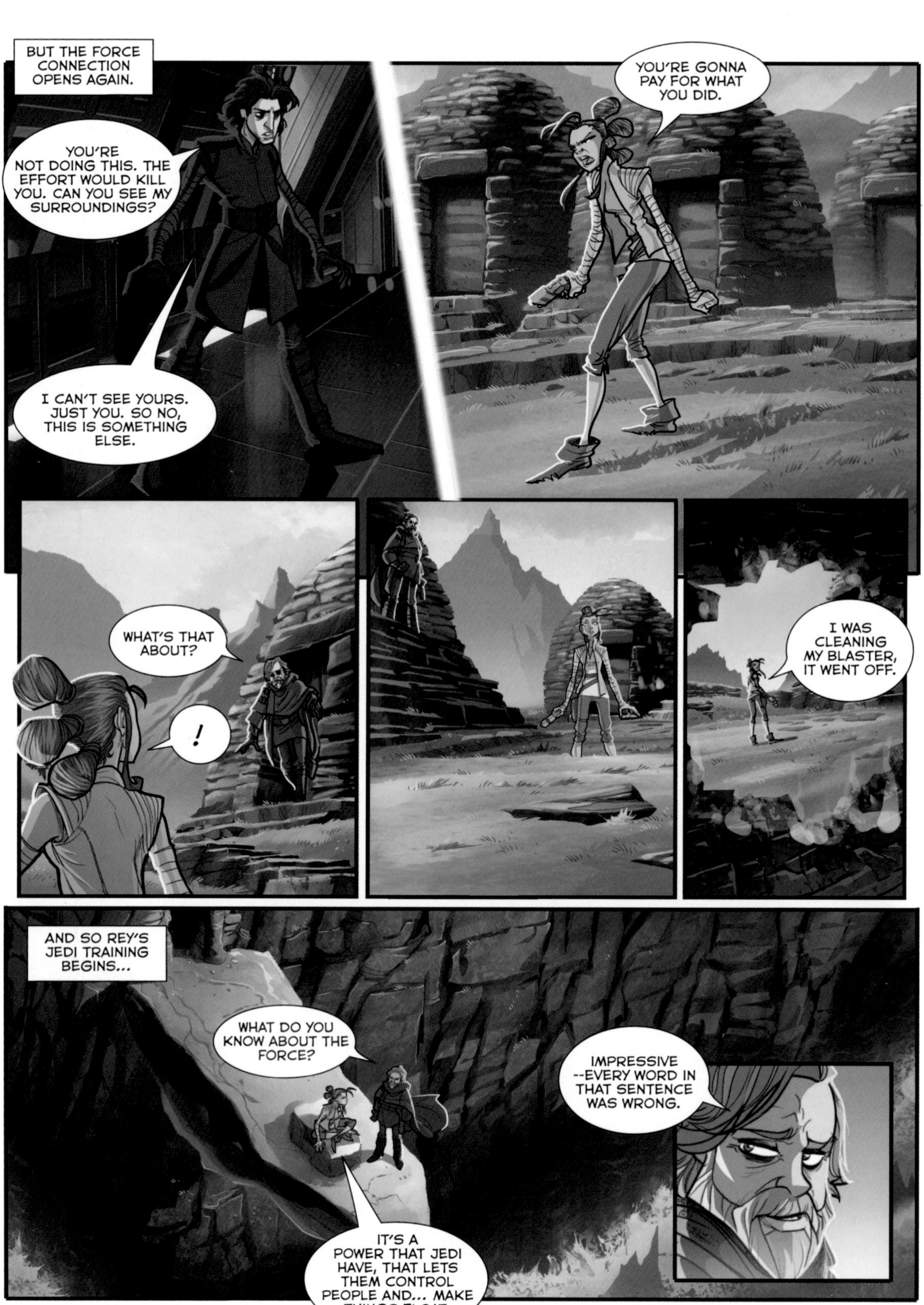
BUT THE FORCE CONNECTION OPENS AGAIN.
YOU'RE NOT DOING THIS. THE EFFORT WOULD KILL YOU. CAN YOU SEE MY SURROUNDINGS?
YOU'RE GONNA PAY FOR WHAT YOU DID.
I CAN'T SEE YOURS. JUST YOU. SO NO, THIS IS SOMETHING ELSE.
WHAT'S THAT ABOUT?
!
I WAS CLEANING MY BLASTER, IT WENT OFF.
AND SO REY'S JEDI TRAINING BEGINS...
WHAT DO YOU KNOW ABOUT THE FORCE?
IT'S A POWER THAT JEDI HAVE, THAT LETS THEM CONTROL PEOPLE AND... MAKE THINGS FLOAT.
IMPRESSIVE --EVERY WORD IN THAT SENTENCE WAS WRONG.

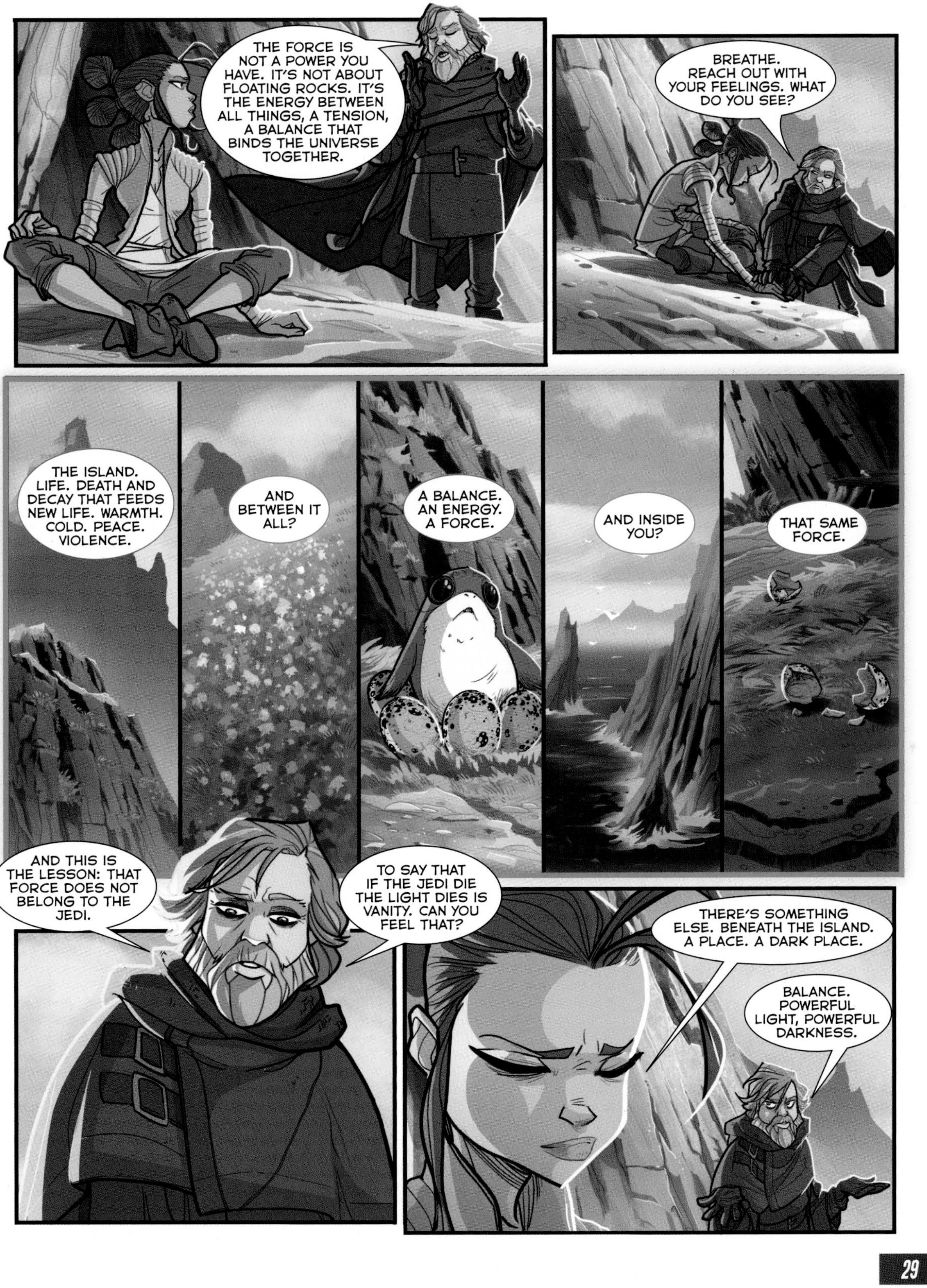
THE FORCE IS NOT A POWER YOU HAVE. IT'S NOT ABOUT FLOATING ROCKS. IT'S THE ENERGY BETWEEN ALL THINGS, A TENSION, A BALANCE THAT BINDS THE UNIVERSE TOGETHER.
BREATHE. REACH OUT WITH YOUR FEELINGS. WHAT DO YOU SEE?
THE ISLAND. LIFE. DEATH AND DECAY THAT FEEDS NEW LIFE. WARMTH. COLD. PEACE. VIOLENCE.
AND BETWEEN IT ALL?
A BALANCE. AN ENERGY. A FORCE.
AND INSIDE YOU?
THAT SAME FORCE.
AND THIS IS THE LESSON: THAT FORCE DOES NOT BELONG TO THE JEDI.
TO SAY THAT IF THE JEDI DIE THE LIGHT DIES IS VANITY. CAN YOU FEEL THAT?
THERE'S SOMETHING ELSE. BENEATH THE ISLAND. A PLACE. A DARK PLACE.
BALANCE. POWERFUL LIGHT, POWERFUL DARKNESS.

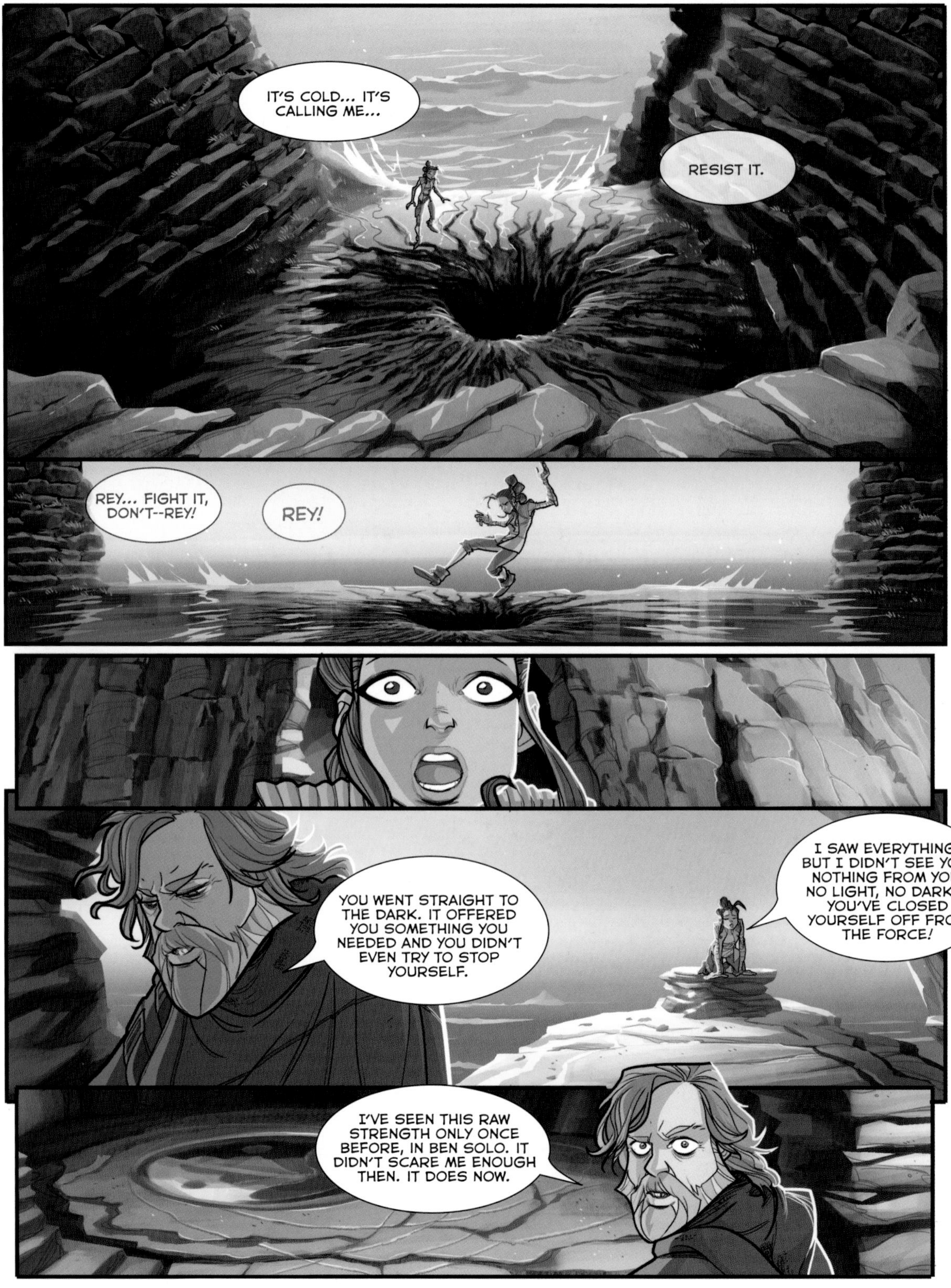

IT'S COLD... IT'S CALLING ME...
RESIST IT.
REY... FIGHT IT, DON'T--REY!
REY!
YOU WENT STRAIGHT TO THE DARK. IT OFFERED YOU SOMETHING YOU NEEDED AND YOU DIDN'T EVEN TRY TO STOP YOURSELF.
I SAW EVERYTHING. BUT I DIDN'T SEE YOU. NOTHING FROM YOU, NO LIGHT, NO DARK... YOU'VE CLOSED YOURSELF OFF FROM THE FORCE!
I'VE SEEN THIS RAW STRENGTH ONLY ONCE BEFORE, IN BEN SOLO. IT DIDN'T SCARE ME ENOUGH THEN. IT DOES NOW.

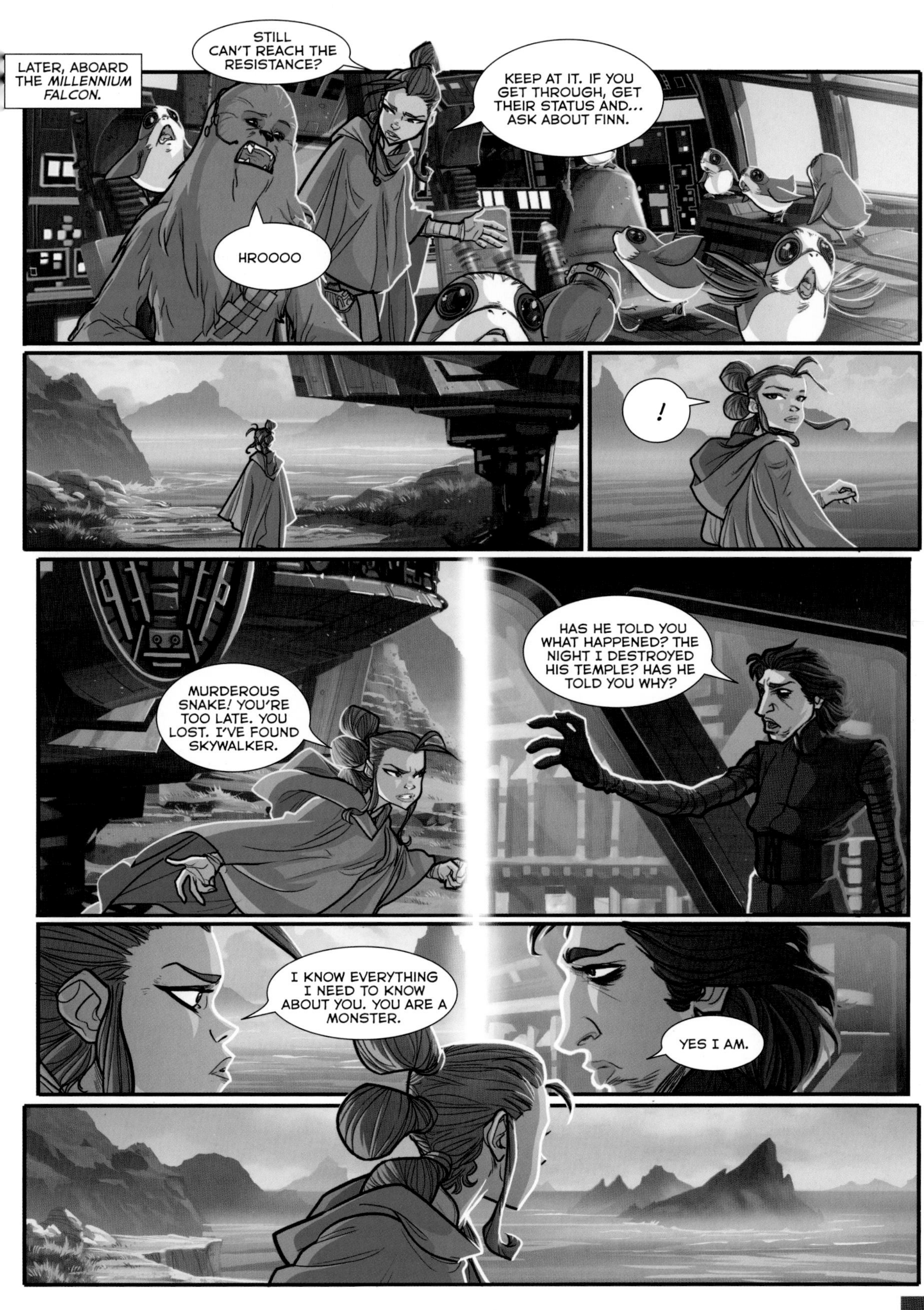
LATER, ABOARD THE *MILLENNIUM FALCON.*
STILL CAN'T REACH THE RESISTANCE?
HROOOO
KEEP AT IT. IF YOU GET THROUGH, GET THEIR STATUS AND... ASK ABOUT FINN.
!
MURDEROUS SNAKE! YOU'RE TOO LATE. YOU LOST. I'VE FOUND SKYWALKER.
HAS HE TOLD YOU WHAT HAPPENED? THE NIGHT I DESTROYED HIS TEMPLE? HAS HE TOLD YOU WHY?
I KNOW EVERYTHING I NEED TO KNOW ABOUT YOU. YOU ARE A MONSTER.
YES I AM.

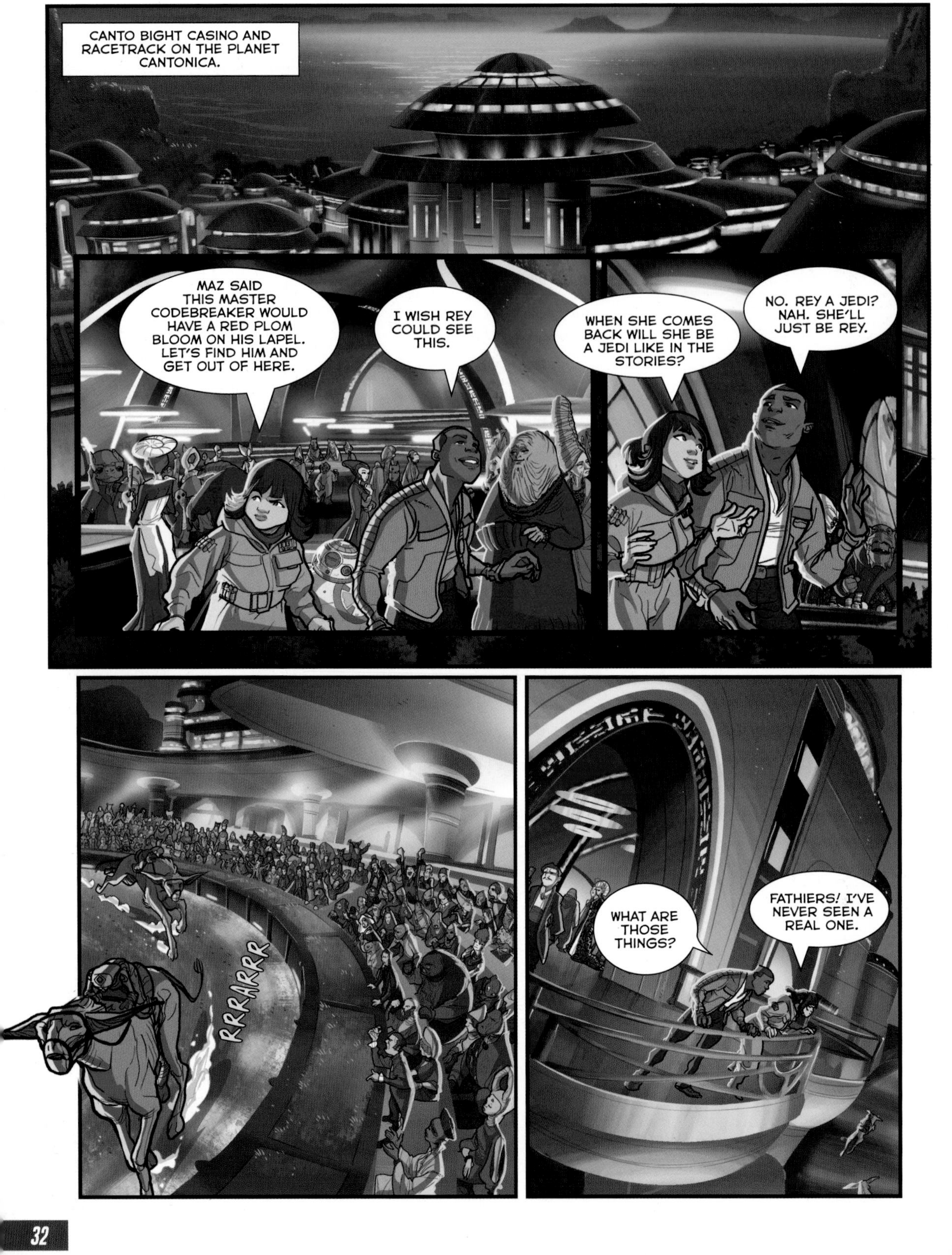
CANTO BIGHT CASINO AND RACETRACK ON THE PLANET CANTONICA.
MAZ SAID THIS MASTER CODEBREAKER WOULD HAVE A RED PLOM BLOOM ON HIS LAPEL. LET'S FIND HIM AND GET OUT OF HERE.
I WISH REY COULD SEE THIS.
WHEN SHE COMES BACK WILL SHE BE A JEDI LIKE IN THE STORIES?
NO. REY A JEDI? NAH. SHE'LL JUST BE REY.
RRRARRR
WHAT ARE THOSE THINGS?
FATHIERS! I'VE NEVER SEEN A REAL ONE.

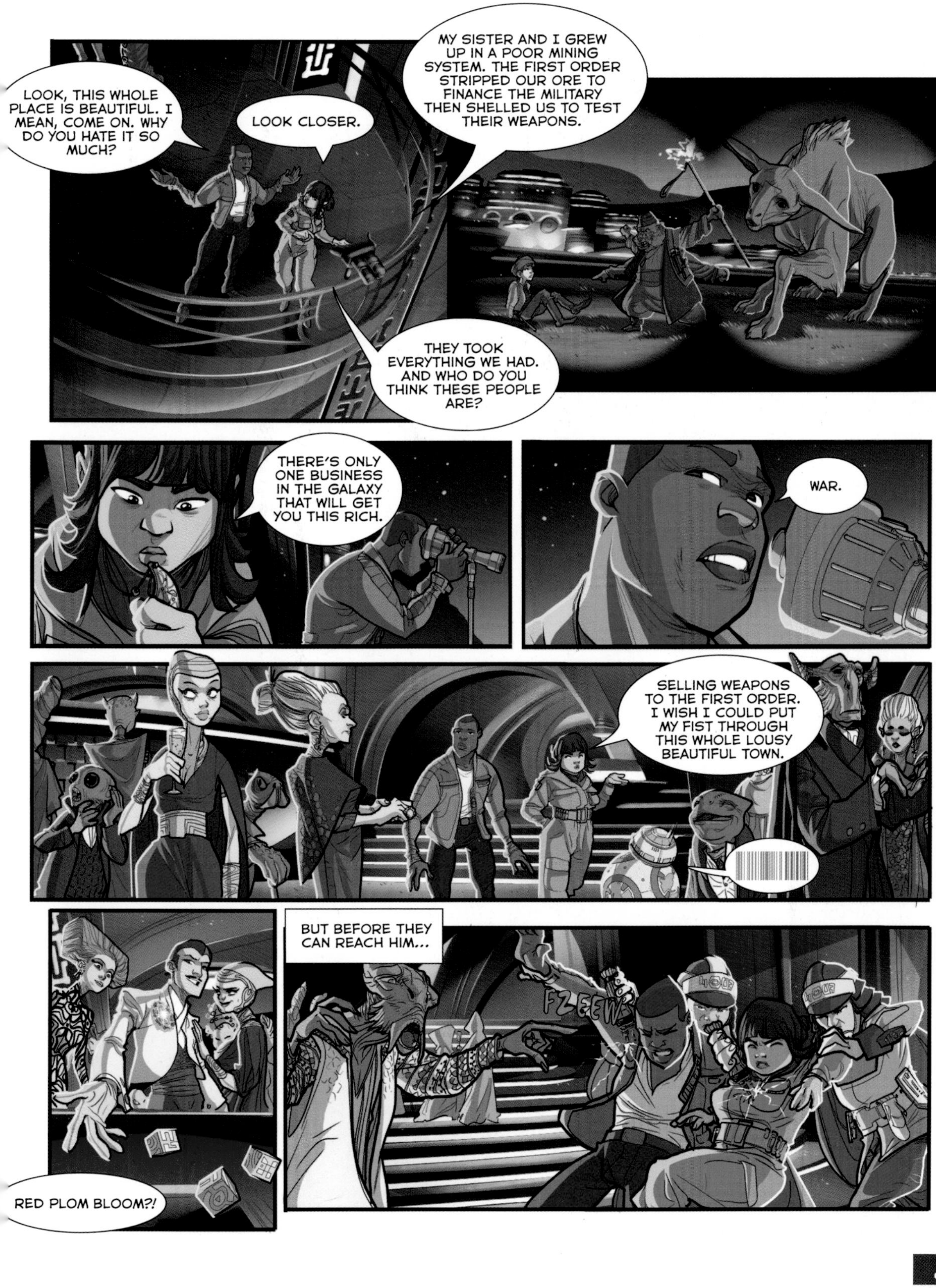

LOOK, THIS WHOLE PLACE IS BEAUTIFUL. I MEAN, COME ON. WHY DO YOU HATE IT SO MUCH?
LOOK CLOSER.
MY SISTER AND I GREW UP IN A POOR MINING SYSTEM. THE FIRST ORDER STRIPPED OUR ORE TO FINANCE THE MILITARY THEN SHELLED US TO TEST THEIR WEAPONS.
THEY TOOK EVERYTHING WE HAD. AND WHO DO YOU THINK THESE PEOPLE ARE?
THERE'S ONLY ONE BUSINESS IN THE GALAXY THAT WILL GET YOU THIS RICH.
WAR.
SELLING WEAPONS TO THE FIRST ORDER. I WISH I COULD PUT MY FIST THROUGH THIS WHOLE LOUSY BEAUTIFUL TOWN.
RED PLOM BLOOM?!
BUT BEFORE THEY CAN REACH HIM...
FZEEW

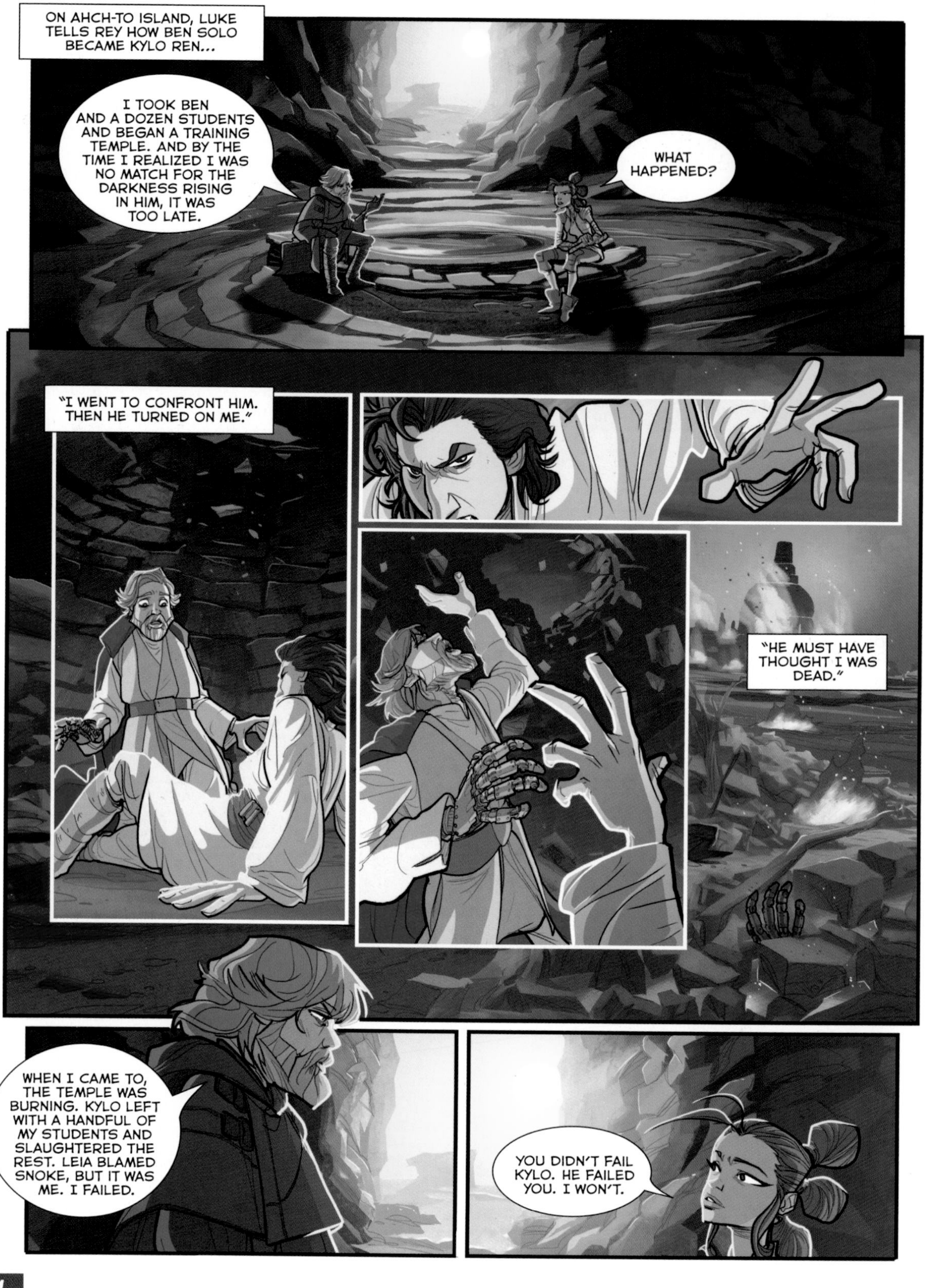
ON AHCH-TO ISLAND, LUKE TELLS REY HOW BEN SOLO BECAME KYLO REN...
I TOOK BEN AND A DOZEN STUDENTS AND BEGAN A TRAINING TEMPLE. AND BY THE TIME I REALIZED I WAS NO MATCH FOR THE DARKNESS RISING IN HIM, IT WAS TOO LATE.
WHAT HAPPENED?
"I WENT TO CONFRONT HIM. THEN HE TURNED ON ME."
"HE MUST HAVE THOUGHT I WAS DEAD."
WHEN I CAME TO, THE TEMPLE WAS BURNING. KYLO LEFT WITH A HANDFUL OF MY STUDENTS AND SLAUGHTERED THE REST. LEIA BLAMED SNOKE, BUT IT WAS ME. I FAILED.
YOU DIDN'T FAIL KYLO. HE FAILED YOU. I WON'T.

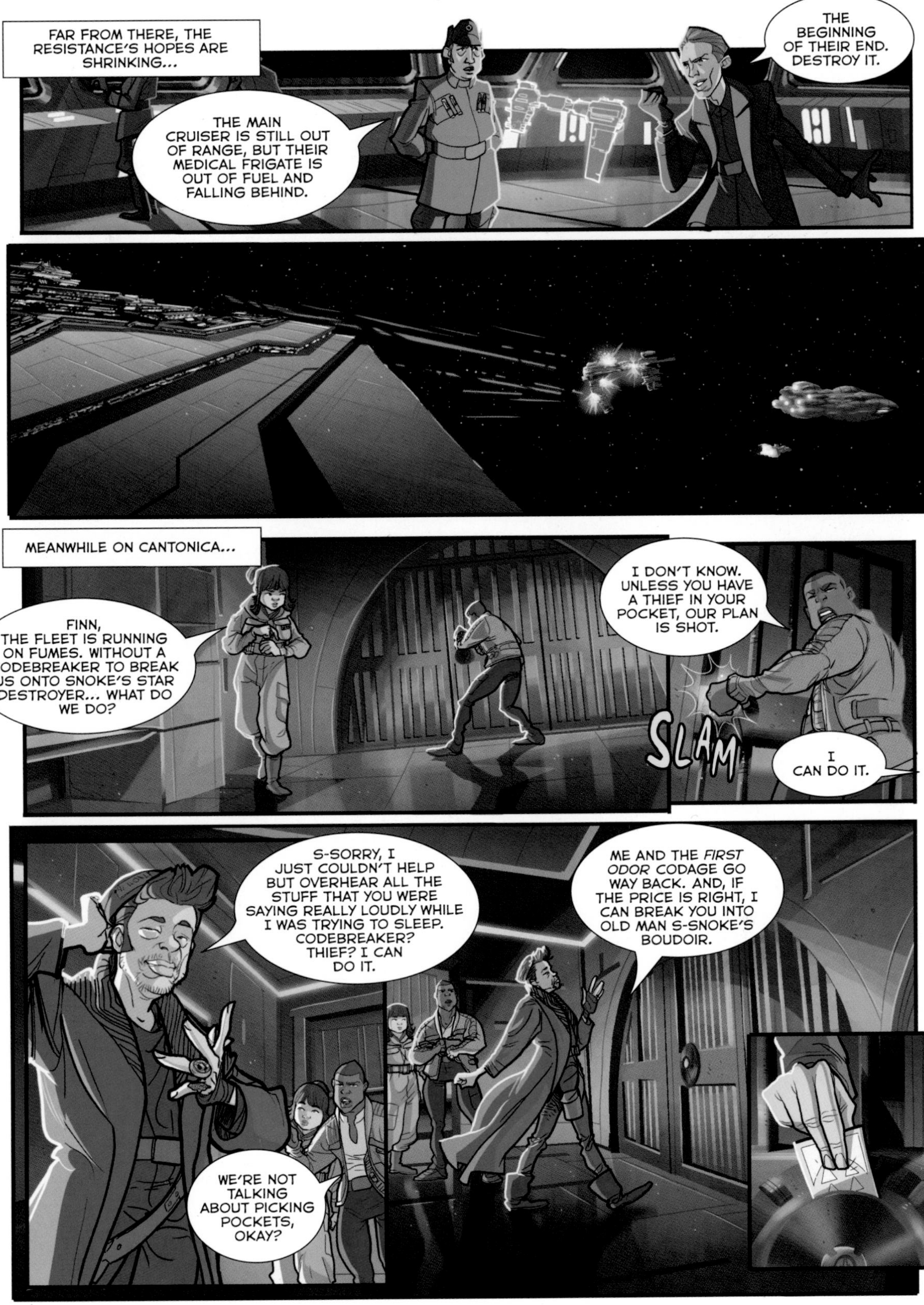
FAR FROM THERE, THE RESISTANCE'S HOPES ARE SHRINKING...
THE MAIN CRUISER IS STILL OUT OF RANGE, BUT THEIR MEDICAL FRIGATE IS OUT OF FUEL AND FALLING BEHIND.
THE BEGINNING OF THEIR END. DESTROY IT.
MEANWHILE ON CANTONICA...
FINN, THE FLEET IS RUNNING ON FUMES. WITHOUT A CODEBREAKER TO BREAK US ONTO SNOKE'S STAR DESTROYER... WHAT DO WE DO?
I DON'T KNOW. UNLESS YOU HAVE A THIEF IN YOUR POCKET, OUR PLAN IS SHOT.
SLAM
I CAN DO IT.
S-SORRY, I JUST COULDN'T HELP BUT OVERHEAR ALL THE STUFF THAT YOU WERE SAYING REALLY LOUDLY WHILE I WAS TRYING TO SLEEP. CODEBREAKER? THIEF? I CAN DO IT.
WE'RE NOT TALKING ABOUT PICKING POCKETS, OKAY?
ME AND THE *FIRST ODOR* CODAGE GO WAY BACK. AND, IF THE PRICE IS RIGHT, I CAN BREAK YOU INTO OLD MAN S-SNOKE'S BOUDOIR.

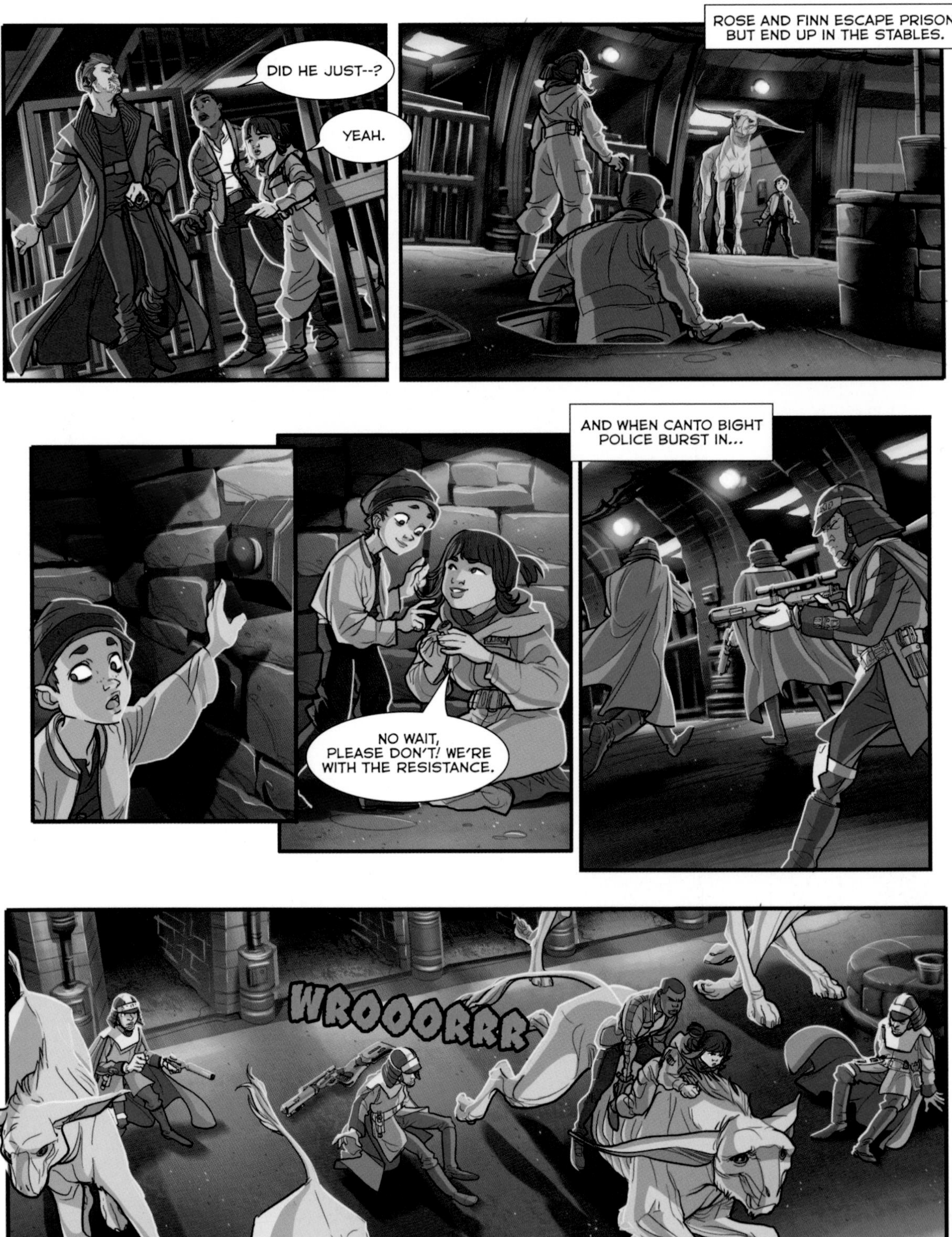
DID HE JUST--?
YEAH.
ROSE AND FINN ESCAPE PRISON, BUT END UP IN THE STABLES.
AND WHEN CANTO BIGHT POLICE BURST IN...
NO WAIT, PLEASE DON'T! WE'RE WITH THE RESISTANCE.
WROOOORRR

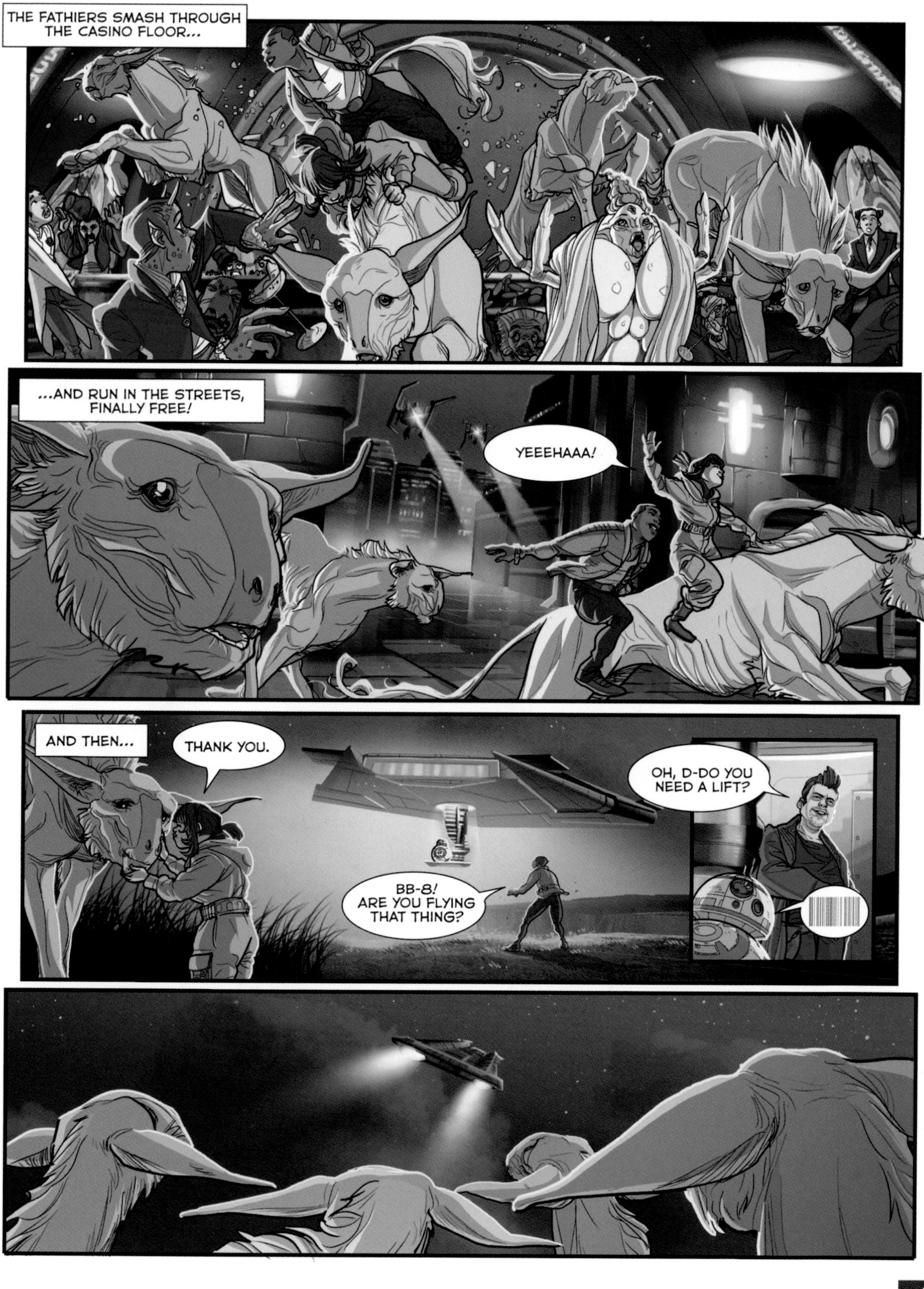
THE FATHIERS SMASH THROUGH THE CASINO FLOOR...
...AND RUN IN THE STREETS, FINALLY FREE!
YEEEHAAA!
AND THEN...
THANK YOU.
BB-8! ARE YOU FLYING THAT THING?
OH, D-DO YOU NEED A LIFT?

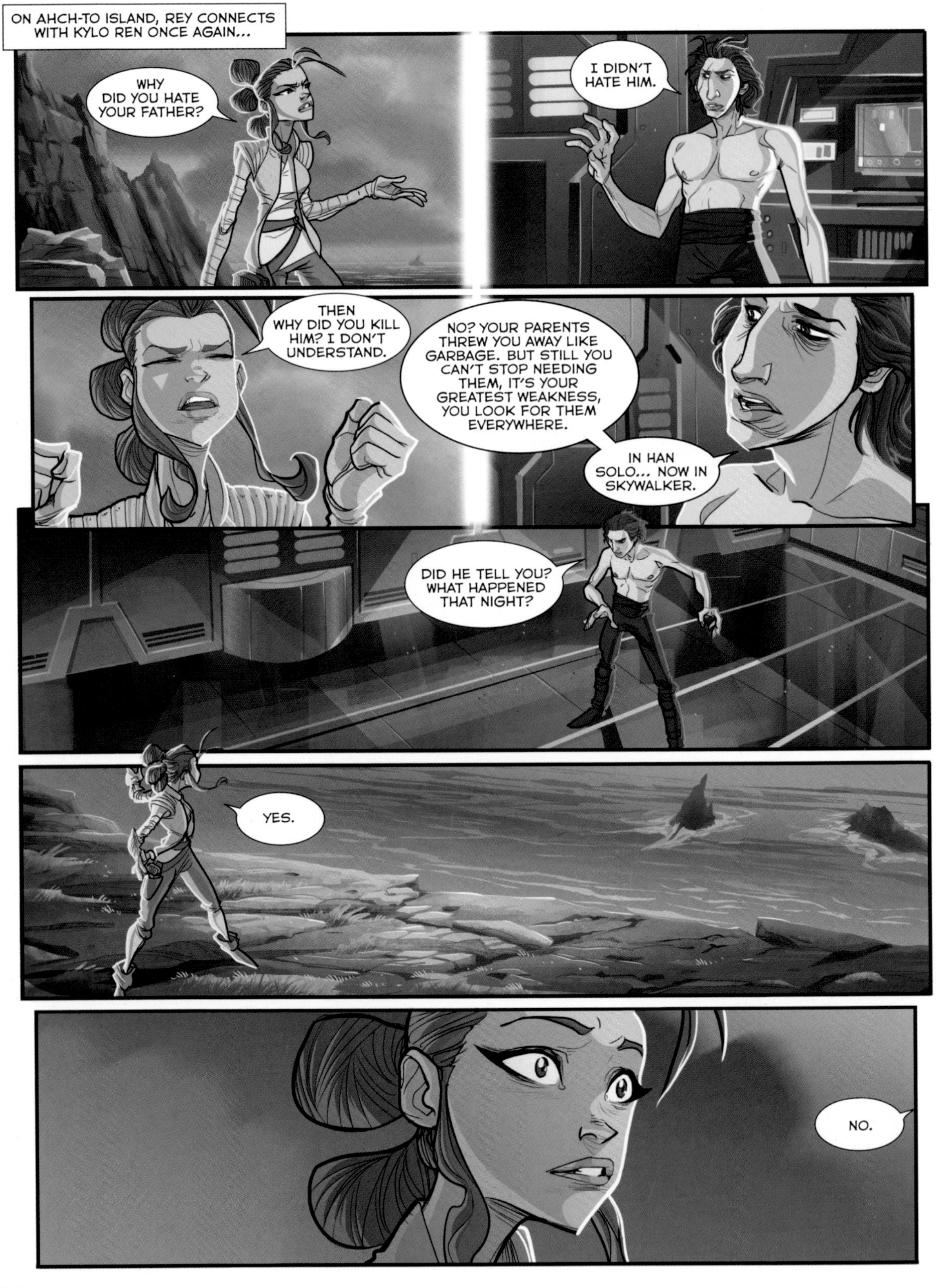
ON AHCH-TO ISLAND, REY CONNECTS WITH KYLO REN ONCE AGAIN...
WHY DID YOU HATE YOUR FATHER?
I DIDN'T HATE HIM.
THEN WHY DID YOU KILL HIM? I DON'T UNDERSTAND.
NO? YOUR PARENTS THREW YOU AWAY LIKE GARBAGE. BUT STILL YOU CAN'T STOP NEEDING THEM, IT'S YOUR GREATEST WEAKNESS, YOU LOOK FOR THEM EVERYWHERE.
IN HAN SOLO... NOW IN SKYWALKER.
DID HE TELL YOU? WHAT HAPPENED THAT NIGHT?
YES.
NO.

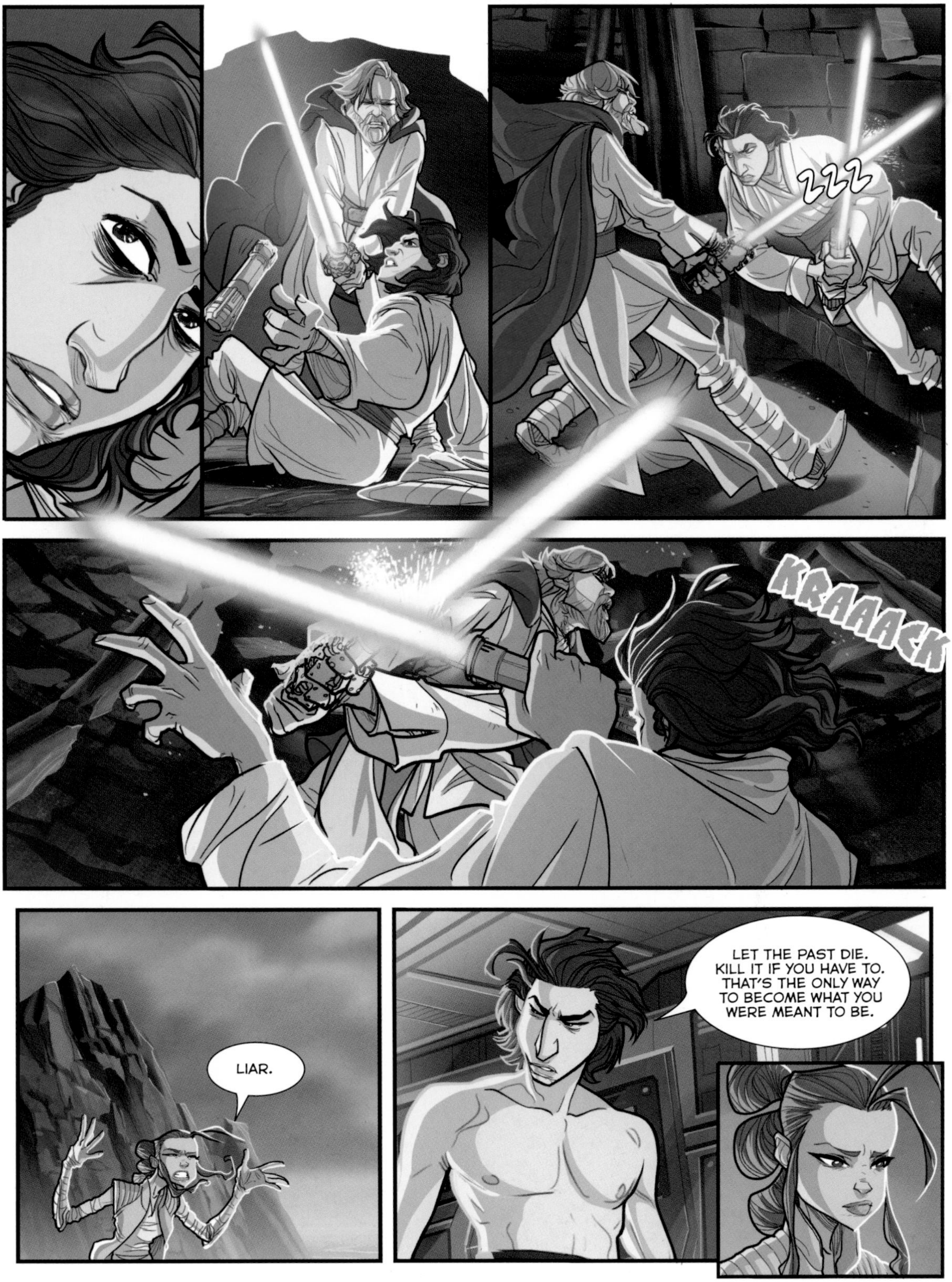
ZZZ
KRAAAACK
LIAR.
LET THE PAST DIE. KILL IT IF YOU HAVE TO. THAT'S THE ONLY WAY TO BECOME WHAT YOU WERE MEANT TO BE.

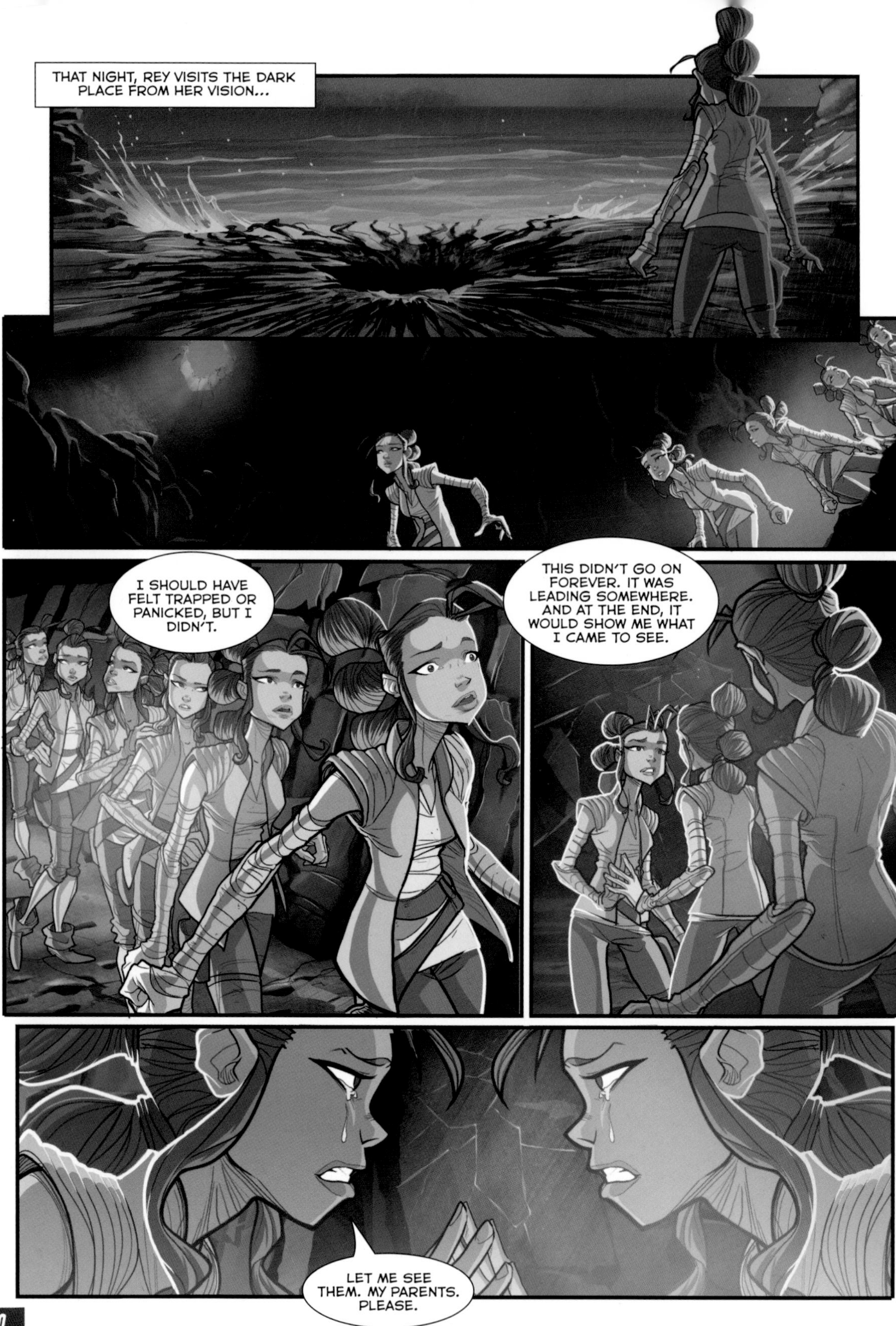
THAT NIGHT, REY VISITS THE DARK PLACE FROM HER VISION...
I SHOULD HAVE FELT TRAPPED OR PANICKED, BUT I DIDN'T.
THIS DIDN'T GO ON FOREVER. IT WAS LEADING SOMEWHERE. AND AT THE END, IT WOULD SHOW ME WHAT I CAME TO SEE.
LET ME SEE THEM. MY PARENTS. PLEASE.

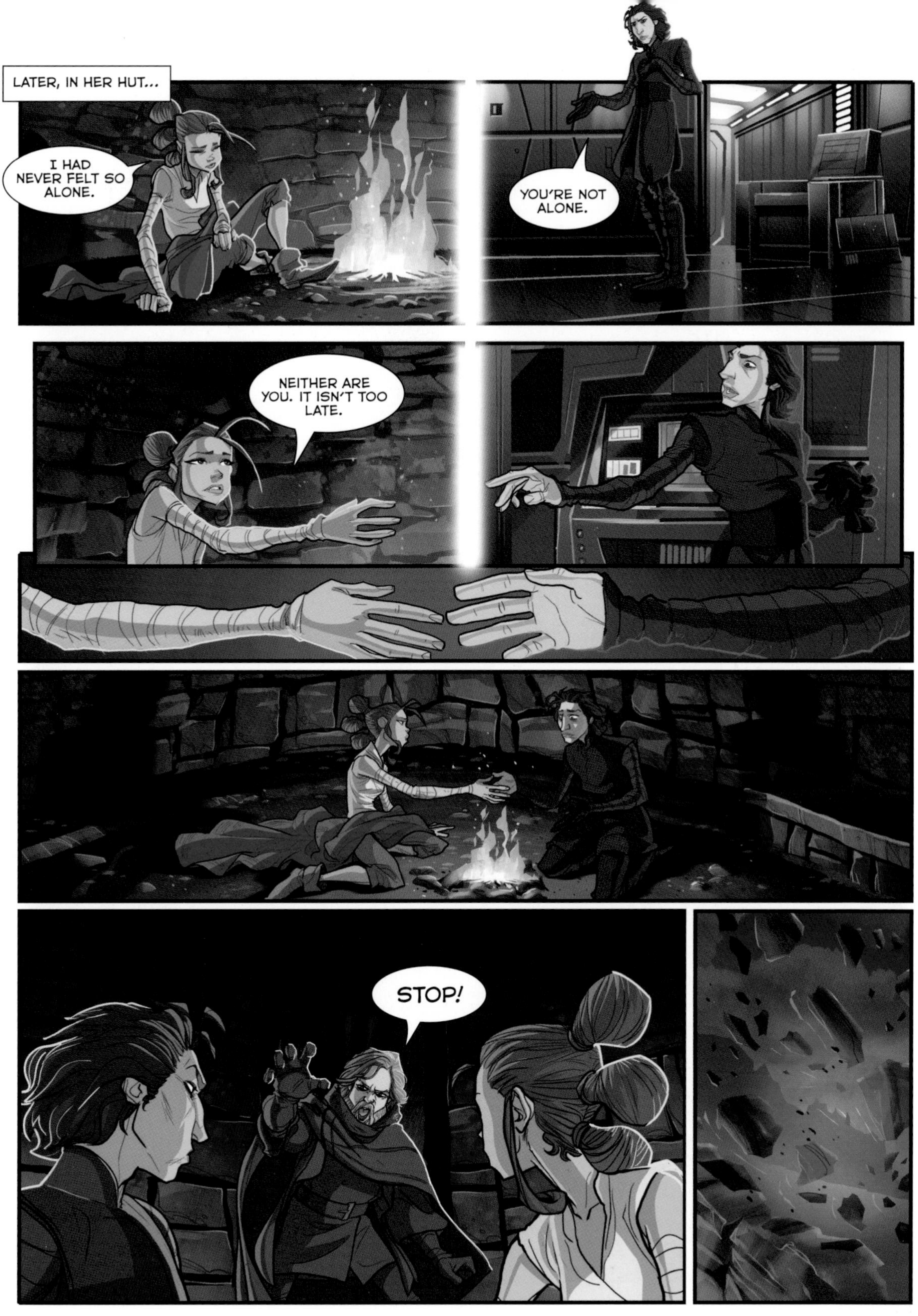
LATER, IN HER HUT...
I HAD NEVER FELT SO ALONE.
YOU'RE NOT ALONE.
NEITHER ARE YOU. IT ISN'T TOO LATE.
STOP!

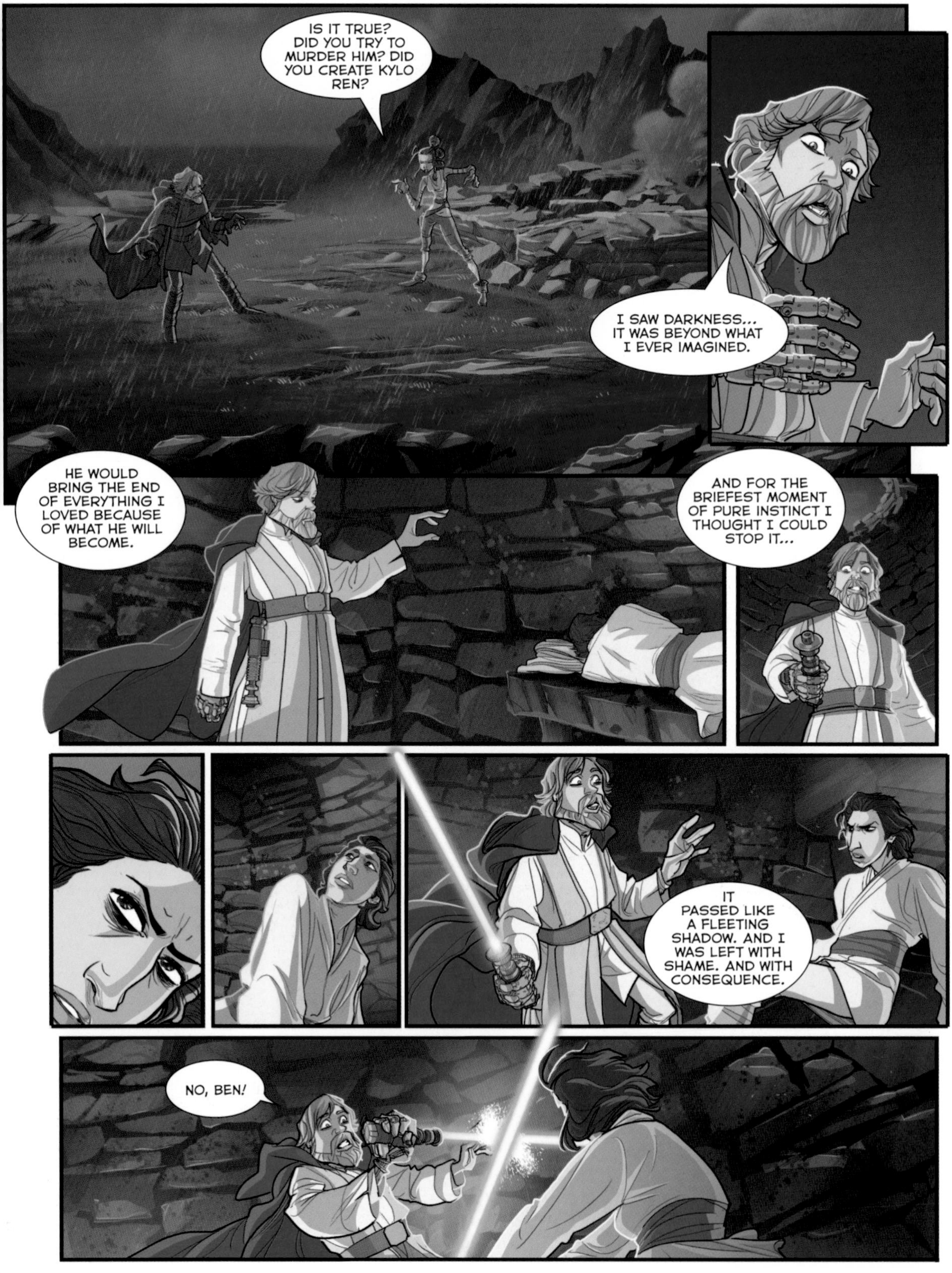
IS IT TRUE? DID YOU TRY TO MURDER HIM? DID YOU CREATE KYLO REN?
I SAW DARKNESS... IT WAS BEYOND WHAT I EVER IMAGINED.
HE WOULD BRING THE END OF EVERYTHING I LOVED BECAUSE OF WHAT HE WILL BECOME.
AND FOR THE BRIEFEST MOMENT OF PURE INSTINCT I THOUGHT I COULD STOP IT...
IT PASSED LIKE A FLEETING SHADOW. AND I WAS LEFT WITH SHAME. AND WITH CONSEQUENCE.
NO, BEN!

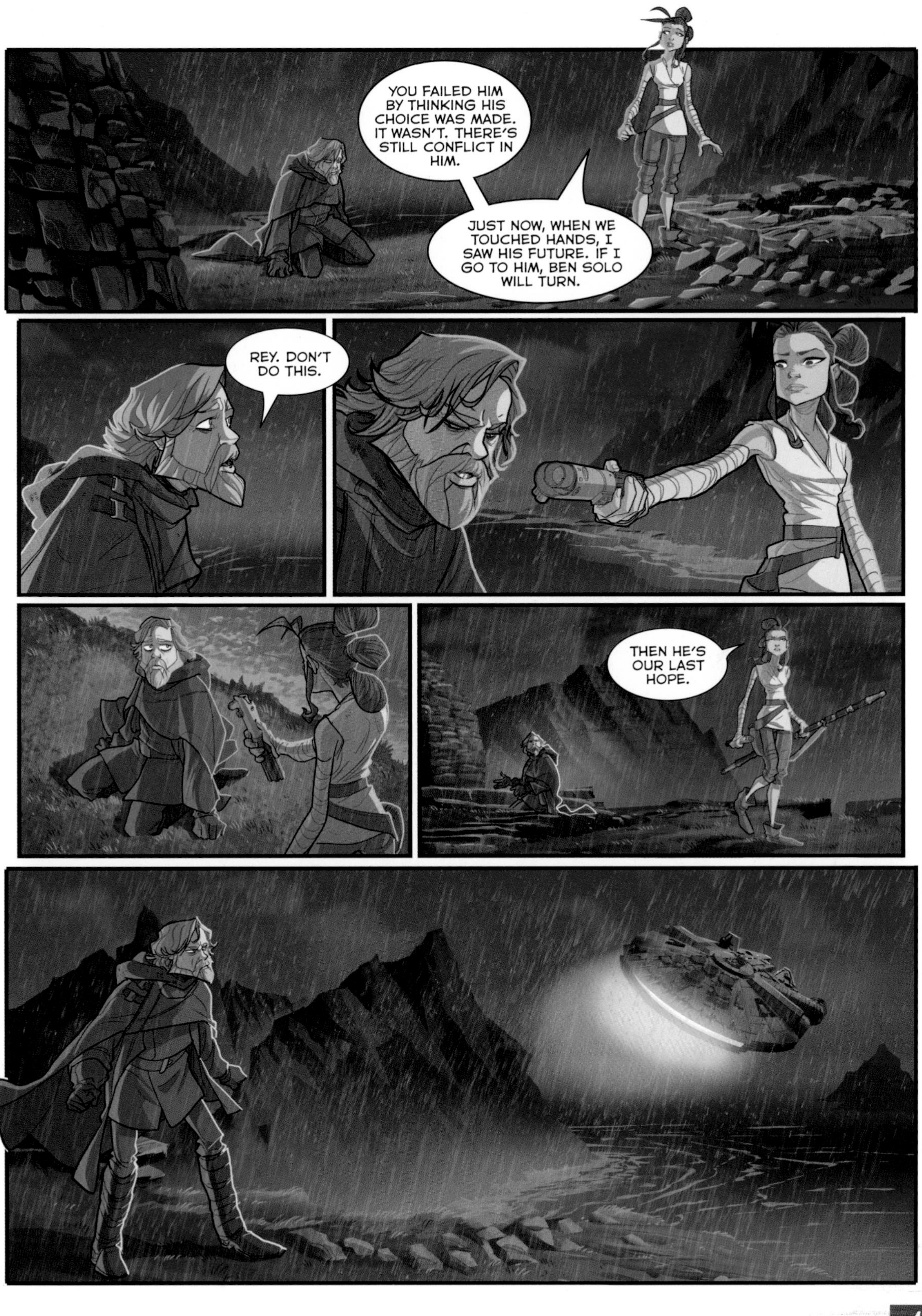
YOU FAILED HIM BY THINKING HIS CHOICE WAS MADE. IT WASN'T. THERE'S STILL CONFLICT IN HIM.
JUST NOW, WHEN WE TOUCHED HANDS, I SAW HIS FUTURE. IF I GO TO HIM, BEN SOLO WILL TURN.
REY. DON'T DO THIS.
THEN HE'S OUR LAST HOPE.

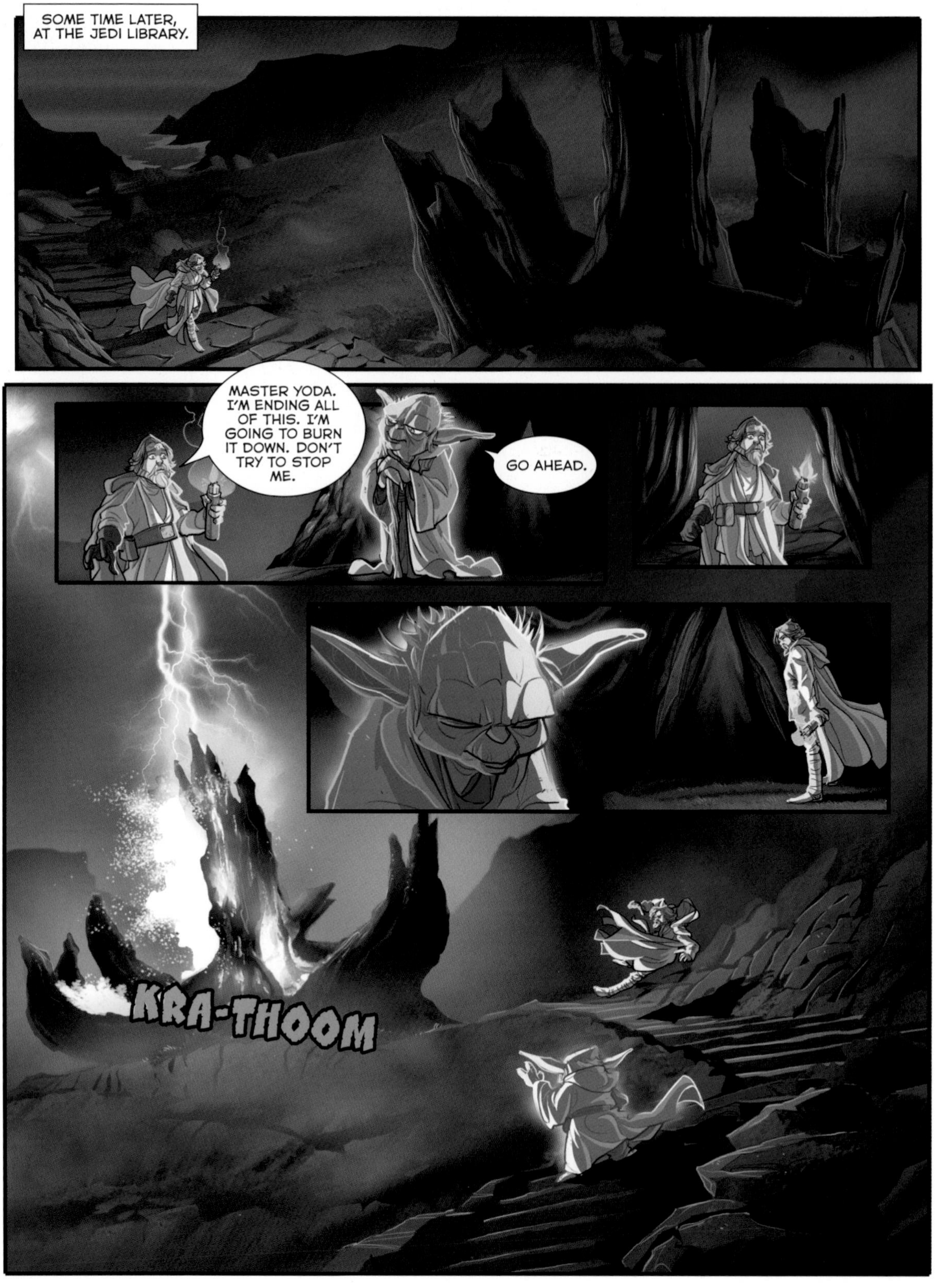
SOME TIME LATER, AT THE JEDI LIBRARY.
MASTER YODA. I'M ENDING ALL OF THIS. I'M GOING TO BURN IT DOWN. DON'T TRY TO STOP ME.
GO AHEAD.
KRA-THOOM

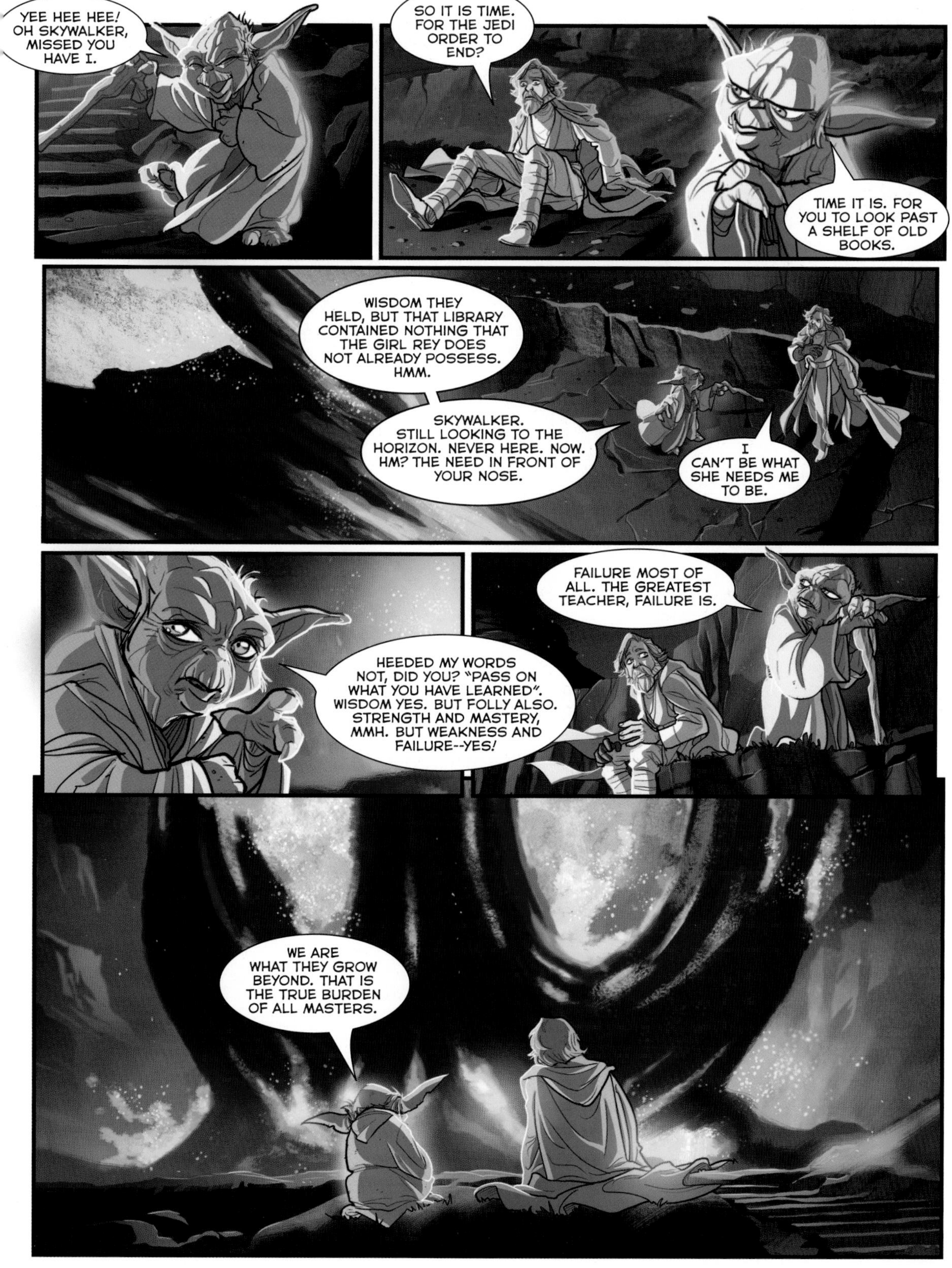
YEE HEE HEE! OH SKYWALKER, MISSED YOU HAVE I.
SO IT IS TIME. FOR THE JEDI ORDER TO END?
TIME IT IS. FOR YOU TO LOOK PAST A SHELF OF OLD BOOKS.
WISDOM THEY HELD, BUT THAT LIBRARY CONTAINED NOTHING THAT THE GIRL REY DOES NOT ALREADY POSSESS. HMM.
SKYWALKER. STILL LOOKING TO THE HORIZON. NEVER HERE. NOW. HM? THE NEED IN FRONT OF YOUR NOSE.
I CAN'T BE WHAT SHE NEEDS ME TO BE.
HEEDED MY WORDS NOT, DID YOU? "PASS ON WHAT YOU HAVE LEARNED". WISDOM YES. BUT FOLLY ALSO. STRENGTH AND MASTERY, MMH. BUT WEAKNESS AND FAILURE--YES!
FAILURE MOST OF ALL. THE GREATEST TEACHER, FAILURE IS.
WE ARE WHAT THEY GROW BEYOND. THAT IS THE TRUE BURDEN OF ALL MASTERS.

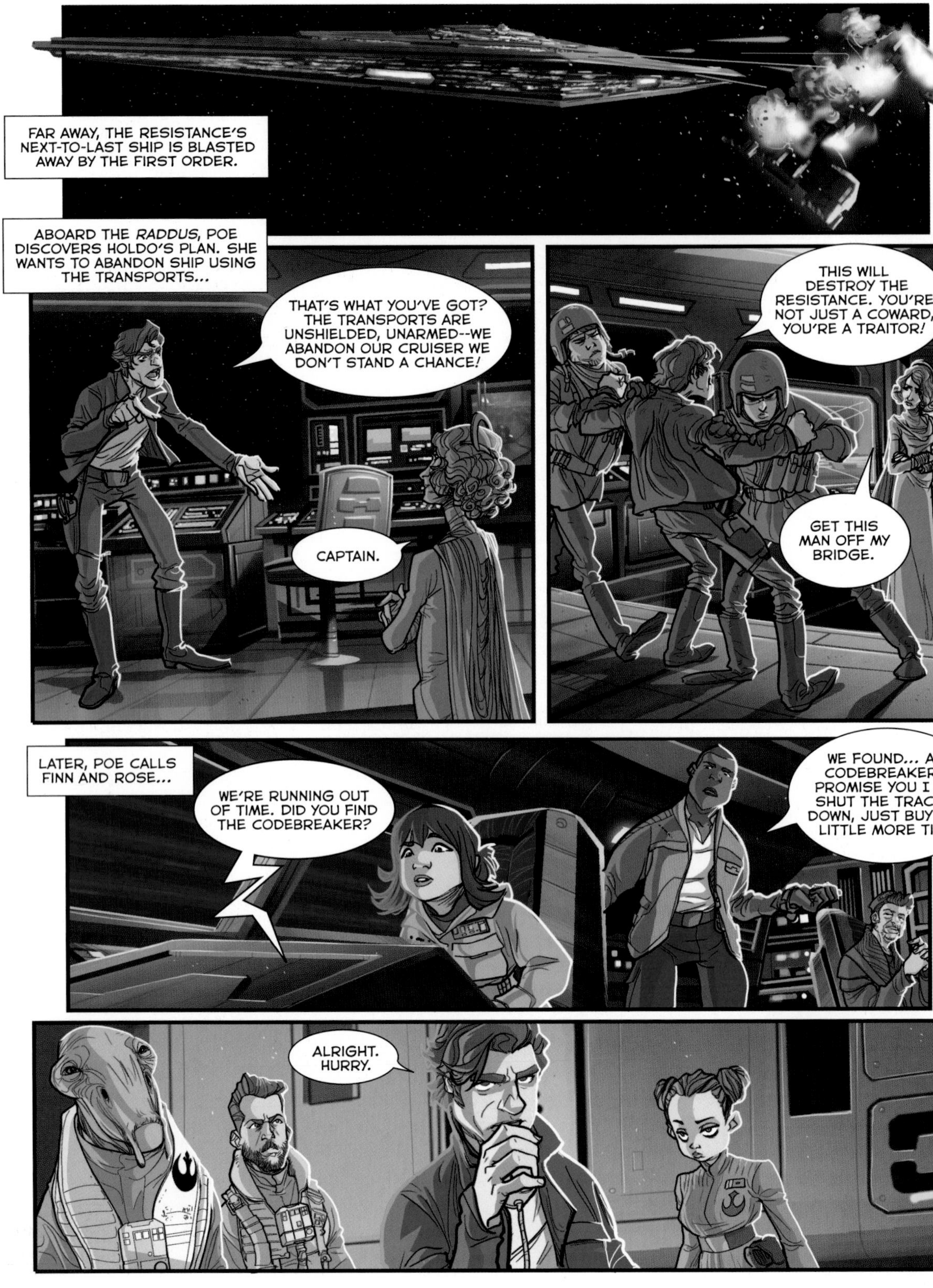
FAR AWAY, THE RESISTANCE'S NEXT-TO-LAST SHIP IS BLASTED AWAY BY THE FIRST ORDER.
ABOARD THE *RADDUS*, POE DISCOVERS HOLDO'S PLAN. SHE WANTS TO ABANDON SHIP USING THE TRANSPORTS...
THAT'S WHAT YOU'VE GOT? THE TRANSPORTS ARE UNSHIELDED, UNARMED--WE ABANDON OUR CRUISER WE DON'T STAND A CHANCE!
CAPTAIN.
THIS WILL DESTROY THE RESISTANCE. YOU'RE NOT JUST A COWARD, YOU'RE A TRAITOR!
GET THIS MAN OFF MY BRIDGE.
LATER, POE CALLS FINN AND ROSE...
WE'RE RUNNING OUT OF TIME. DID YOU FIND THE CODEBREAKER?
WE FOUND... A... CODEBREAKER. I PROMISE YOU I CAN SHUT THE TRACKER DOWN, JUST BUY US A LITTLE MORE TIME.
ALRIGHT. HURRY.

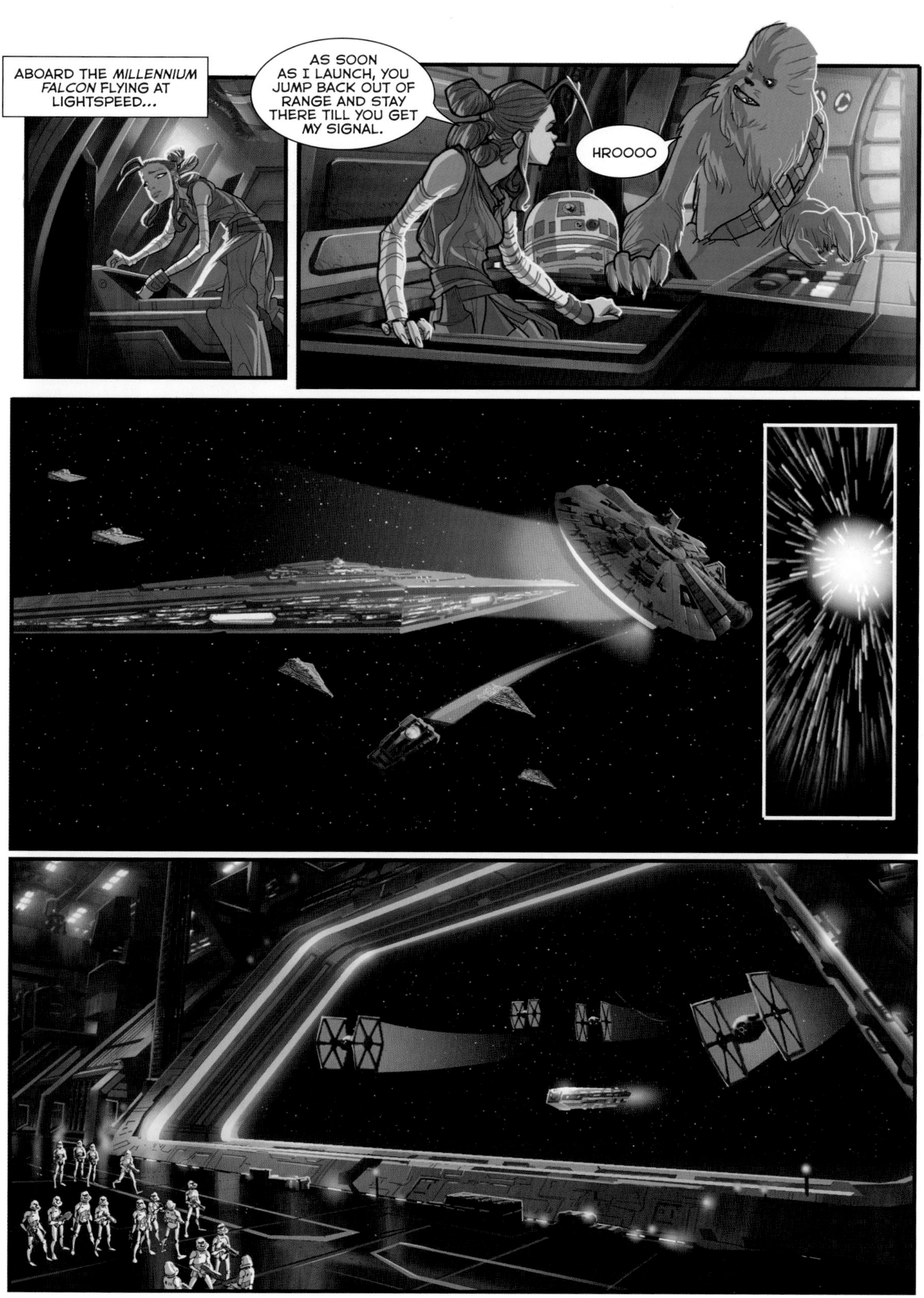
ABOARD THE MILLENNIUM FALCON FLYING AT LIGHTSPEED...
AS SOON AS I LAUNCH, YOU JUMP BACK OUT OF RANGE AND STAY THERE TILL YOU GET MY SIGNAL.
HROOOO

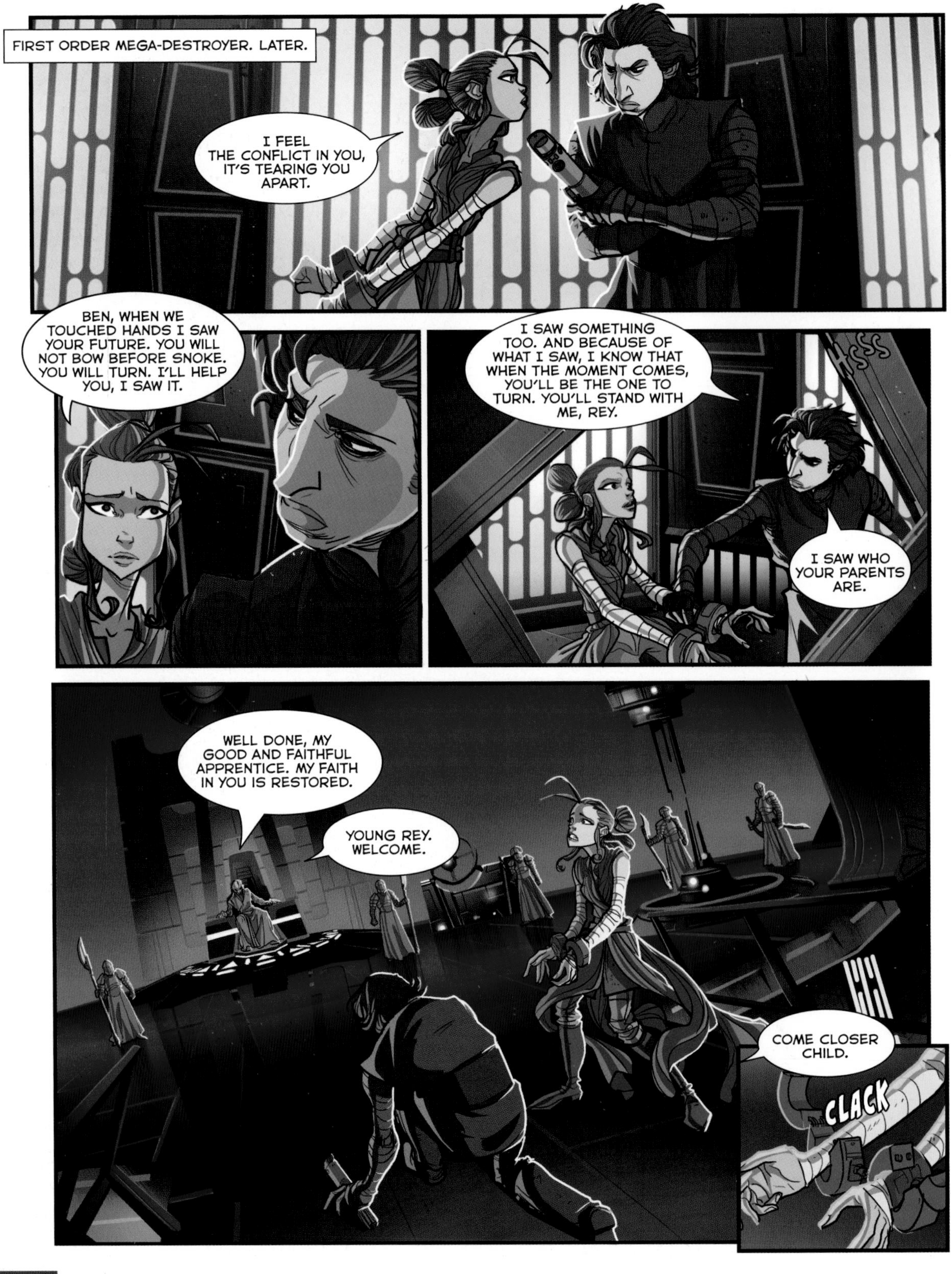
FIRST ORDER MEGA-DESTROYER. LATER.
I FEEL THE CONFLICT IN YOU, IT'S TEARING YOU APART.
BEN, WHEN WE TOUCHED HANDS I SAW YOUR FUTURE. YOU WILL NOT BOW BEFORE SNOKE. YOU WILL TURN. I'LL HELP YOU, I SAW IT.
I SAW SOMETHING TOO. AND BECAUSE OF WHAT I SAW, I KNOW THAT WHEN THE MOMENT COMES, YOU'LL BE THE ONE TO TURN. YOU'LL STAND WITH ME, REY.
I SAW WHO YOUR PARENTS ARE.
WELL DONE, MY GOOD AND FAITHFUL APPRENTICE. MY FAITH IN YOU IS RESTORED.
YOUNG REY. WELCOME.
COME CLOSER CHILD.
CLACK

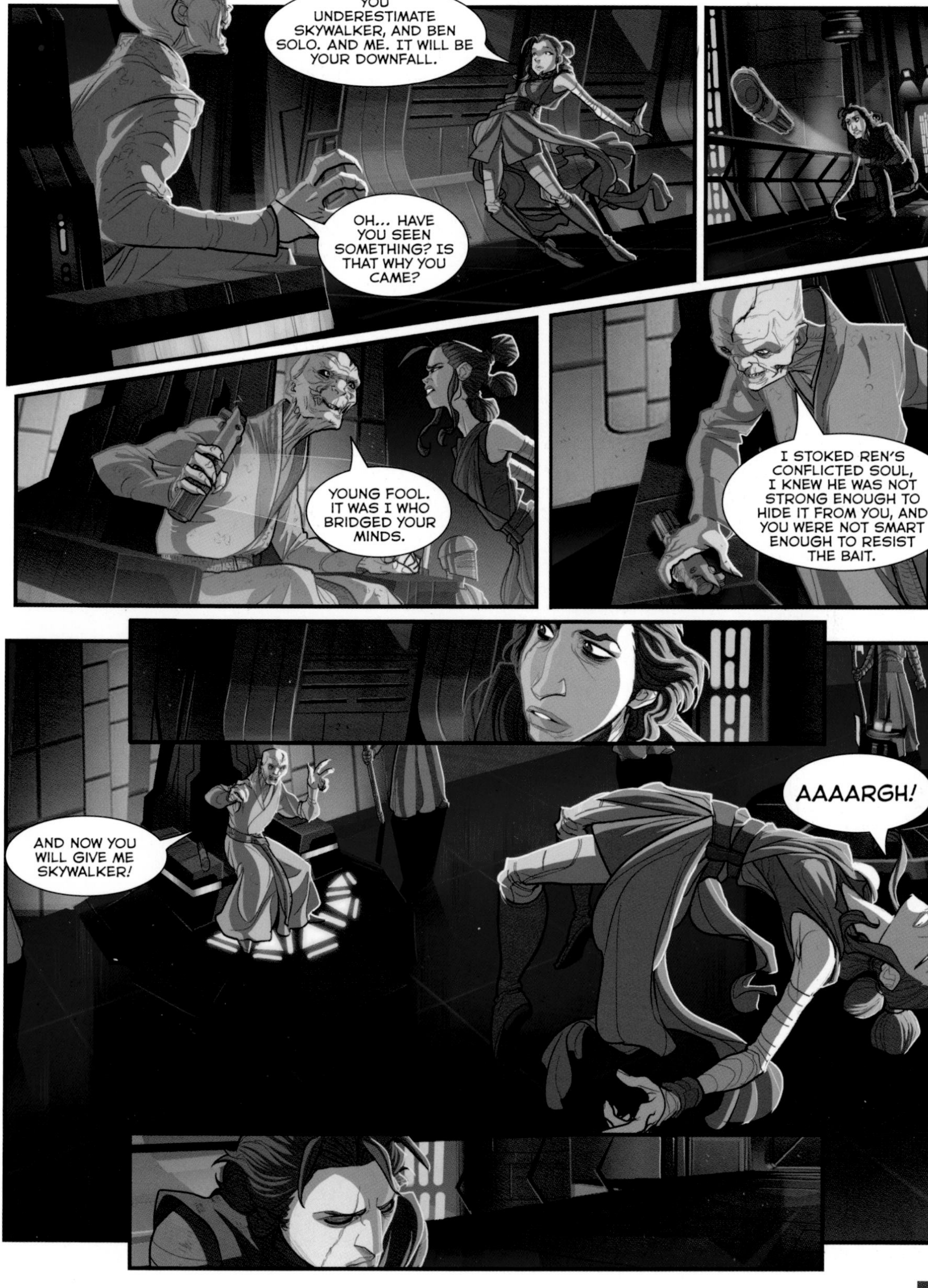
YOU UNDERESTIMATE SKYWALKER, AND BEN SOLO. AND ME. IT WILL BE YOUR DOWNFALL.
OH... HAVE YOU SEEN SOMETHING? IS THAT WHY YOU CAME?
YOUNG FOOL. IT WAS I WHO BRIDGED YOUR MINDS.
I STOKED REN'S CONFLICTED SOUL, I KNEW HE WAS NOT STRONG ENOUGH TO HIDE IT FROM YOU, AND YOU WERE NOT SMART ENOUGH TO RESIST THE BAIT.
AAAARGH!
AND NOW YOU WILL GIVE ME SKYWALKER!

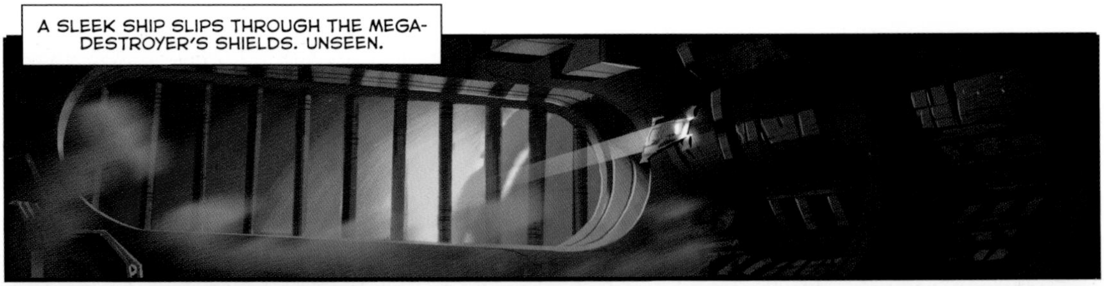
A SLEEK SHIP SLIPS THROUGH THE MEGA-DESTROYER'S SHIELDS. UNSEEN.

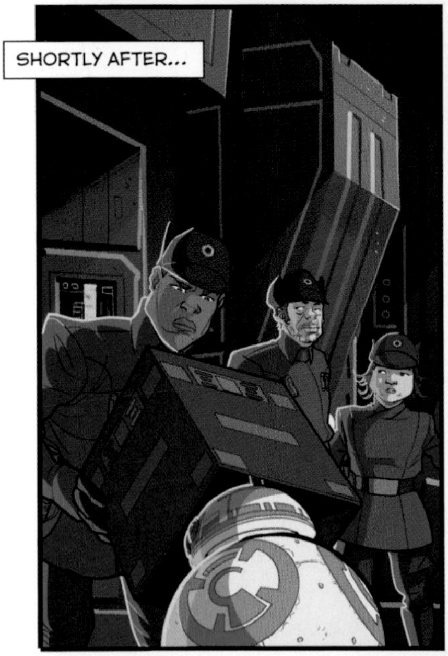
SHORTLY AFTER...

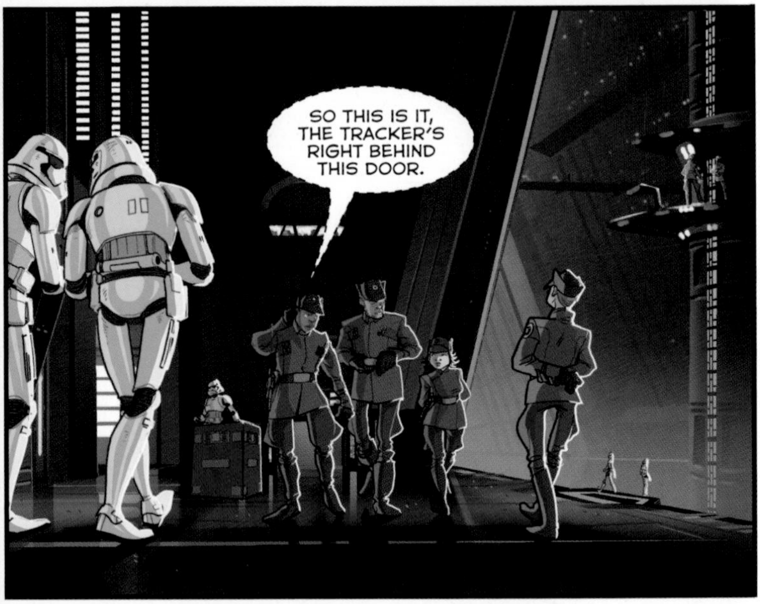
SO THIS IS IT, THE TRACKER'S RIGHT BEHIND THIS DOOR.

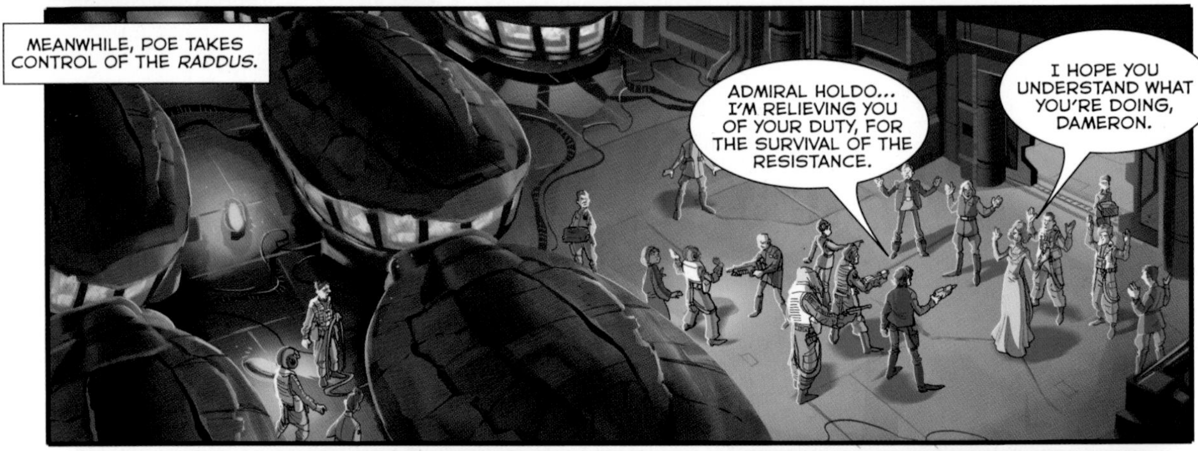
MEANWHILE, POE TAKES CONTROL OF THE *RADDUS*.
ADMIRAL HOLDO... I'M RELIEVING YOU OF YOUR DUTY, FOR THE SURVIVAL OF THE RESISTANCE.
I HOPE YOU UNDERSTAND WHAT YOU'RE DOING, DAMERON.

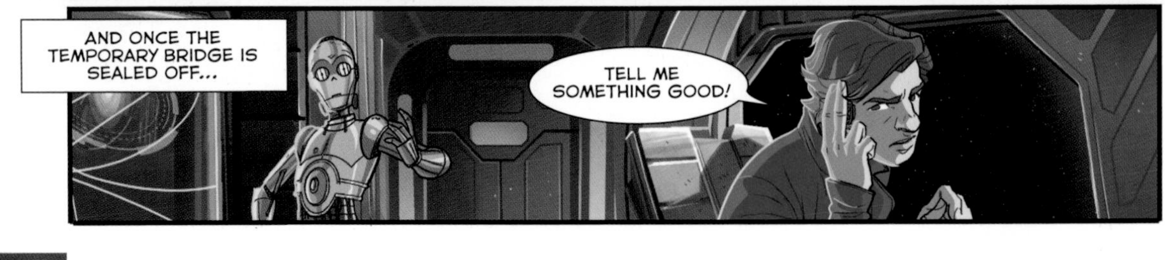
AND ONCE THE TEMPORARY BRIDGE IS SEALED OFF...
TELL ME SOMETHING GOOD!

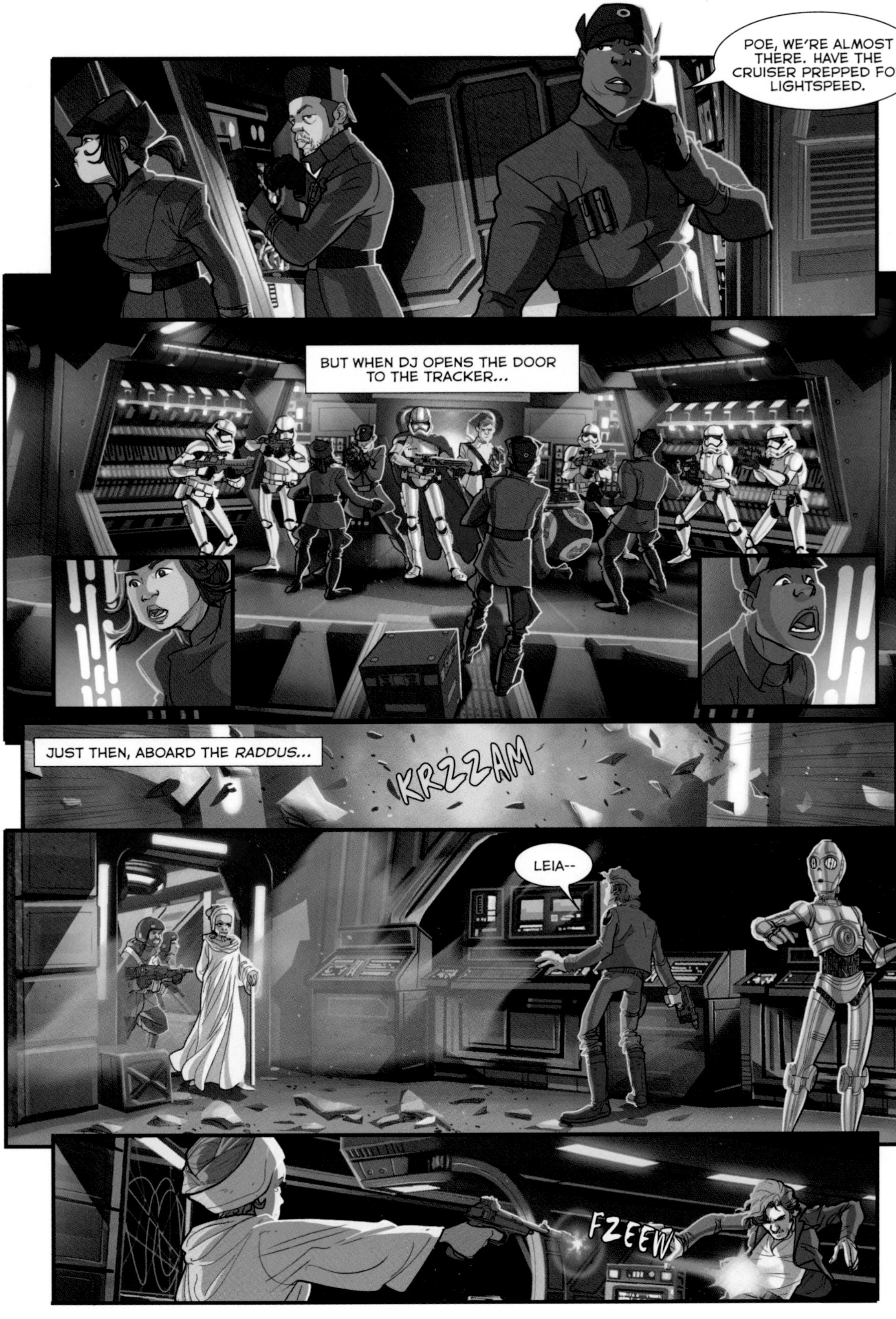
POE, WE'RE ALMOST THERE. HAVE THE CRUISER PREPPED FOR LIGHTSPEED.
BUT WHEN DJ OPENS THE DOOR TO THE TRACKER...
JUST THEN, ABOARD THE *RADDUS*...
KRZZAM
LEIA--
FZEEW

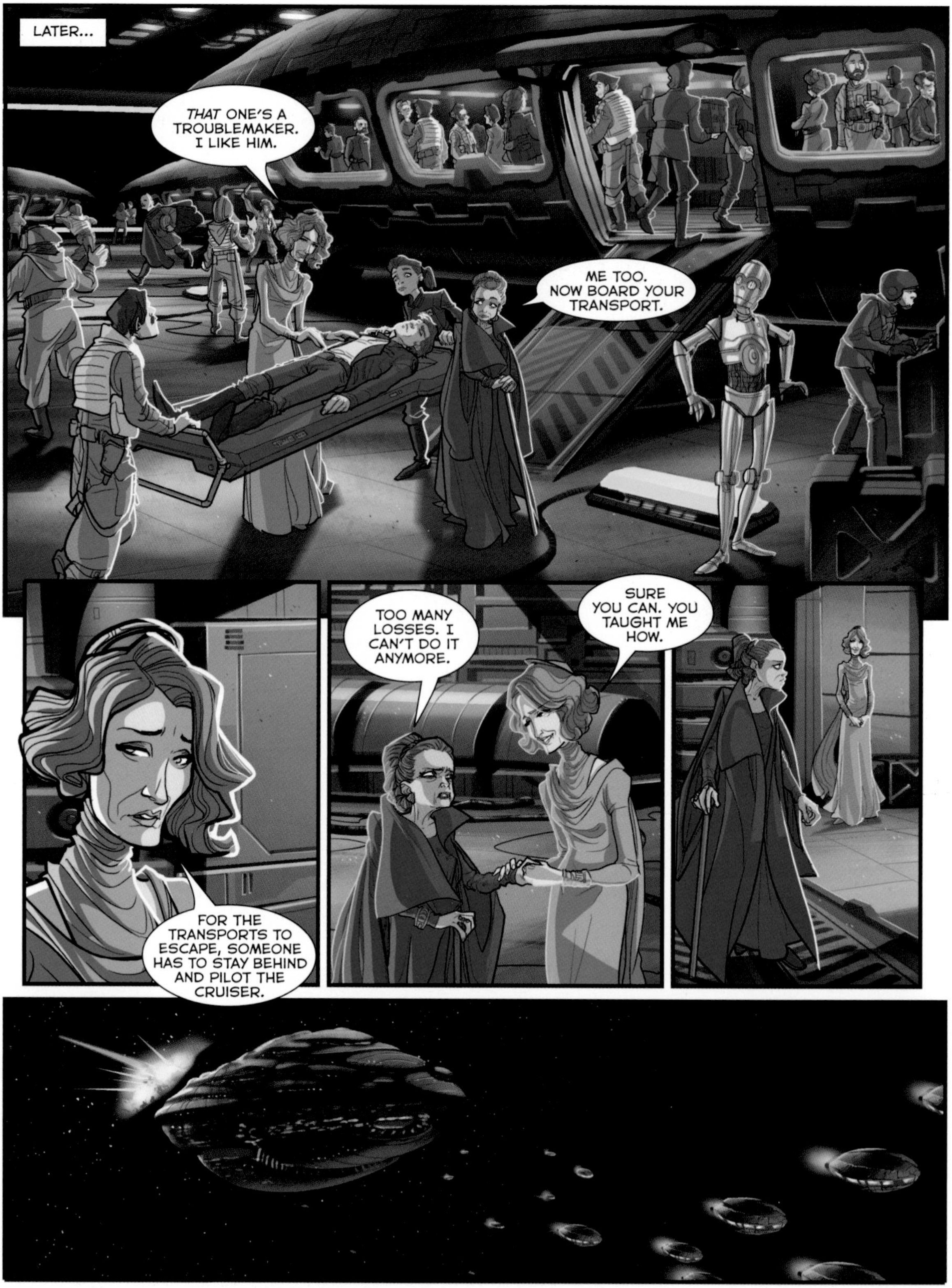
LATER...
THAT ONE'S A TROUBLEMAKER. I LIKE HIM.
ME TOO. NOW BOARD YOUR TRANSPORT.
FOR THE TRANSPORTS TO ESCAPE, SOMEONE HAS TO STAY BEHIND AND PILOT THE CRUISER.
TOO MANY LOSSES. I CAN'T DO IT ANYMORE.
SURE YOU CAN. YOU TAUGHT ME HOW.

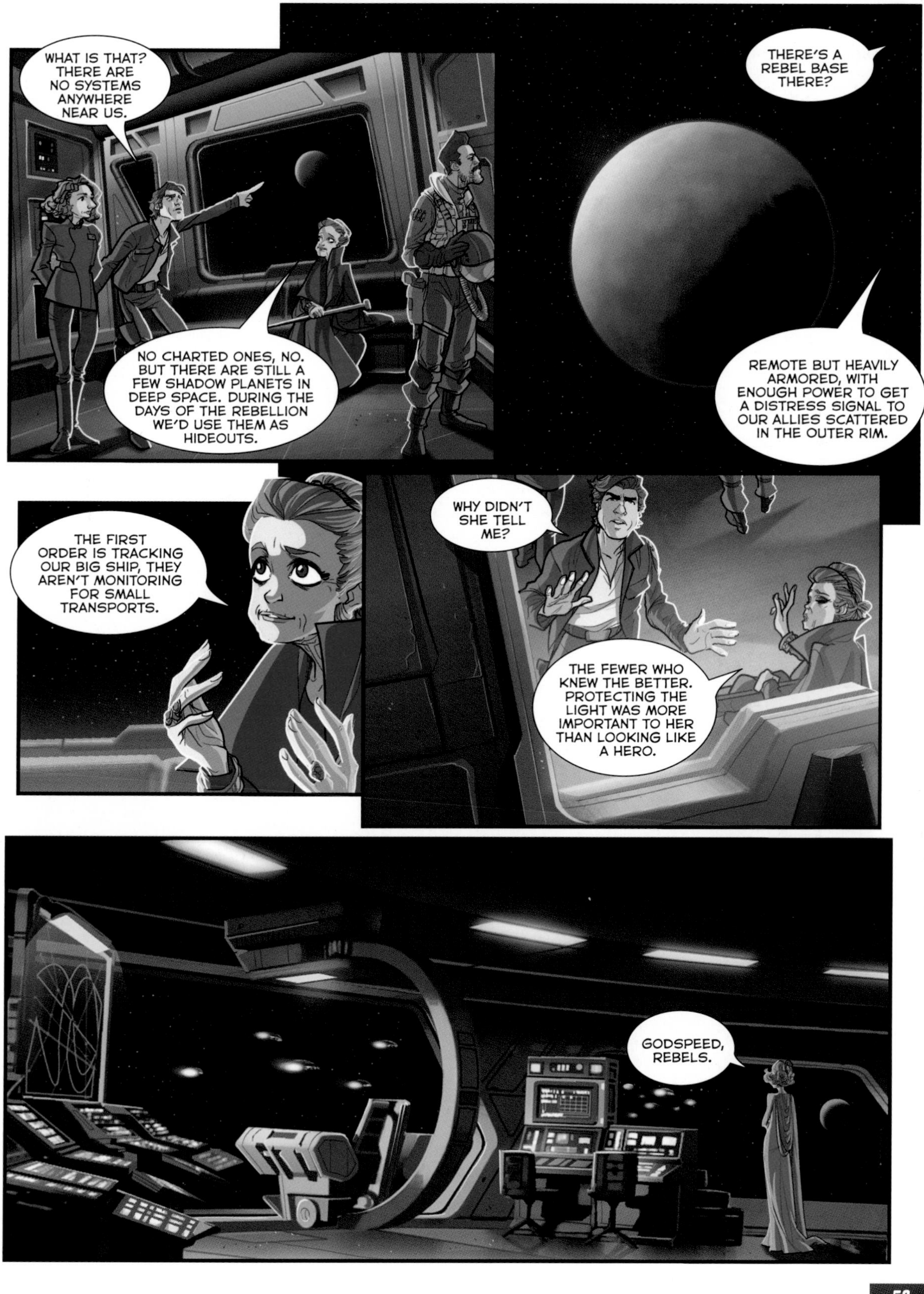
WHAT IS THAT? THERE ARE NO SYSTEMS ANYWHERE NEAR US.
NO CHARTED ONES, NO. BUT THERE ARE STILL A FEW SHADOW PLANETS IN DEEP SPACE. DURING THE DAYS OF THE REBELLION WE'D USE THEM AS HIDEOUTS.
THERE'S A REBEL BASE THERE?
REMOTE BUT HEAVILY ARMORED, WITH ENOUGH POWER TO GET A DISTRESS SIGNAL TO OUR ALLIES SCATTERED IN THE OUTER RIM.
THE FIRST ORDER IS TRACKING OUR BIG SHIP, THEY AREN'T MONITORING FOR SMALL TRANSPORTS.
WHY DIDN'T SHE TELL ME?
THE FEWER WHO KNEW THE BETTER. PROTECTING THE LIGHT WAS MORE IMPORTANT TO HER THAN LOOKING LIKE A HERO.
GODSPEED, REBELS.

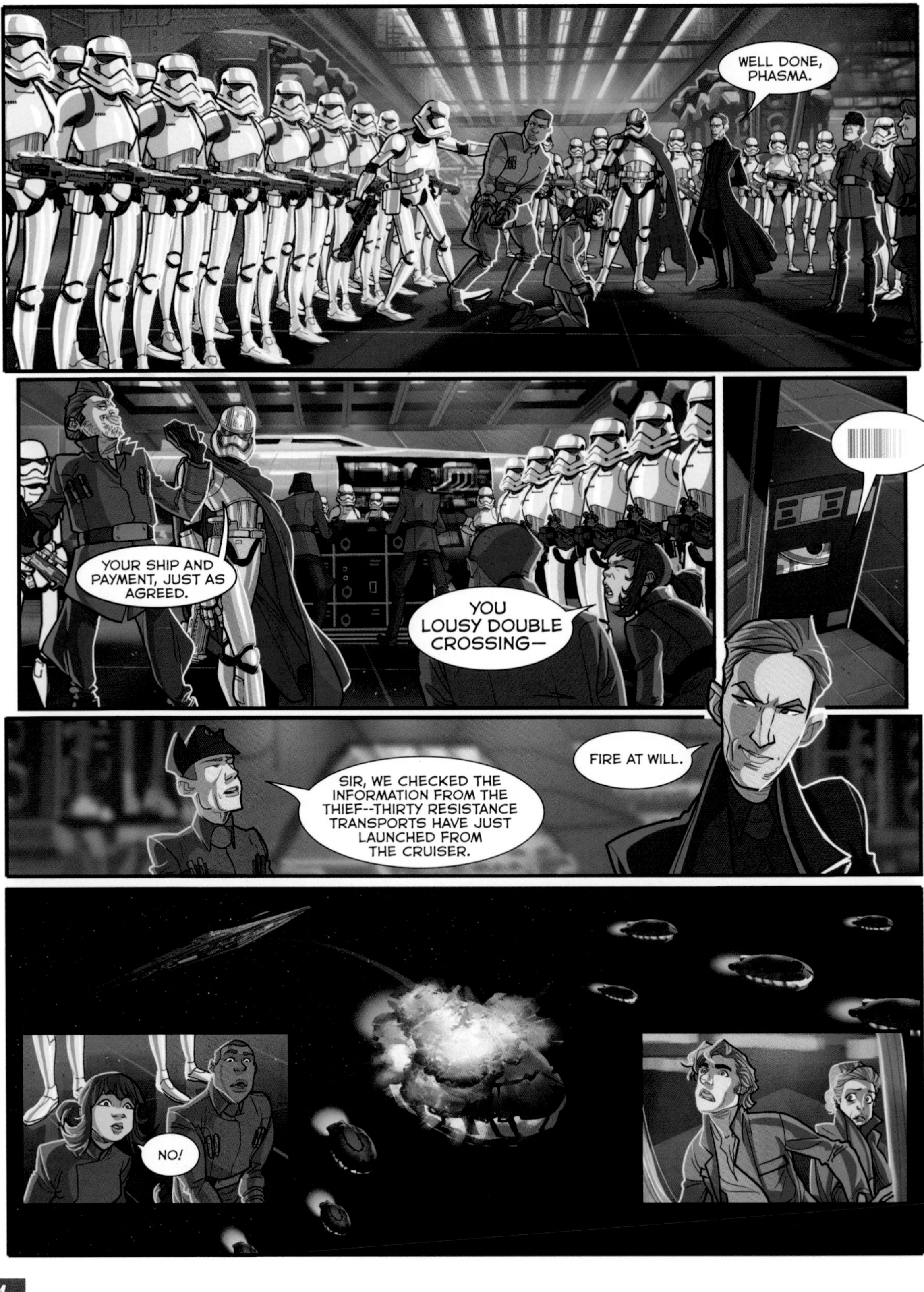
WELL DONE, PHASMA.
YOUR SHIP AND PAYMENT, JUST AS AGREED.
YOU LOUSY DOUBLE CROSSING—
FIRE AT WILL.
SIR, WE CHECKED THE INFORMATION FROM THE THIEF--THIRTY RESISTANCE TRANSPORTS HAVE JUST LAUNCHED FROM THE CRUISER.
NO!

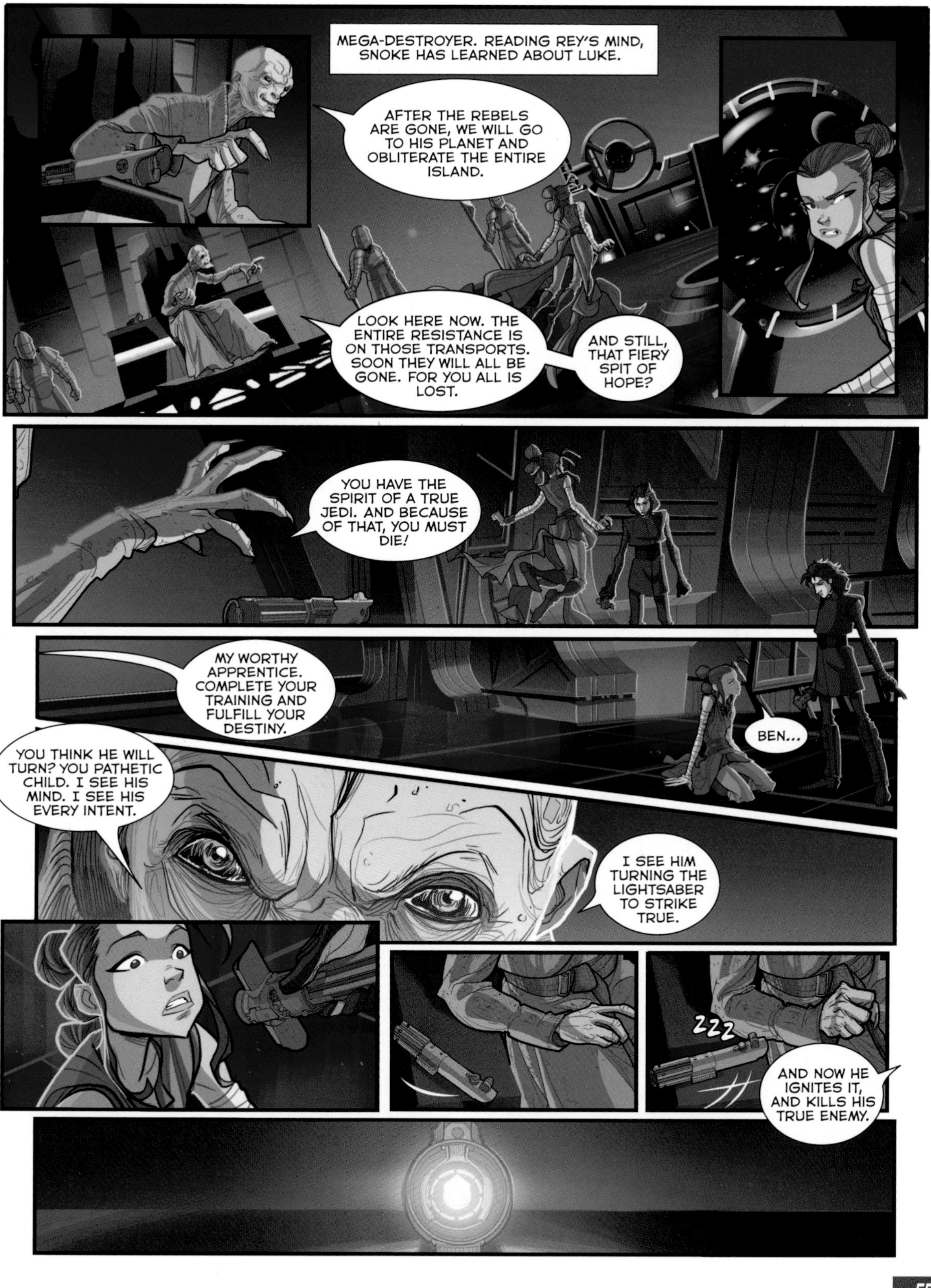

MEGA-DESTROYER. READING REY'S MIND, SNOKE HAS LEARNED ABOUT LUKE.
AFTER THE REBELS ARE GONE, WE WILL GO TO HIS PLANET AND OBLITERATE THE ENTIRE ISLAND.
LOOK HERE NOW. THE ENTIRE RESISTANCE IS ON THOSE TRANSPORTS. SOON THEY WILL ALL BE GONE. FOR YOU ALL IS LOST.
AND STILL, THAT FIERY SPIT OF HOPE?
YOU HAVE THE SPIRIT OF A TRUE JEDI. AND BECAUSE OF THAT, YOU MUST DIE!
MY WORTHY APPRENTICE. COMPLETE YOUR TRAINING AND FULFILL YOUR DESTINY.
BEN...
YOU THINK HE WILL TURN? YOU PATHETIC CHILD. I SEE HIS MIND. I SEE HIS EVERY INTENT.
I SEE HIM TURNING THE LIGHTSABER TO STRIKE TRUE.
ZZZ
AND NOW HE IGNITES IT, AND KILLS HIS TRUE ENEMY.

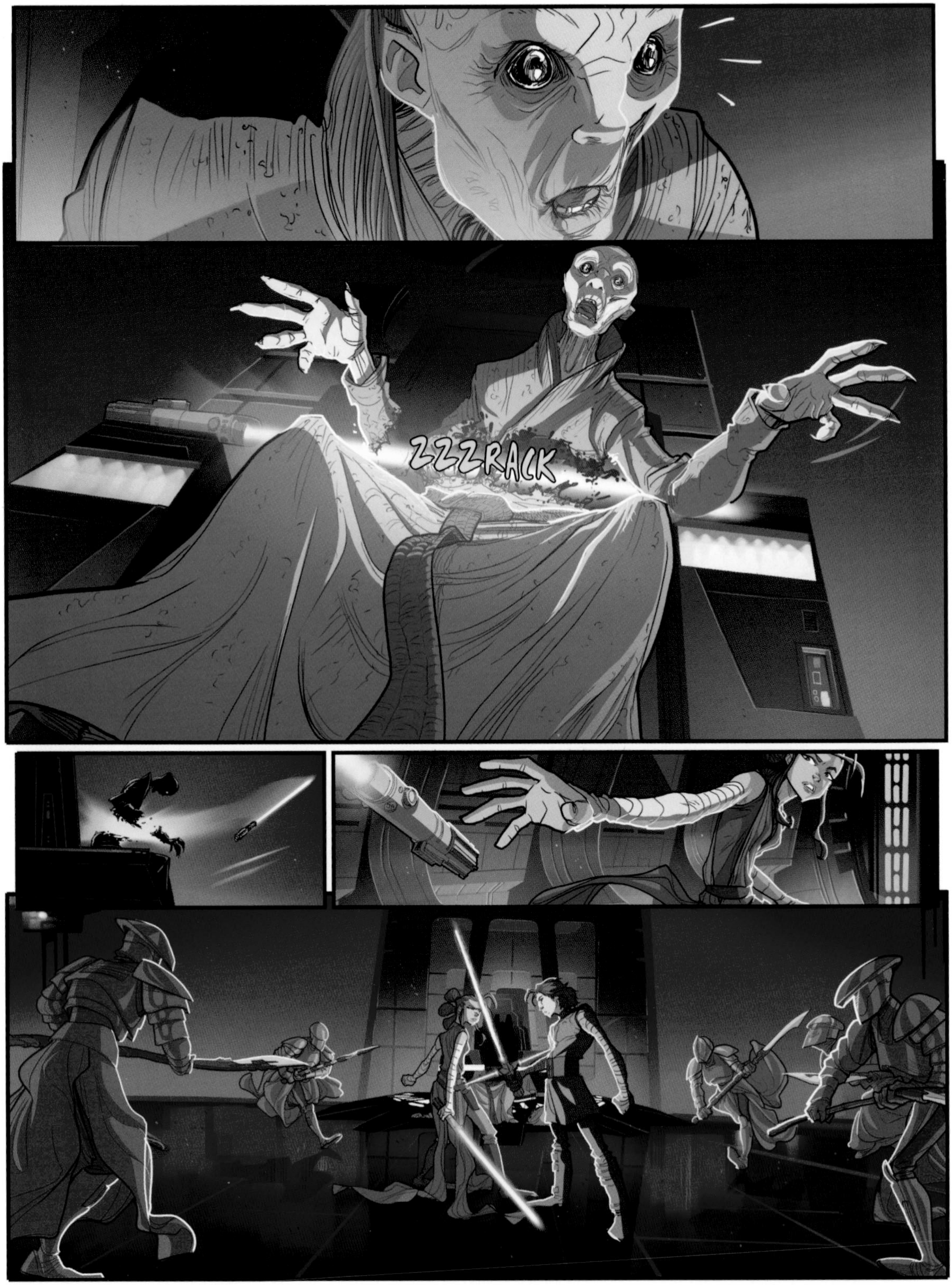
ZZZRACK

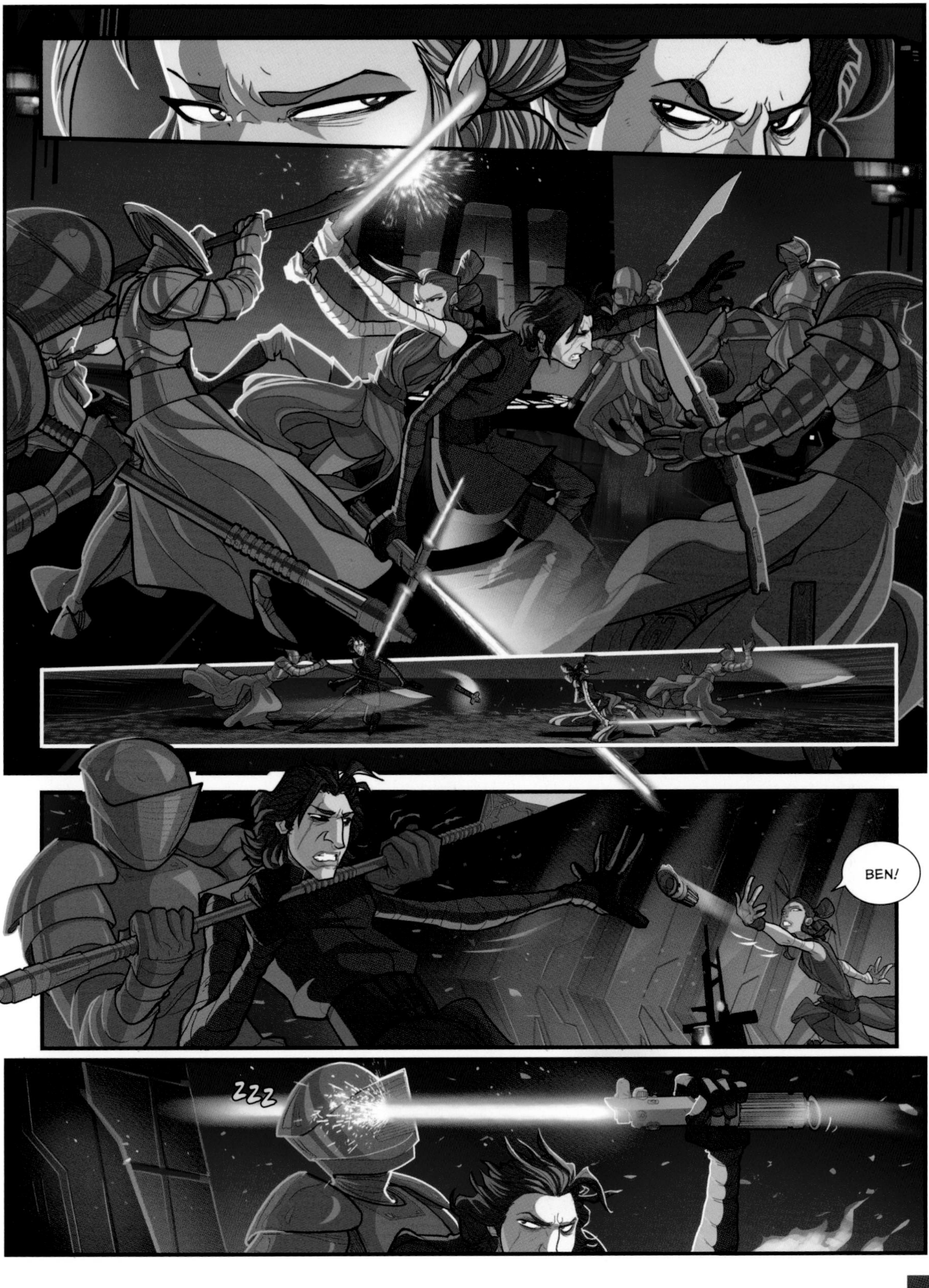
BEN!
ZZZ

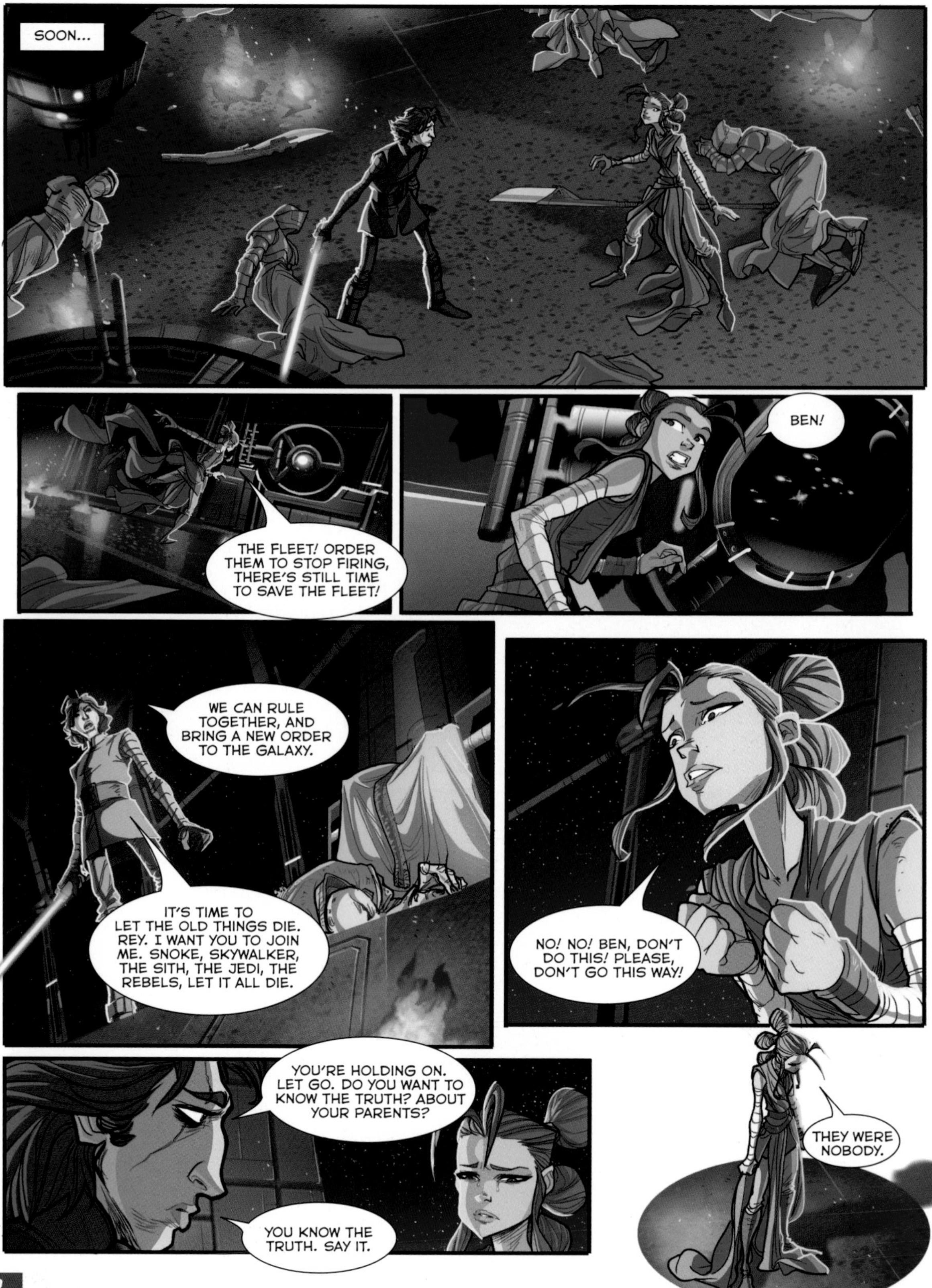
SOON...
THE FLEET! ORDER THEM TO STOP FIRING, THERE'S STILL TIME TO SAVE THE FLEET!
BEN!
WE CAN RULE TOGETHER, AND BRING A NEW ORDER TO THE GALAXY.
IT'S TIME TO LET THE OLD THINGS DIE. REY. I WANT YOU TO JOIN ME. SNOKE, SKYWALKER, THE SITH, THE JEDI, THE REBELS, LET IT ALL DIE.
NO! NO! BEN, DON'T DO THIS! PLEASE, DON'T GO THIS WAY!
YOU'RE HOLDING ON. LET GO. DO YOU WANT TO KNOW THE TRUTH? ABOUT YOUR PARENTS?
YOU KNOW THE TRUTH. SAY IT.
THEY WERE NOBODY.

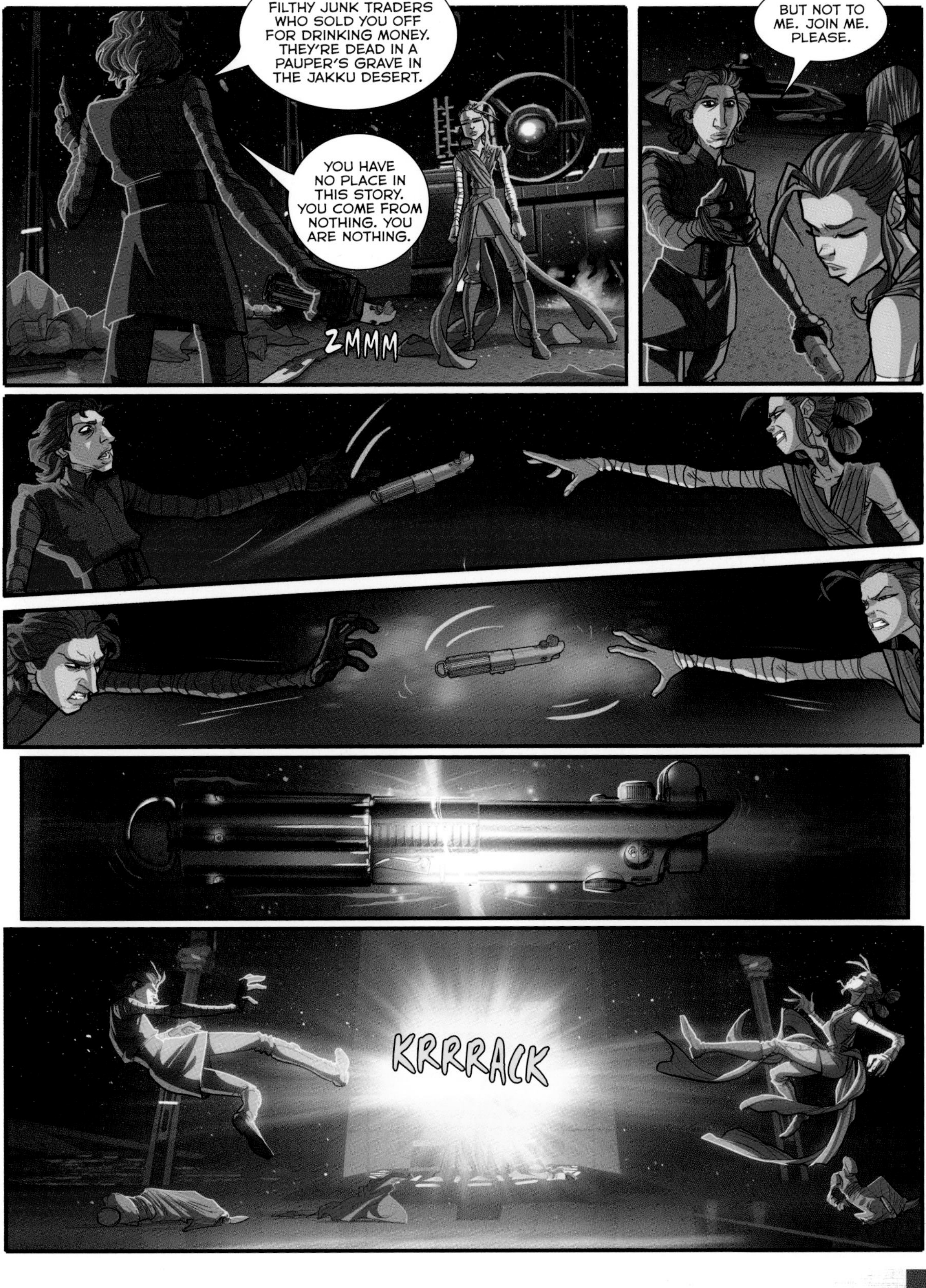

THEY WERE FILTHY JUNK TRADERS WHO SOLD YOU OFF FOR DRINKING MONEY. THEY'RE DEAD IN A PAUPER'S GRAVE IN THE JAKKU DESERT.
YOU HAVE NO PLACE IN THIS STORY. YOU COME FROM NOTHING. YOU ARE NOTHING.
ZMMM
BUT NOT TO ME. JOIN ME. PLEASE.
KRRRACK

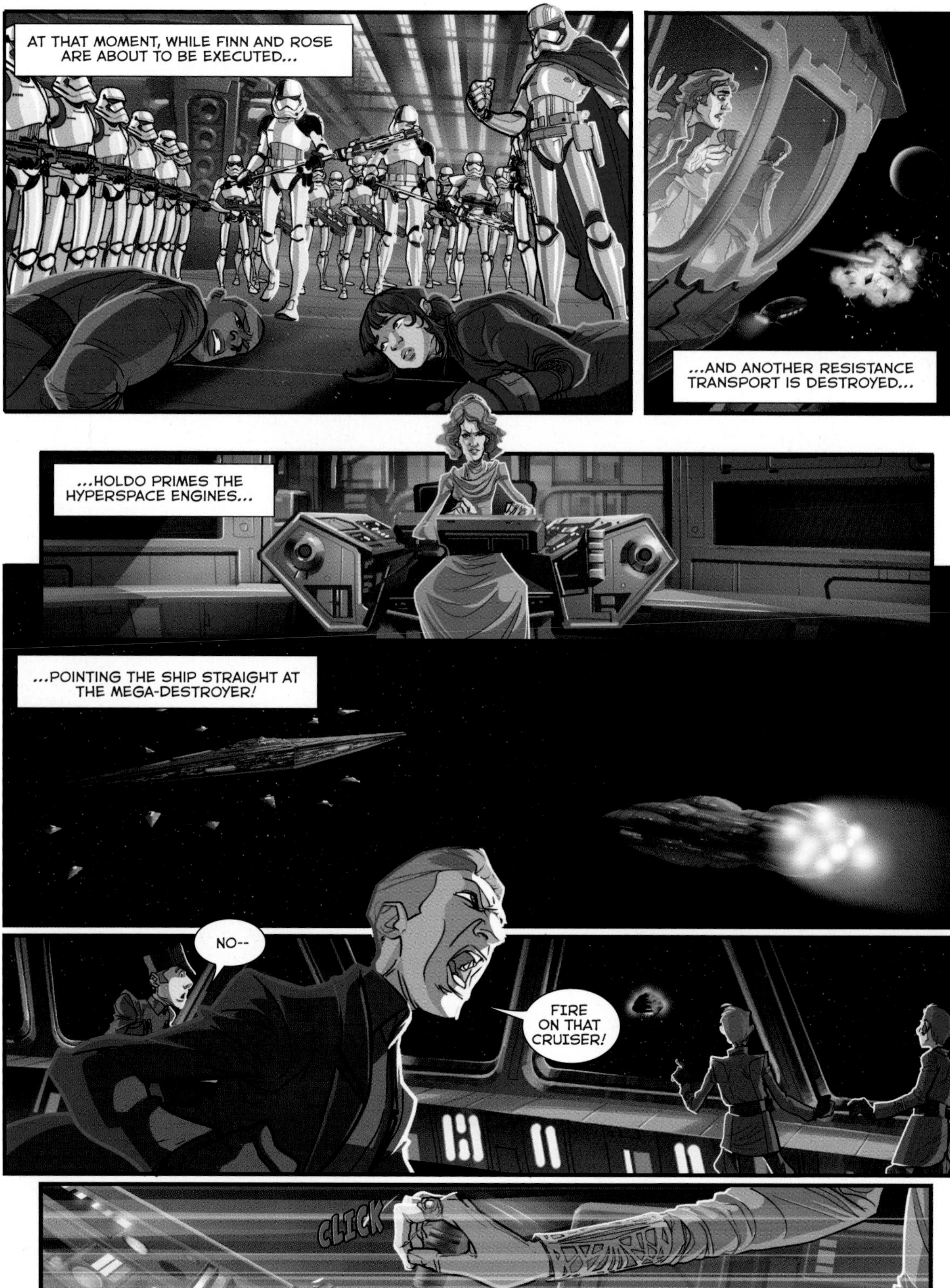
AT THAT MOMENT, WHILE FINN AND ROSE ARE ABOUT TO BE EXECUTED...
...AND ANOTHER RESISTANCE TRANSPORT IS DESTROYED...
...HOLDO PRIMES THE HYPERSPACE ENGINES...
...POINTING THE SHIP STRAIGHT AT THE MEGA-DESTROYER!
NO--
FIRE ON THAT CRUISER!
CLICK

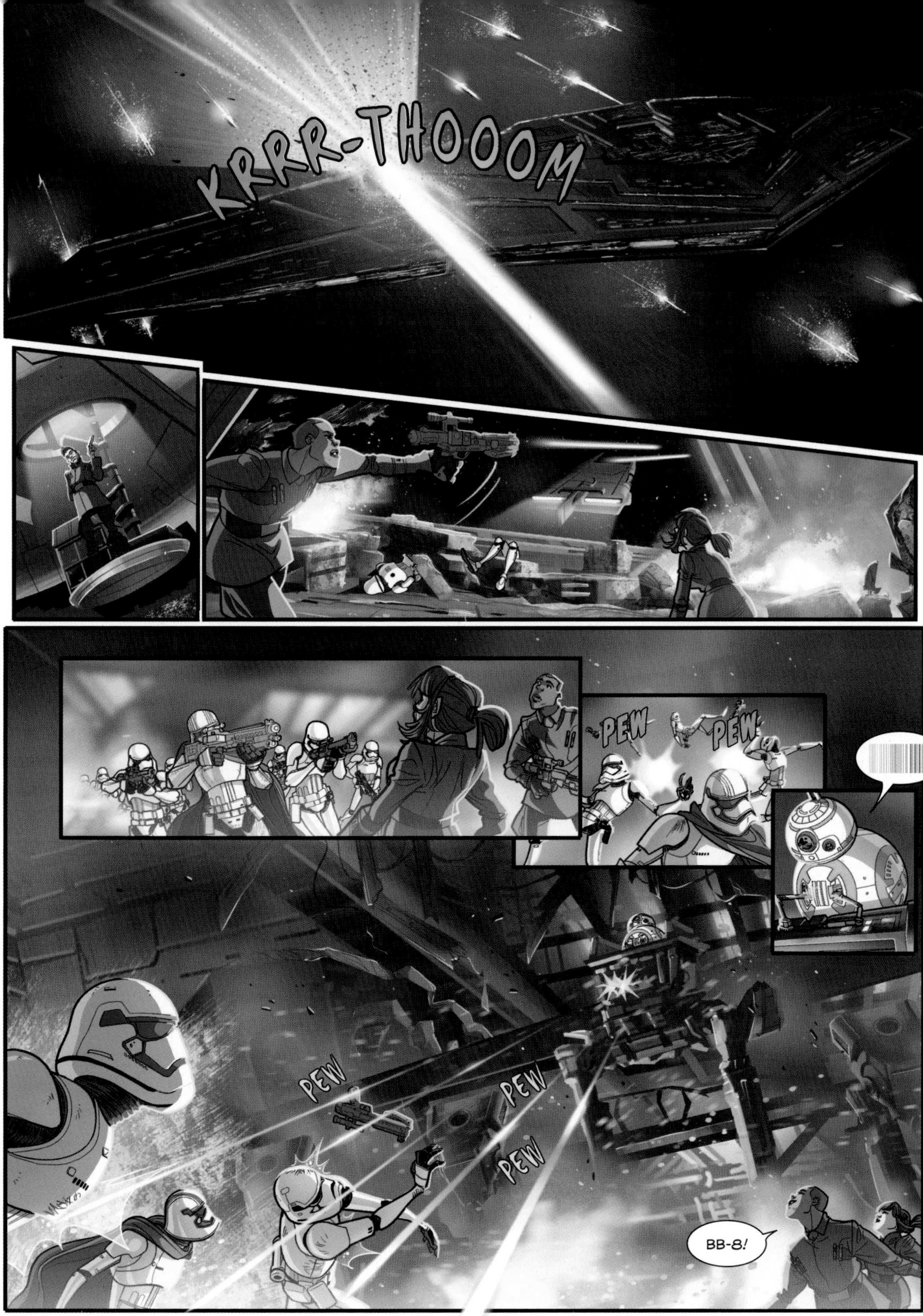
KRRR-THOOOM
PEW
PEW
PEW
PEW
PEW
BB-8!

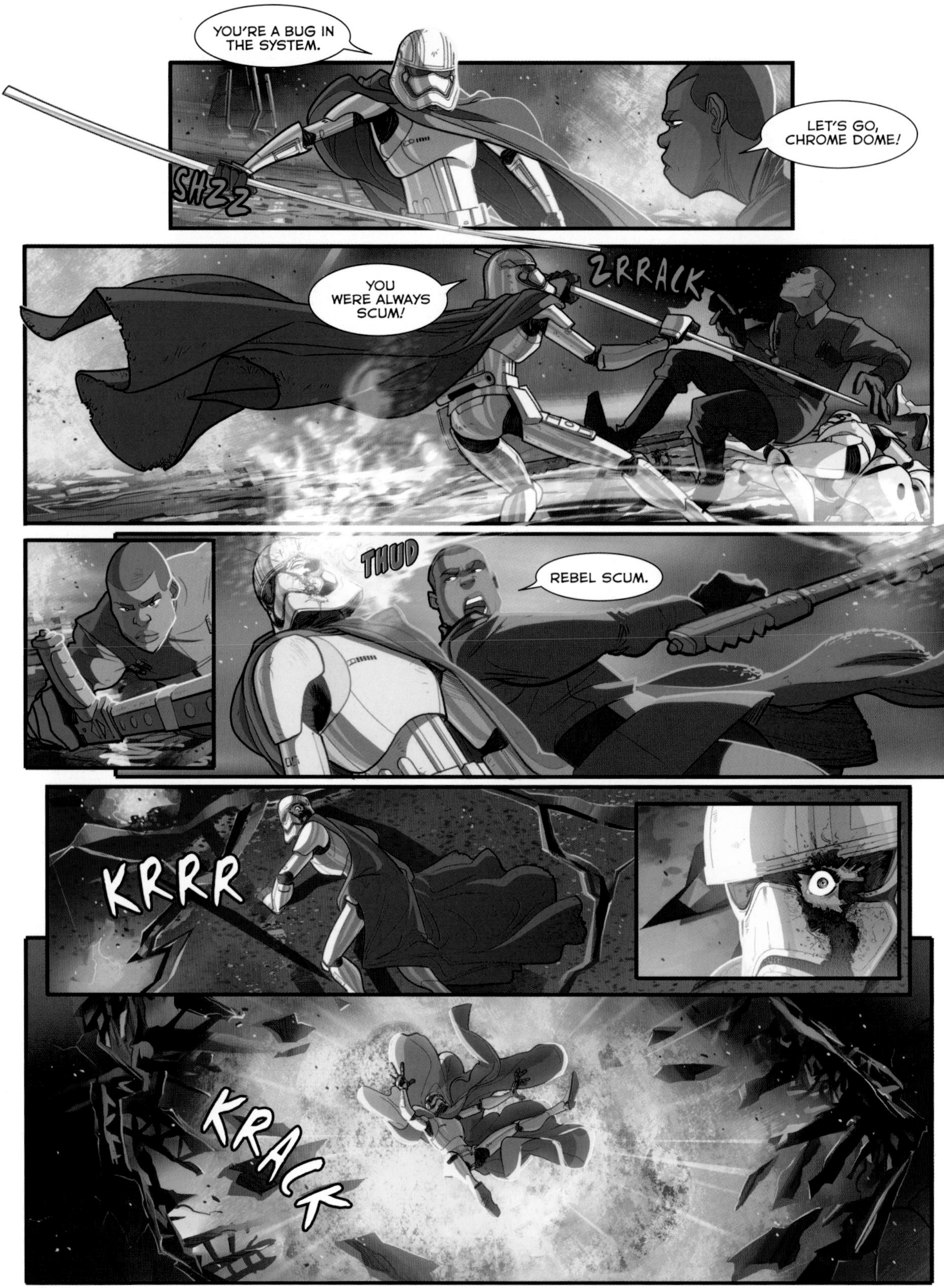
YOU'RE A BUG IN THE SYSTEM.
SHZZ
LET'S GO, CHROME DOME!
YOU WERE ALWAYS SCUM!
ZRRACK
THUD
REBEL SCUM.
KRRR
KRACK

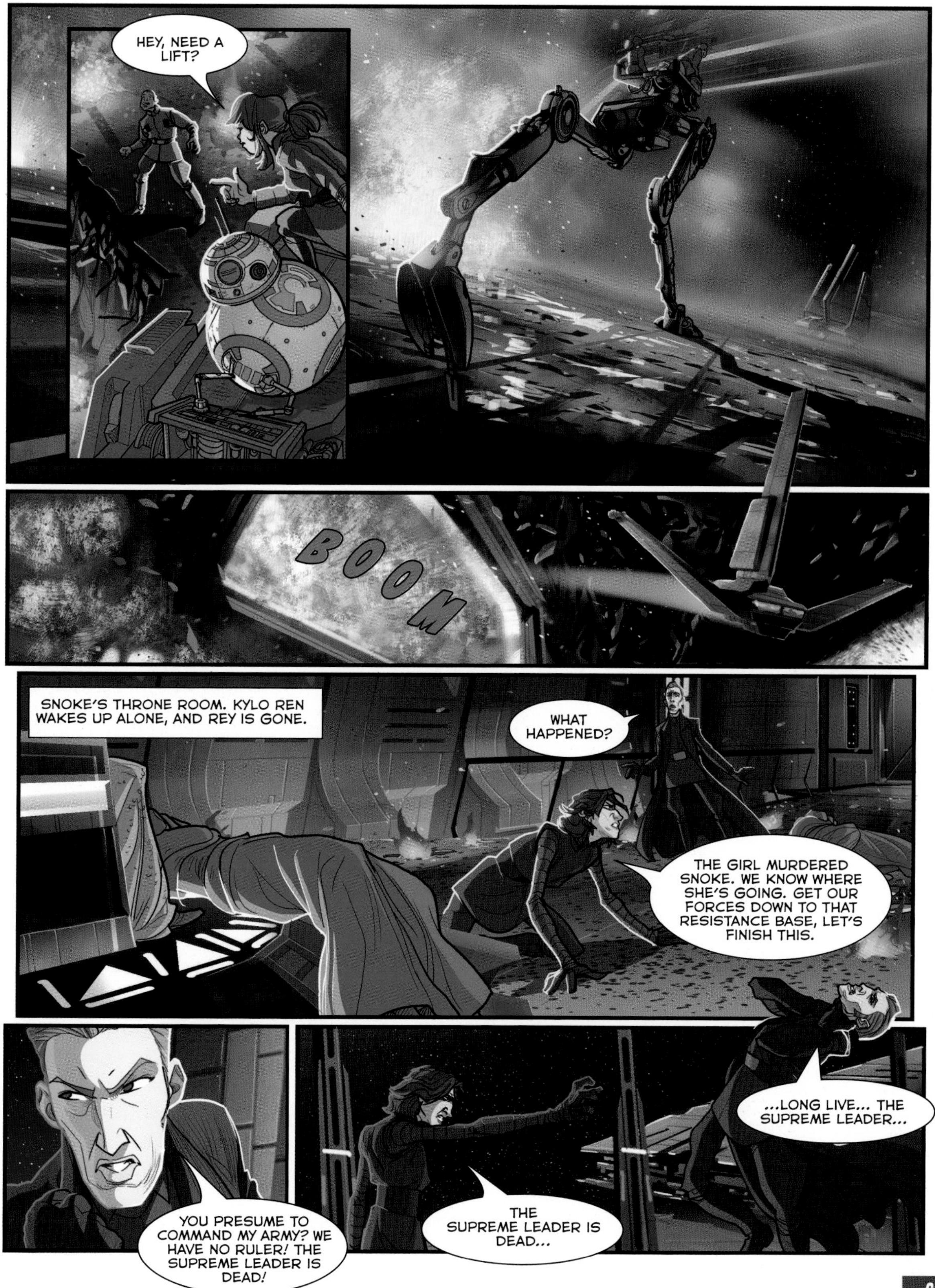
HEY, NEED A LIFT?
BOOM
SNOKE'S THRONE ROOM. KYLO REN WAKES UP ALONE, AND REY IS GONE.
WHAT HAPPENED?
THE GIRL MURDERED SNOKE. WE KNOW WHERE SHE'S GOING. GET OUR FORCES DOWN TO THAT RESISTANCE BASE, LET'S FINISH THIS.
YOU PRESUME TO COMMAND MY ARMY? WE HAVE NO RULER! THE SUPREME LEADER IS DEAD!
THE SUPREME LEADER IS DEAD...
...LONG LIVE... THE SUPREME LEADER...

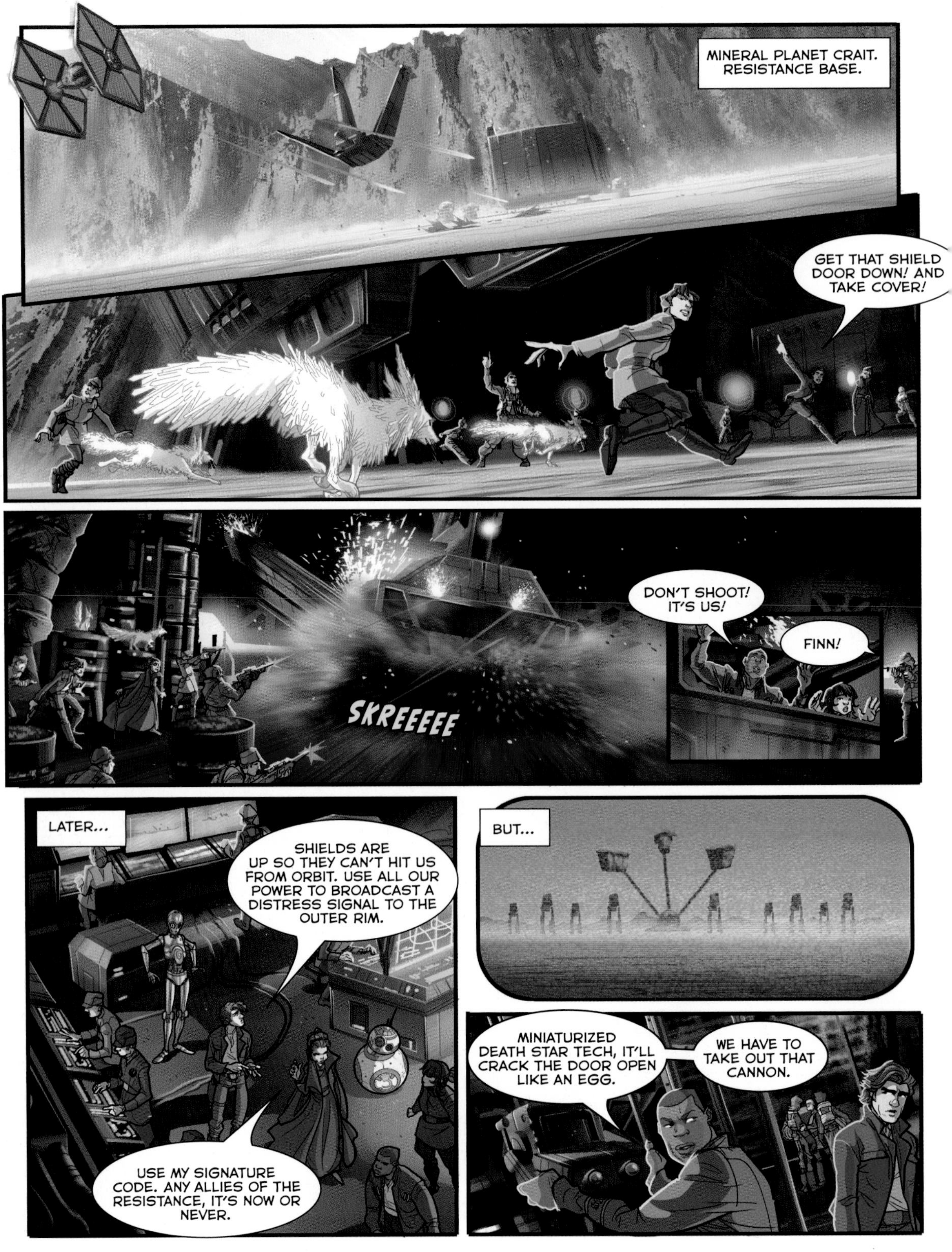
MINERAL PLANET CRAIT. RESISTANCE BASE.
GET THAT SHIELD DOOR DOWN! AND TAKE COVER!
DON'T SHOOT! IT'S US!
FINN!
SKREEEEE
LATER...
SHIELDS ARE UP SO THEY CAN'T HIT US FROM ORBIT. USE ALL OUR POWER TO BROADCAST A DISTRESS SIGNAL TO THE OUTER RIM.
USE MY SIGNATURE CODE. ANY ALLIES OF THE RESISTANCE, IT'S NOW OR NEVER.
BUT...
MINIATURIZED DEATH STAR TECH, IT'LL CRACK THE DOOR OPEN LIKE AN EGG.
WE HAVE TO TAKE OUT THAT CANNON.

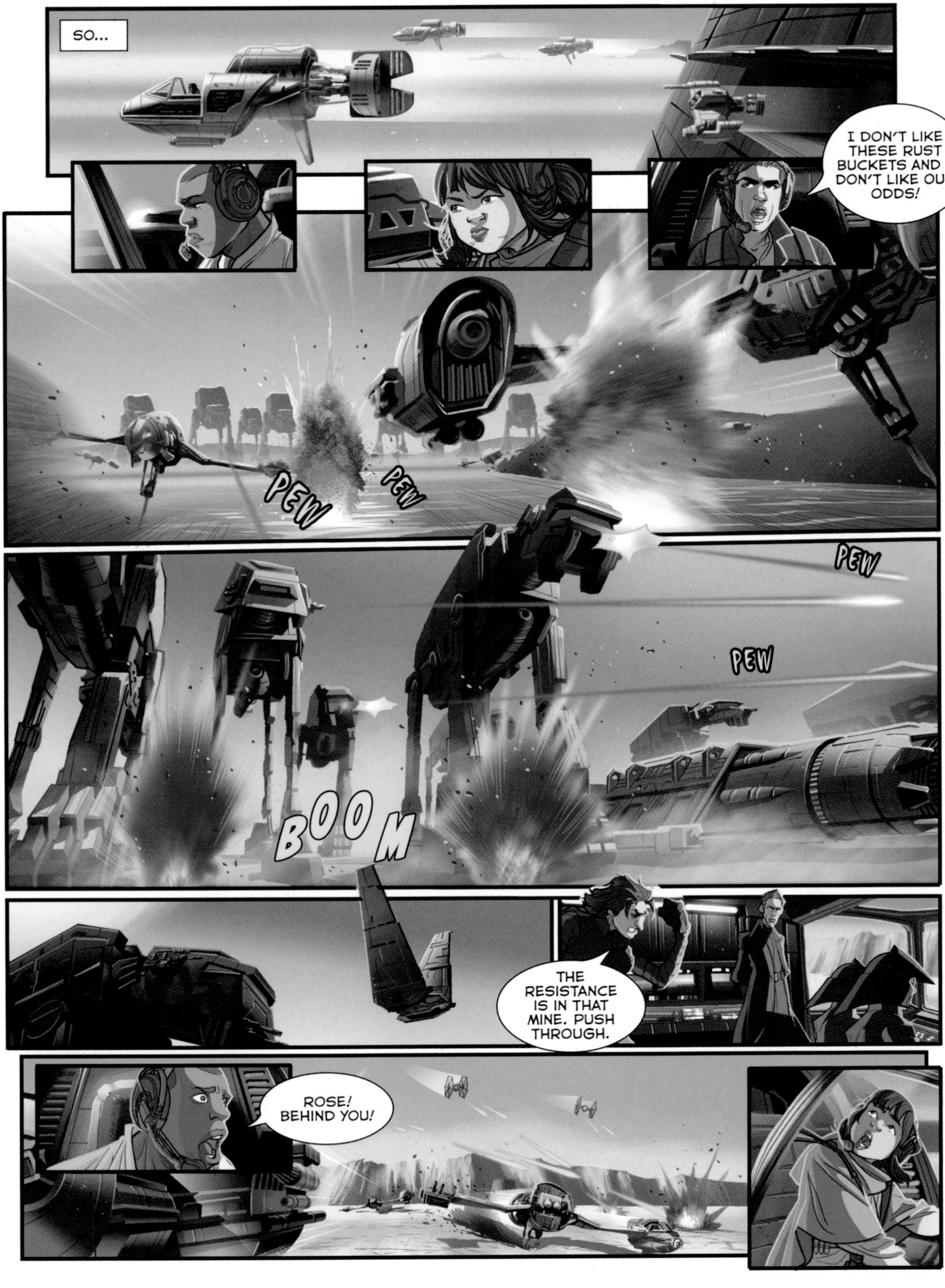
SO...
I DON'T LIKE THESE RUST BUCKETS AND I DON'T LIKE OUR ODDS!
PEW
PEW
PEW
PEW
BOOM
THE RESISTANCE IS IN THAT MINE. PUSH THROUGH.
ROSE! BEHIND YOU!

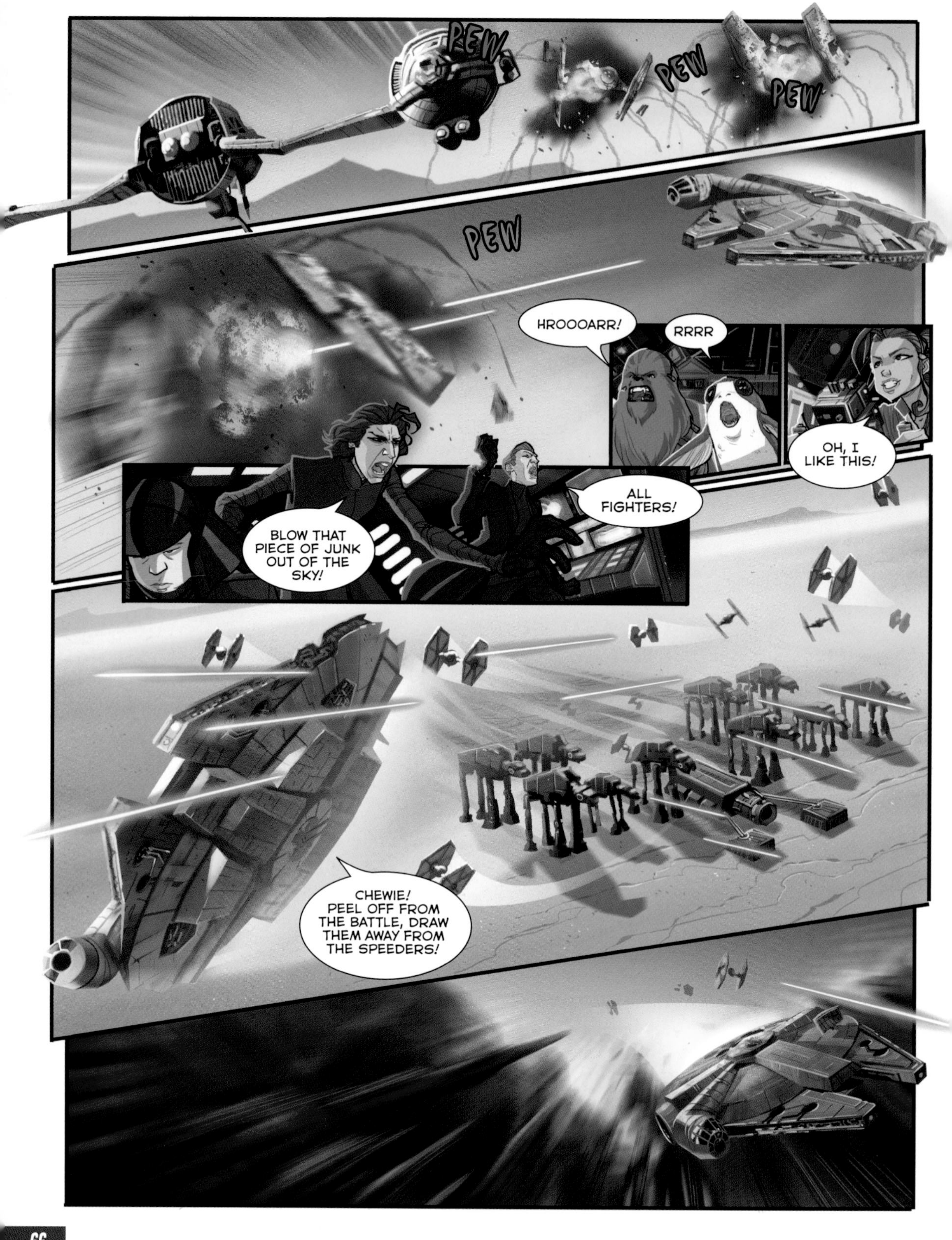
PEW
PEW
PEW
PEW
HROOOARR!
RRRR
OH, I LIKE THIS!
ALL FIGHTERS!
BLOW THAT PIECE OF JUNK OUT OF THE SKY!
CHEWIE! PEEL OFF FROM THE BATTLE, DRAW THEM AWAY FROM THE SPEEDERS!

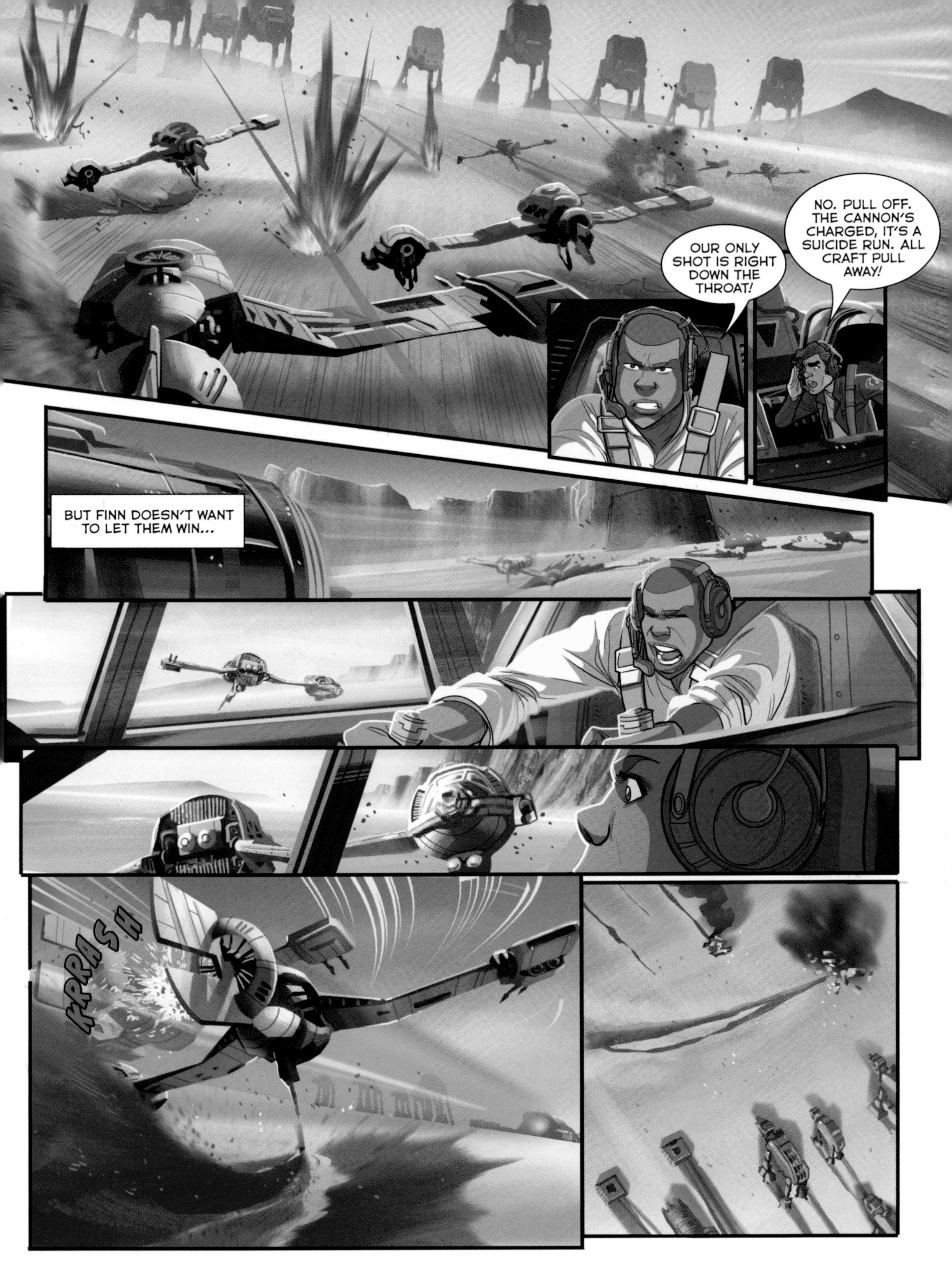
OUR ONLY SHOT IS RIGHT DOWN THE THROAT!
NO. PULL OFF. THE CANNON'S CHARGED, IT'S A SUICIDE RUN. ALL CRAFT PULL AWAY!
BUT FINN DOESN'T WANT TO LET THEM WIN...
KRRASH

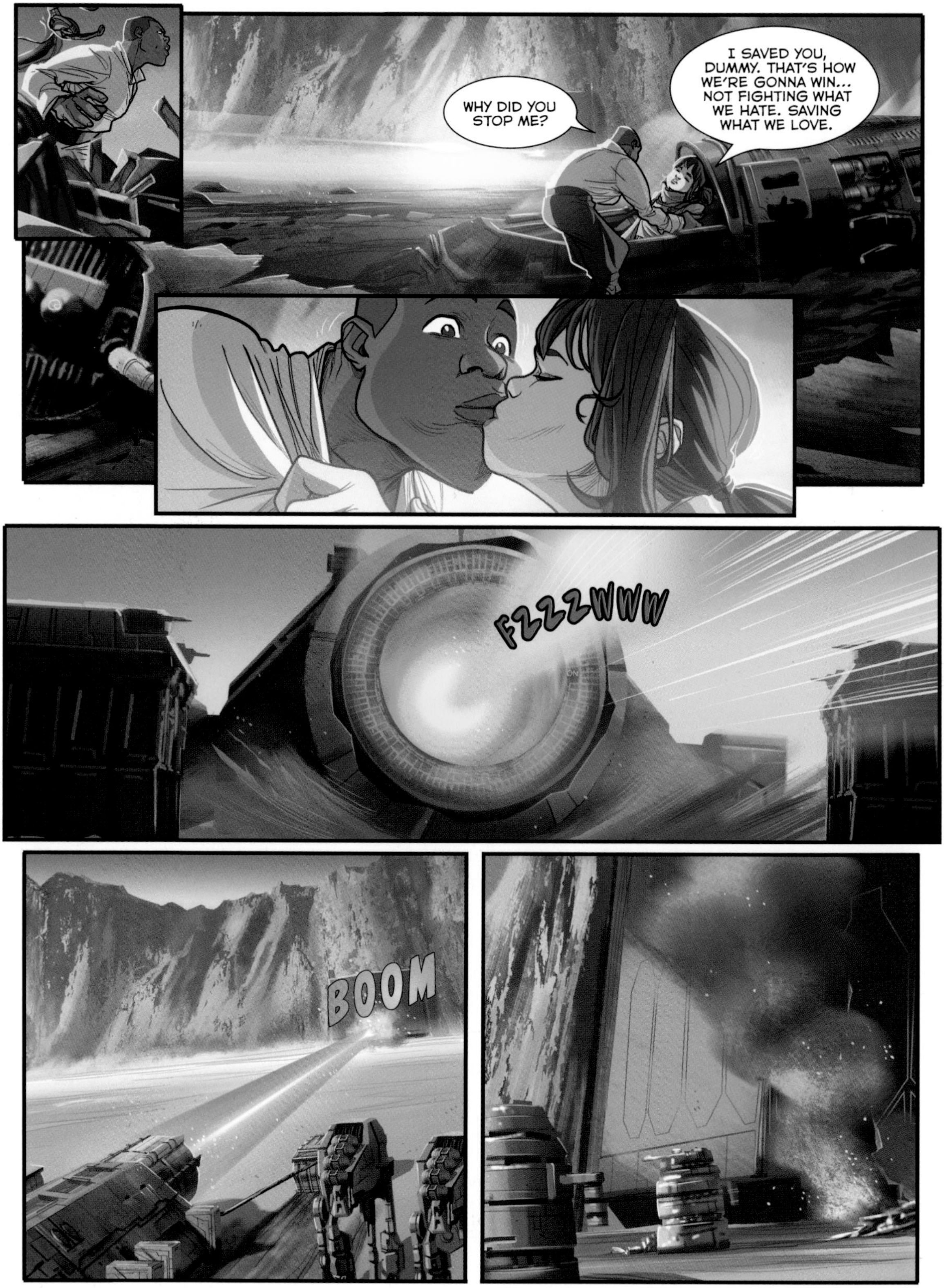
WHY DID YOU STOP ME?
I SAVED YOU, DUMMY. THAT'S HOW WE'RE GONNA WIN... NOT FIGHTING WHAT WE HATE. SAVING WHAT WE LOVE.
FZZZWWW
BOOM

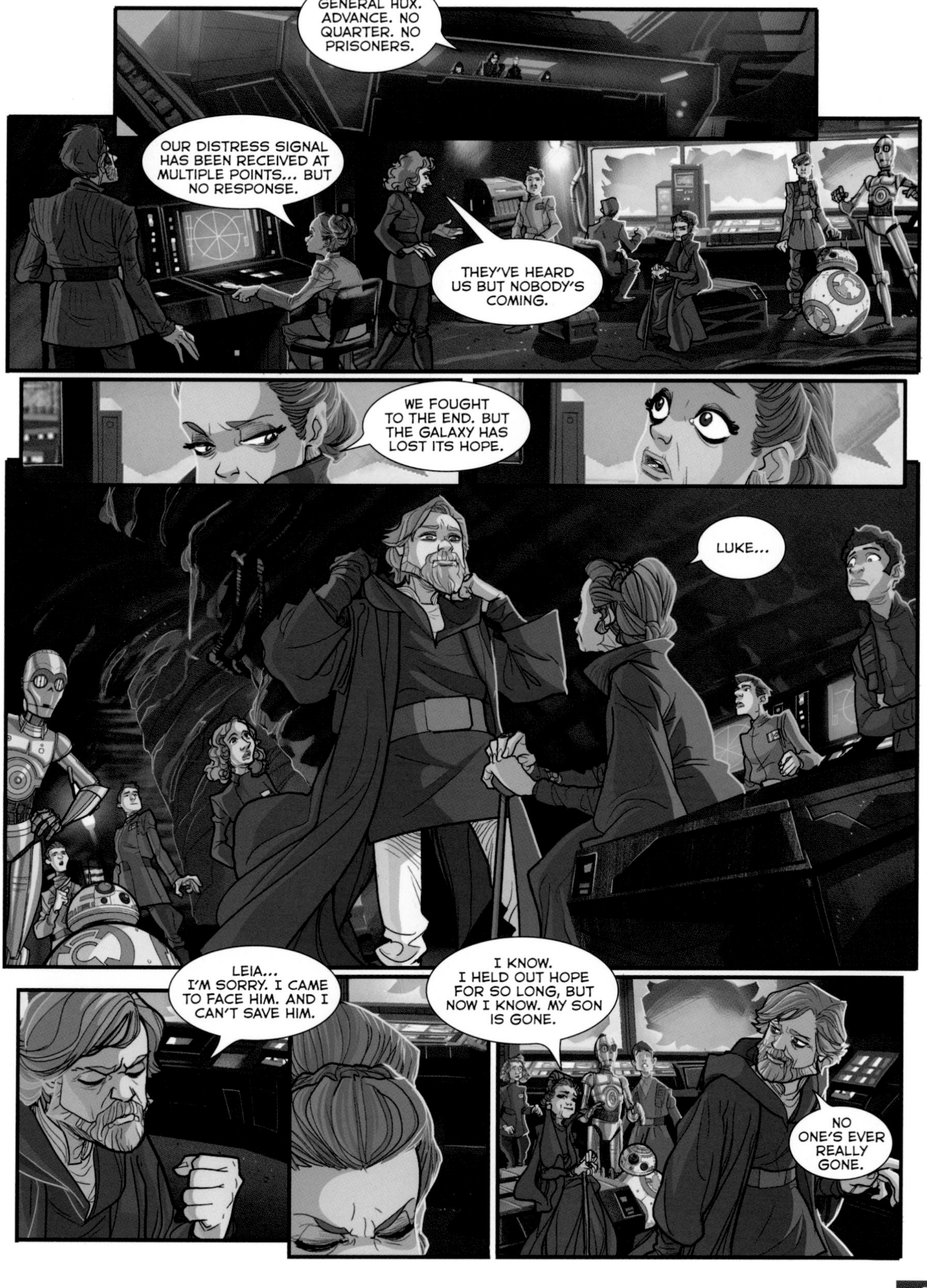
GENERAL HUX. ADVANCE. NO QUARTER. NO PRISONERS.
OUR DISTRESS SIGNAL HAS BEEN RECEIVED AT MULTIPLE POINTS... BUT NO RESPONSE.
THEY'VE HEARD US BUT NOBODY'S COMING.
WE FOUGHT TO THE END. BUT THE GALAXY HAS LOST ITS HOPE.
LUKE...
LEIA... I'M SORRY. I CAME TO FACE HIM. AND I CAN'T SAVE HIM.
I KNOW. I HELD OUT HOPE FOR SO LONG, BUT NOW I KNOW. MY SON IS GONE.
NO ONE'S EVER REALLY GONE.

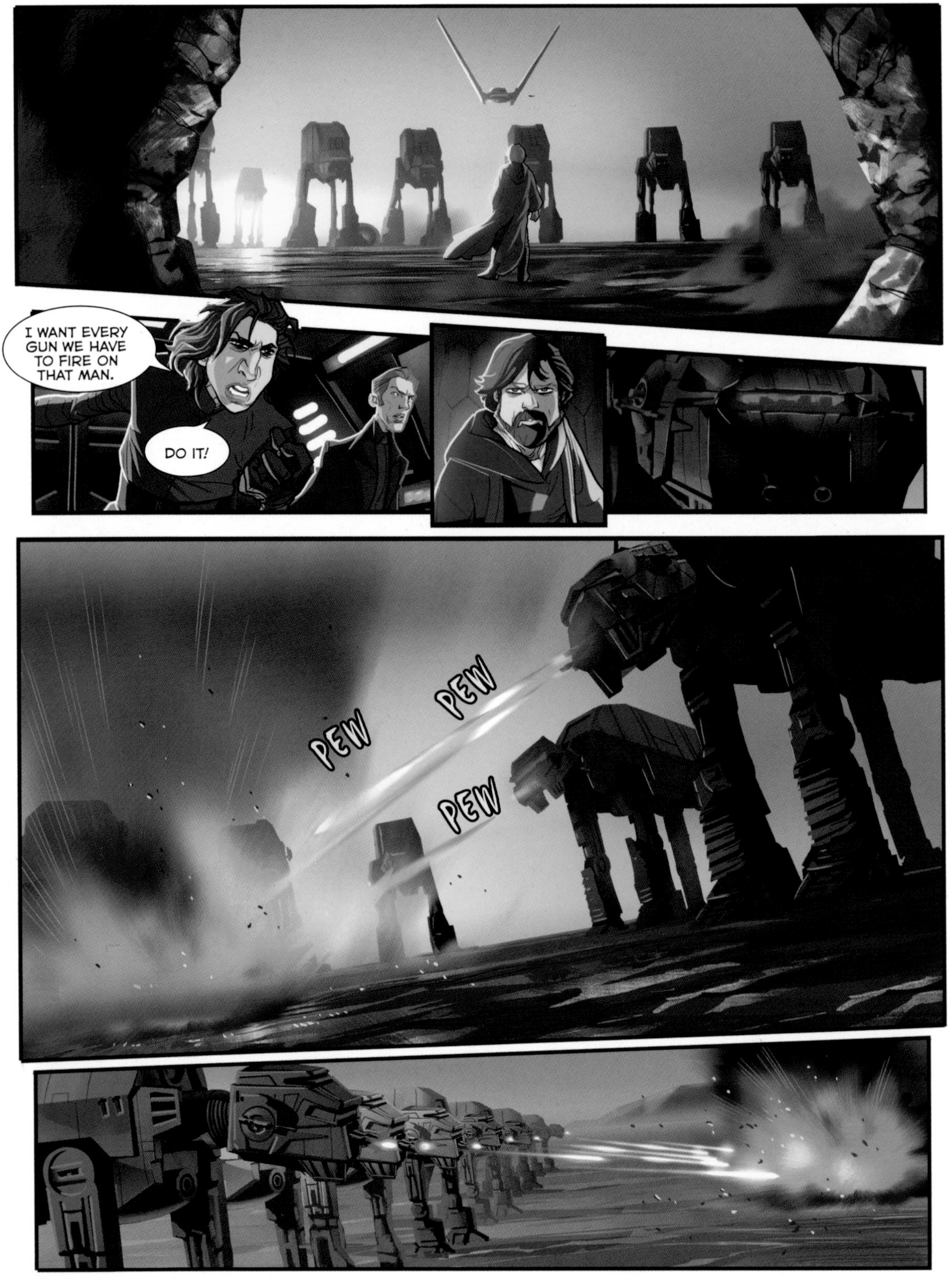
I WANT EVERY GUN WE HAVE TO FIRE ON THAT MAN.
DO IT!
PEW
PEW
PEW

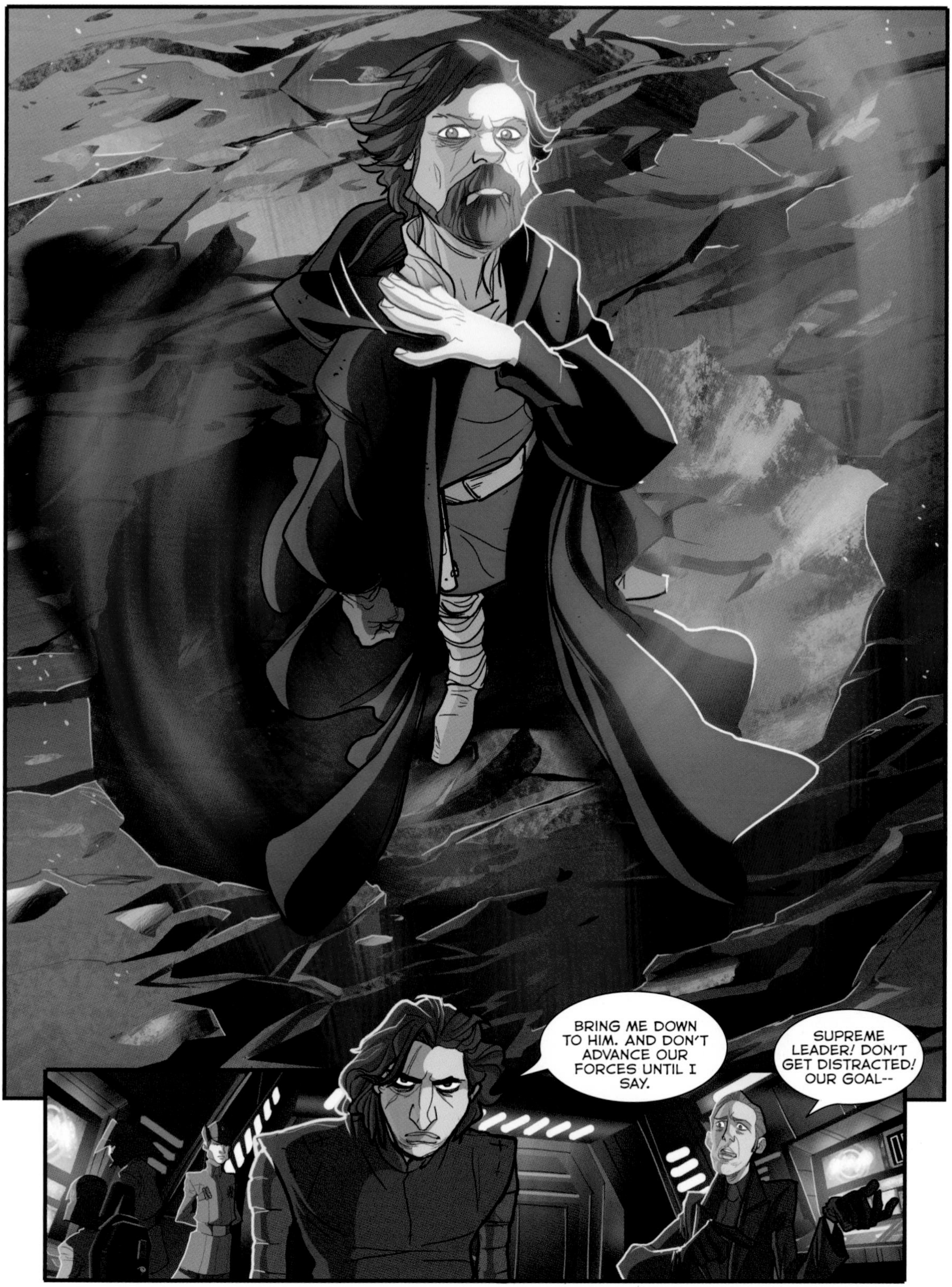
BRING ME DOWN TO HIM. AND DON'T ADVANCE OUR FORCES UNTIL I SAY.
SUPREME LEADER! DON'T GET DISTRACTED! OUR GOAL--

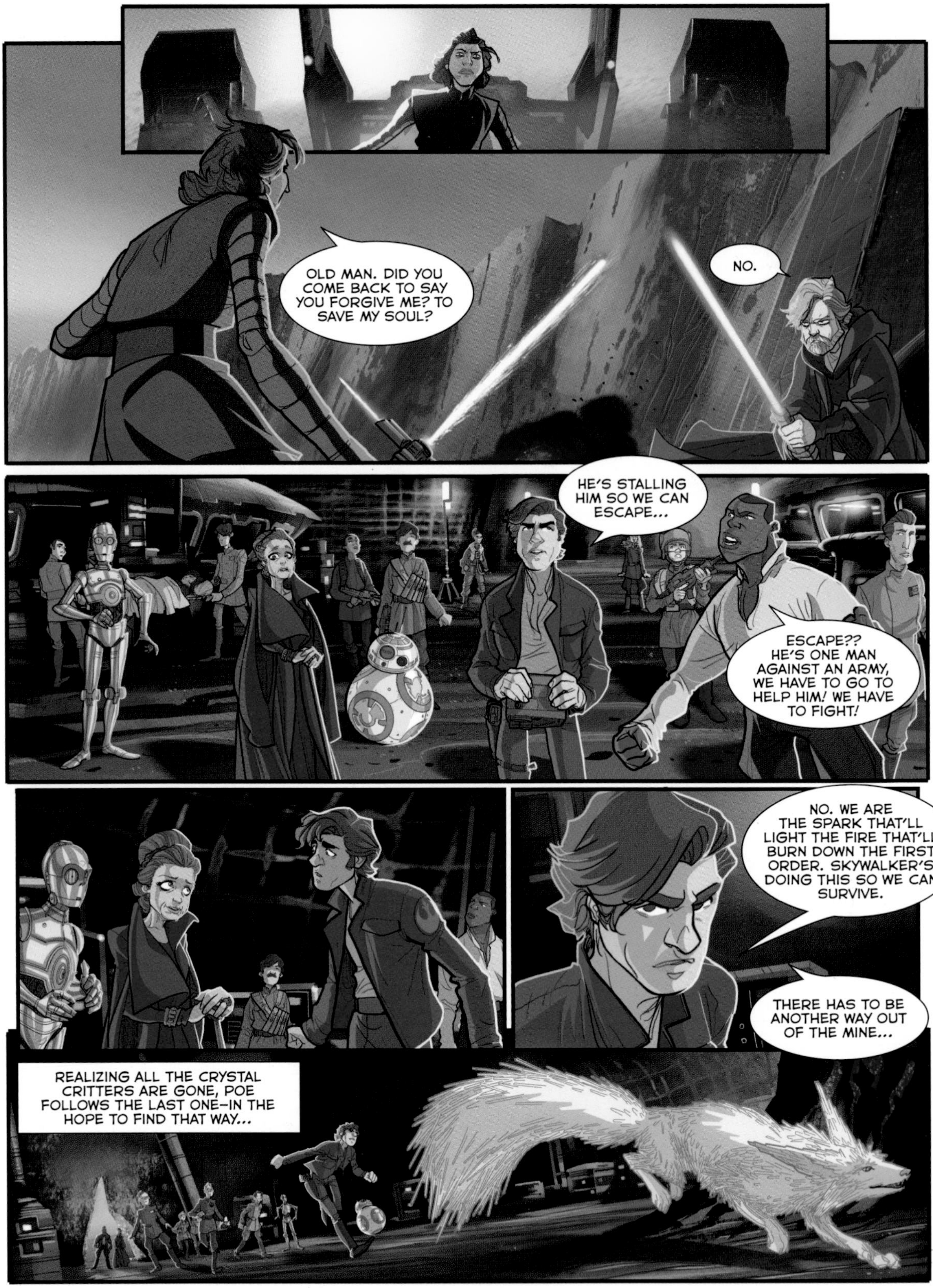
OLD MAN. DID YOU COME BACK TO SAY YOU FORGIVE ME? TO SAVE MY SOUL?
NO.
HE'S STALLING HIM SO WE CAN ESCAPE...
ESCAPE?? HE'S ONE MAN AGAINST AN ARMY, WE HAVE TO GO TO HELP HIM! WE HAVE TO FIGHT!
NO. WE ARE THE SPARK THAT'LL LIGHT THE FIRE THAT'LL BURN DOWN THE FIRST ORDER. SKYWALKER'S DOING THIS SO WE CAN SURVIVE.
THERE HAS TO BE ANOTHER WAY OUT OF THE MINE...
REALIZING ALL THE CRYSTAL CRITTERS ARE GONE, POE FOLLOWS THE LAST ONE—IN THE HOPE TO FIND THAT WAY...

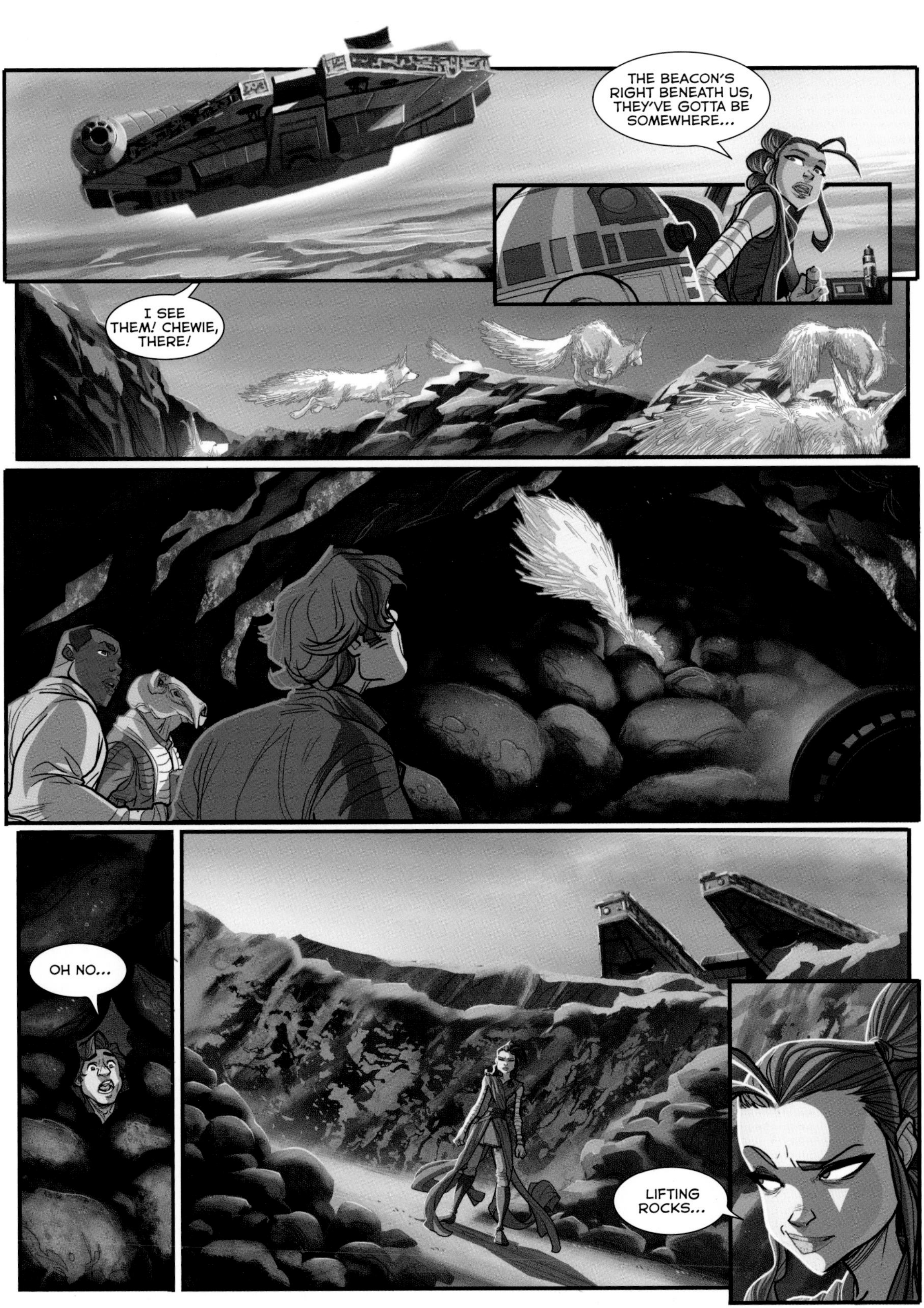
THE BEACON'S RIGHT BENEATH US, THEY'VE GOTTA BE SOMEWHERE...
I SEE THEM! CHEWIE, THERE!
OH NO...
LIFTING ROCKS...

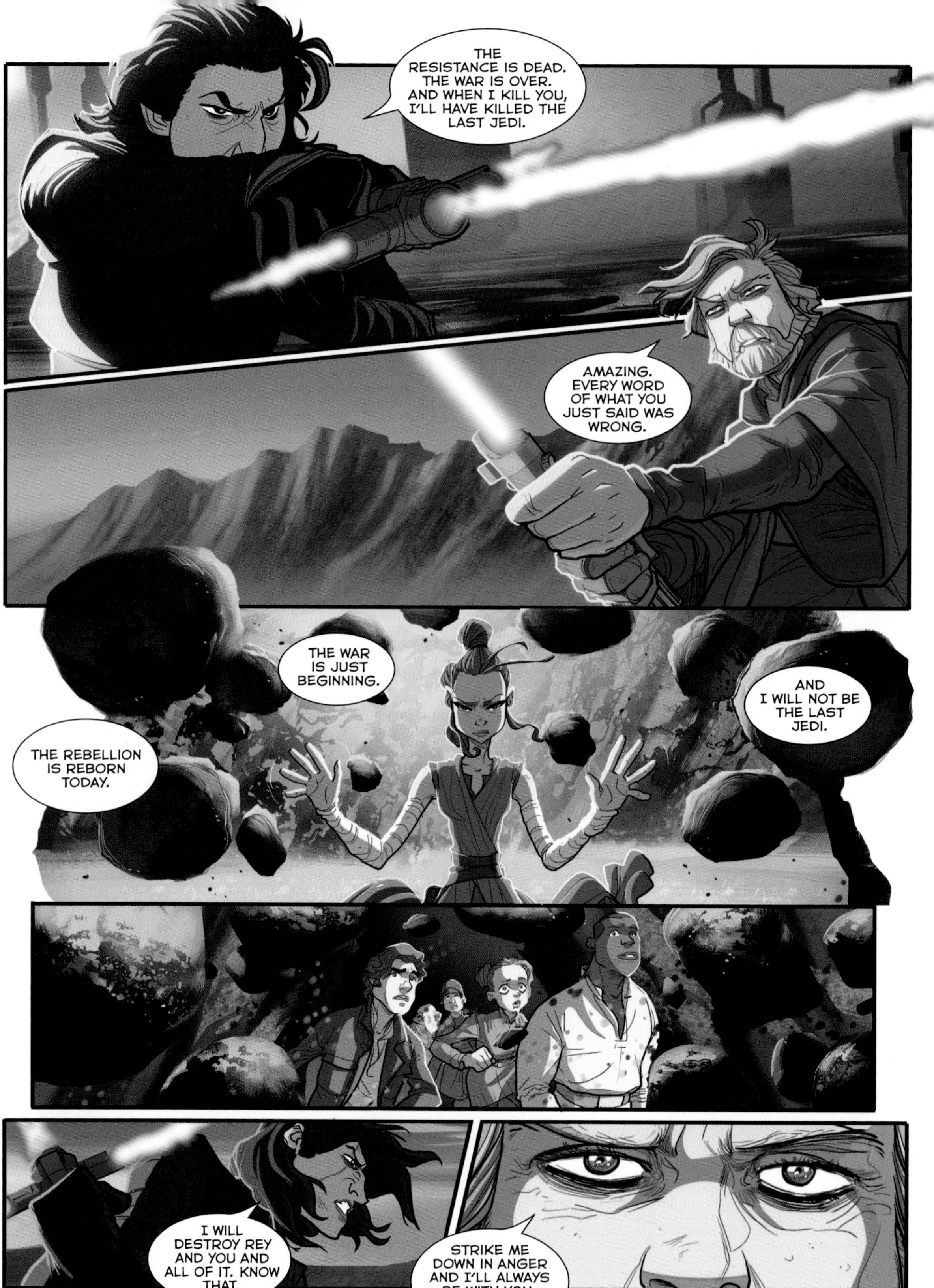
THE RESISTANCE IS DEAD. THE WAR IS OVER. AND WHEN I KILL YOU, I'LL HAVE KILLED THE LAST JEDI.
AMAZING. EVERY WORD OF WHAT YOU JUST SAID WAS WRONG.
THE REBELLION IS REBORN TODAY.
THE WAR IS JUST BEGINNING.
AND I WILL NOT BE THE LAST JEDI.
I WILL DESTROY REY AND YOU AND ALL OF IT. KNOW THAT.
STRIKE ME DOWN IN ANGER AND I'LL ALWAYS BE WITH YOU. JUST LIKE YOUR FATHER.

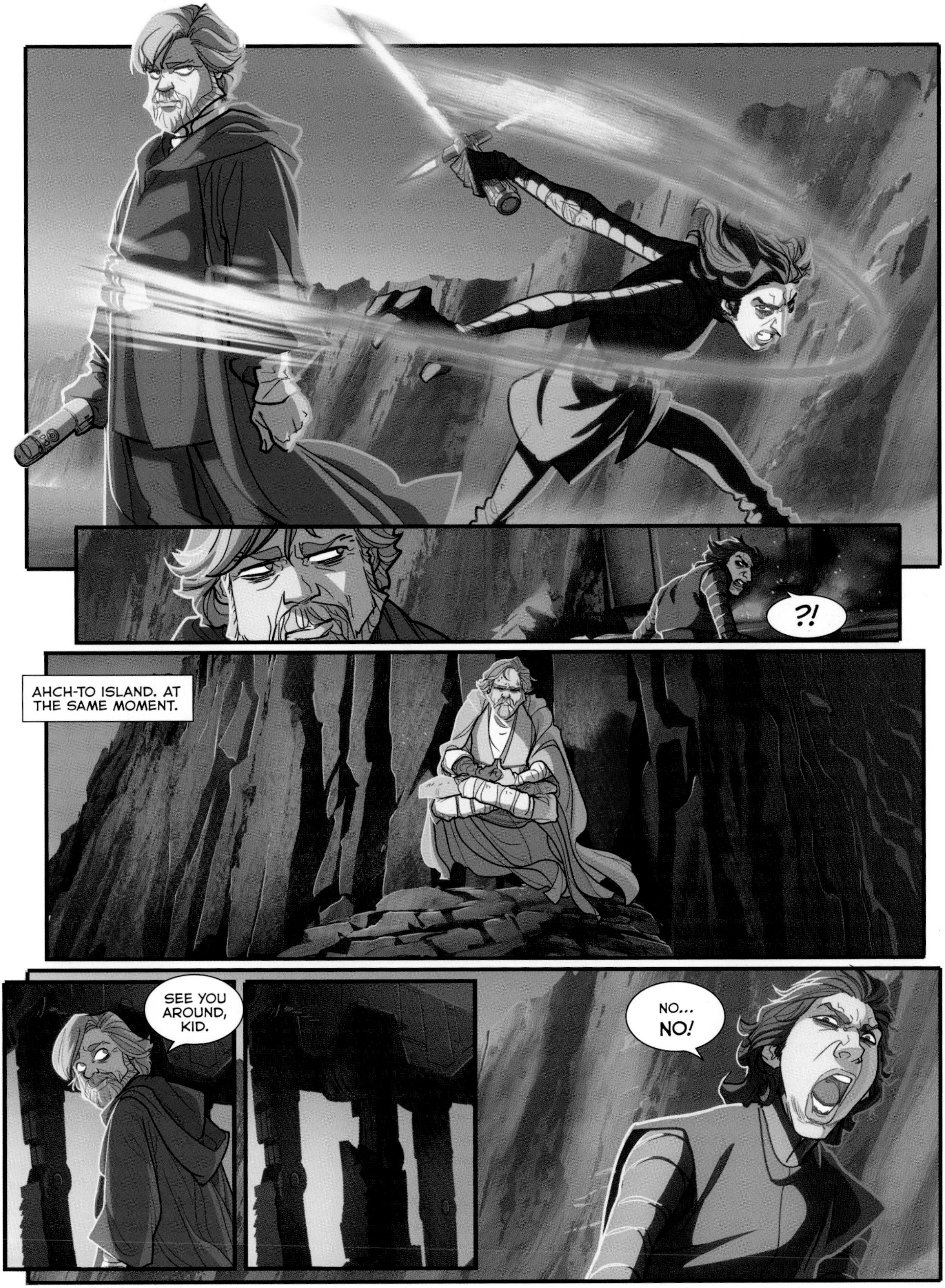
?!
AHCH-TO ISLAND. AT THE SAME MOMENT.
SEE YOU AROUND, KID.
NO... NO!

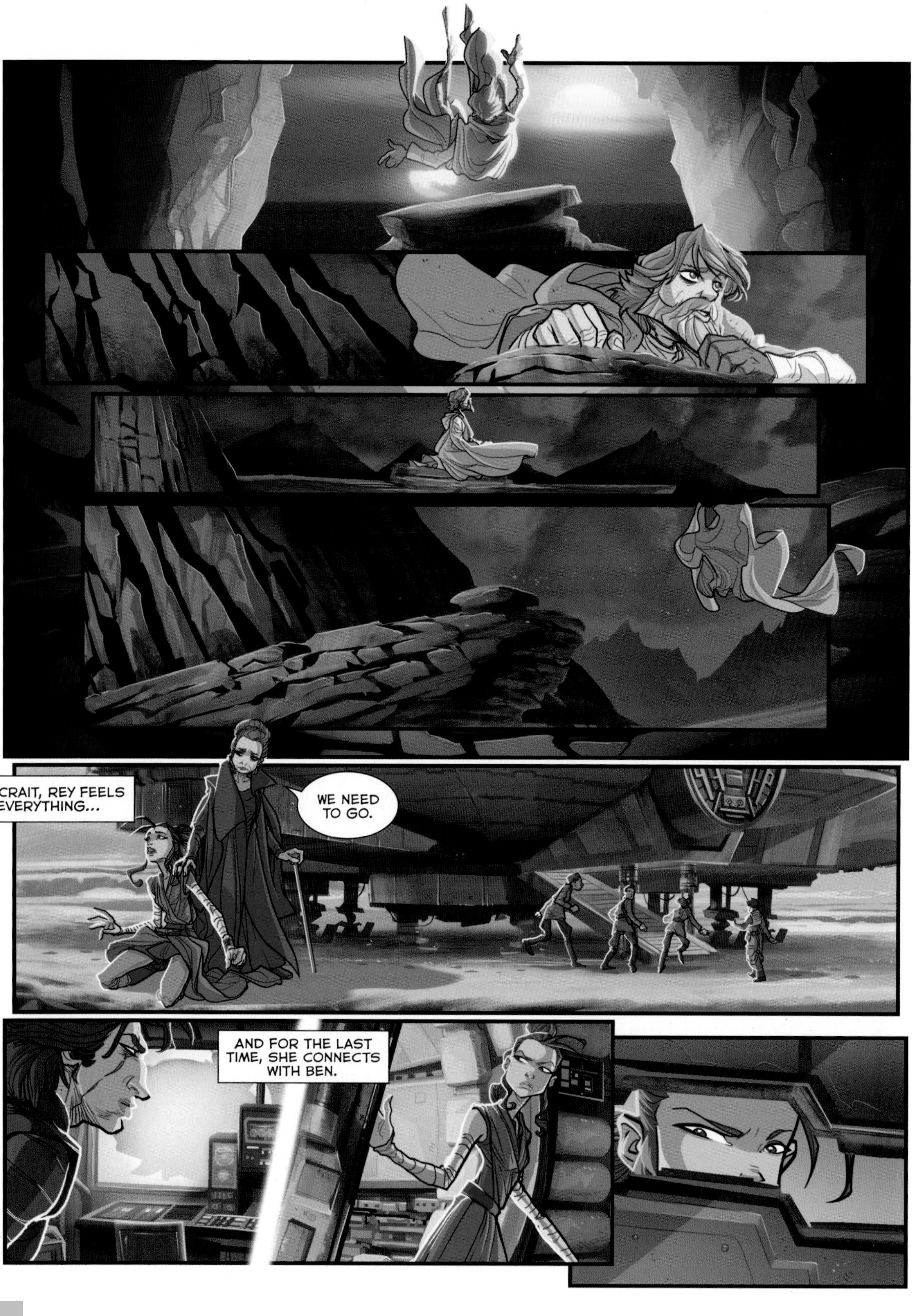
ON CRAIT, REY FEELS EVERYTHING...
WE NEED TO GO.
AND FOR THE LAST TIME, SHE CONNECTS WITH BEN.

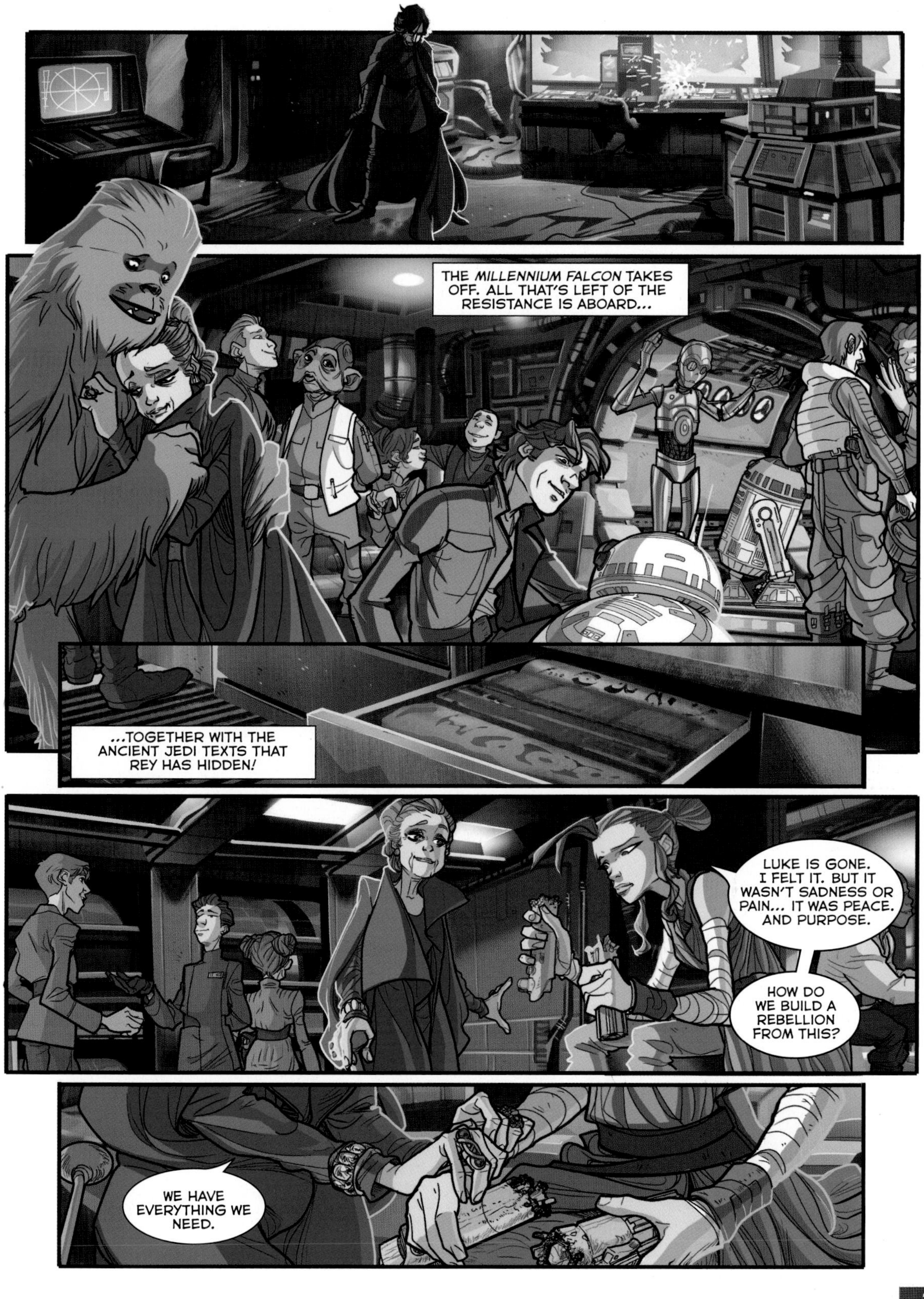
THE *MILLENNIUM FALCON* TAKES OFF. ALL THAT'S LEFT OF THE RESISTANCE IS ABOARD...
...TOGETHER WITH THE ANCIENT JEDI TEXTS THAT REY HAS HIDDEN!
LUKE IS GONE. I FELT IT. BUT IT WASN'T SADNESS OR PAIN... IT WAS PEACE. AND PURPOSE.
HOW DO WE BUILD A REBELLION FROM THIS?
WE HAVE EVERYTHING WE NEED.

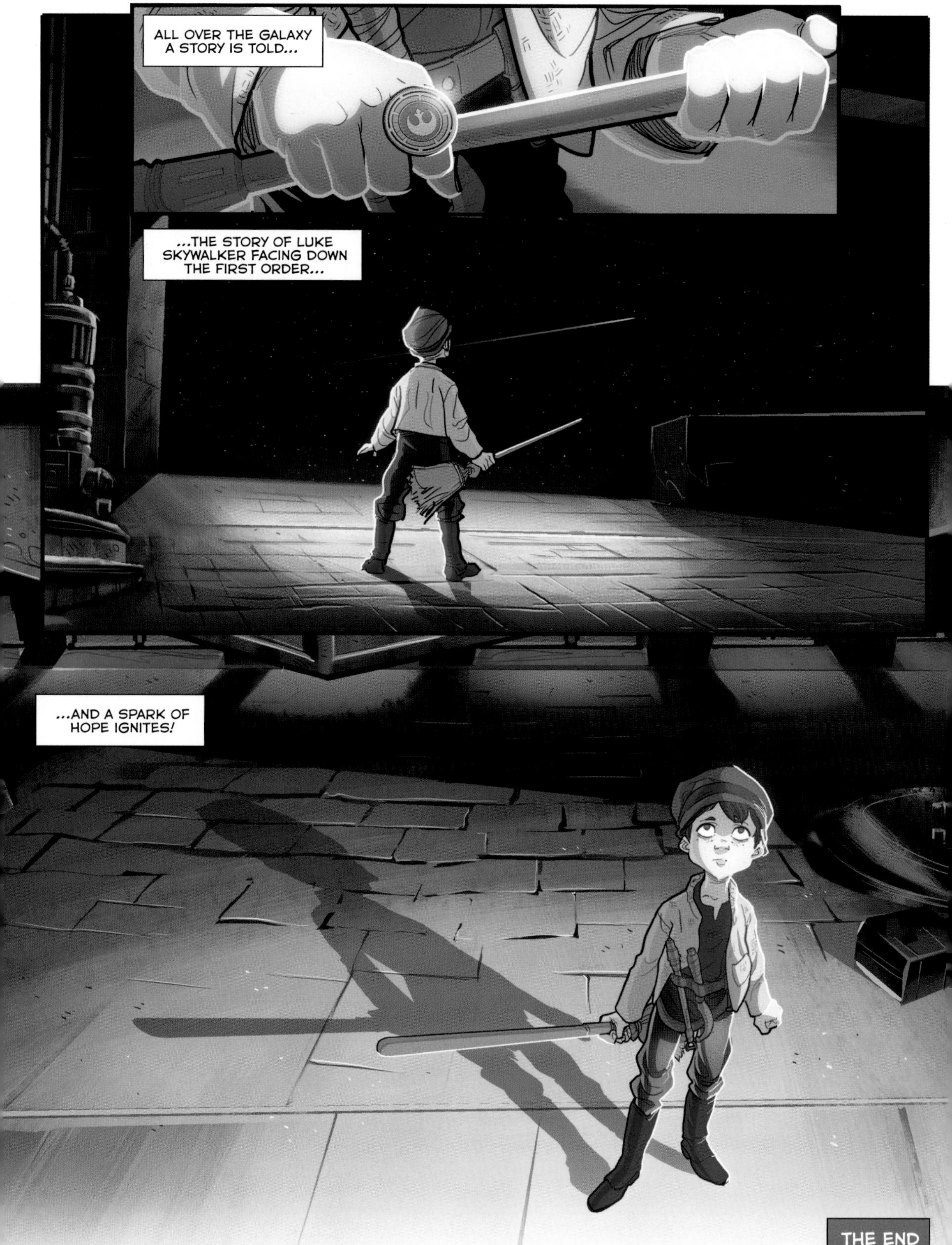
ALL OVER THE GALAXY A STORY IS TOLD...
...THE STORY OF LUKE SKYWALKER FACING DOWN THE FIRST ORDER...
...AND A SPARK OF HOPE IGNITES!
THE END

"YOU ASKED ME WHY I CAME HERE? I CAME TO THIS ISLAND TO DIE. IT'S TIME FOR THE JEDI TO END."

LUKE SKYWALKER

CREDITS

Manuscript Adaptation
Alessandro Ferrari

Character Studies
Igor Chimisso

Layout
Stefano Simeone

Clean Up and Ink
Igor Chimisso

Paint (background and settings)
Massimo Rocca

Paint (characters)
Kawaii Creative Studio

Cover
Eric Jones

Special Thanks to
Michael Siglain, Jennifer Heddle,
James Waugh, Pablo Hidalgo,
Leland Chee, Matt Martin

Editorial Director
Bianca Coletti

Editorial Team
Guido Frazzini (Director, Comics),
Stefano Ambrosio (Executive Editor, New IP),
Carlotta Quattrocolo (Executive Editor, Franchise),
Camilla Vedove (Senior Manager, Editorial
Development),
Behnoosh Khalili (Senior Editor),
Julie Dorris (Senior Editor)

Design
Enrico Soave (*Senior Designer*)

Art
Ken Shue (VP, Global Art),
Roberto Santillo (Creative Director),
Marco Ghiglione (Creative Manager),
Manny Mederos (Creative Manager),
Stefano Attardi (Illustration Manager)

Portfolio Management
Olivia Ciancarelli (*Director*)

Business & Marketing
Mariantonietta Galla (Senior Manager, Franchise),
Virpi Korhonen (Editorial Manager)

For IDW:
Editors
Justin Eisinger and Alonzo Simon

Collection Design
Clyde Grapa

Based on a story by Rian Johnson

Based on characters created by George Lucas

For international rights, contact licensing@idwpublishing.com

ISBN: 978-1-68405-231-8

23 22 21 20   2 3 4 5

Chris Ryall, President & Publisher/CCO • **Cara Morrison**, Chief Financial Officer • **Matthew Ruzicka**, Chief Accounting Officer • **David Hedgecock**, Associate Publisher • **John Barber**, Editor-in-Chief • **Justin Eisinger**, Editorial Director, Graphic Novels and Collections • **Scott Dunbier**, Director, Special Projects • **Jerry Bennington**, VP of New Product Development • **Lorelei Bunjes**, VP of Technology & Information Services • **Jud Meyers**, Sales Director • **Anna Morrow**, Marketing Director • **Tara McCrillis**, Director of Design & Production • **Mike Ford**, Director of Operations • **Shauna Monteforte**, Manufacturing Operations Director • **Rebekah Cahalin**, General Manager

Ted Adams and Robbie Robbins, IDW Founders

www.IDWPUBLISHING.com

Facebook: facebook.com/idwpublishing • Twitter: @idwpublishing • YouTube: youtube.com/idwpublishing
Tumblr: tumblr.idwpublishing.com • Instagram: instagram.com/idwpublishing